THE
PORTER ROCKWELL
CHRONICLES
VOL. 1

OTHER BOOKS BY THE AUTHOR:
Porter Rockwell: A Biography (1986)
Rockwell: U.S. Marshal, A Novel (1987)

Richard Lloyd Dewey

THE
PORTER ROCKWELL
CHRONICLES

Vol. 1

STRATFORD
BOOKS

The Porter Rockwell Chronicles
Vol. 1

Book Cover Photography: Larry Brukiewa

ISBN: 0-9616024-6-5
The Porter Rockwell Chronicles, Vol. 1

Stratford Books, L.C.
Eastern States Office
4308 37th Road North
Arlington, Virginia 22207

Stratford Books, L.C.
Western States Office
P.O. Box 1371
Provo, UT 84603-1371

First Printing: December, 1999
Second Printing: February, 2000
Third Printing: December, 2000
Fourth Printing: October, 2001

This book is printed on acid-free paper.

Printed in the United States of America

To Tina Annette Dewey,
David Christopher Dewey,
and Heather Annette Dewey,
my first treasures.

THE
PORTER ROCKWELL
CHRONICLES
VOL. I

PART I

Journey

CHAPTER 1

W inter had slid unobtrusively into a sultry spring. The countryside of Manchester, New York was alive with chirping birds and budding trees.

Upon finishing his morning chores, young Porter Rockwell, age six, drifted across a meadow in the warmth of noon to the stream a mile from his farmhouse. After baiting a hook, he flung his pole and sat on a boulder, waiting for the first bite. An hour passed. At first he thought it was his imagination but soon caught the sound of horse hooves thundering in the distance. Looking through the trees he descried five boys age 14 hitching their animals to trees and walking toward the stream.

Presently they were upon him.

"Zeke saw you head this way an hour ago," said the largest lad. "He's collecting fishing poles for the needy."

"And we're the needy," said Ezekiel, their leader.

The others chuckled.

"You stealing it?" said Porter.

"No, just borrowing it for good," said Ezekiel.

"Why?" said Porter.

"You giving us lip, boy?" said the largest.

"I think boys with lip oughta be taught a lesson," said Ezekiel. He then grabbed Porter and pulled him up. He pushed him to the first boy, who latched onto his collar and shoved him away. Porter went splashing backwards into the stream. It was apparent to Porter the boys had been drinking. They were a bit slow and clumsy, and their eyes were glazed over.

The five laughed and turned away.

Ezekiel grabbed the fishing pole.

Westward they walked, but got no more than 30 yards when suddenly the largest lad was tackled from behind and fell straight forward.

Porter wrestled him on the ground. When the others realized what had happened they broke out yelling. The boy wrestling Porter pushed him away and stood.

Ezekiel strode up to Porter and kicked him. "I reckon we oughta teach this worm to respect his elders. He ain't gonna walk for a month by the time I get finished with him."

"Or me when I get through with him!" said the largest lad.

All five surrounded Porter. He stood, facing them, and watched them come slowly at him. Suddenly he spotted an opening between two of them where he could dash into thick woods and possibly escape, but the arrogant expression on Ezekiel so infuriated him that he knew he had no alternative: He lowered his head and ran into the mocking, bigger boy and butted him in the stomach with a loud groan. Ezekiel had the wind knocked out of him, but Porter, still afoot, turned to face another — then was kicked in the chin. The young Rockwell flew backwards onto the ground, his mouth bleeding. The other four boys surrounded Ezekiel, who lay gasping for breath.

Porter flew back to his feet, lowered his head again, and ran at the largest lad. But the lad lowered his fist and cold-cocked him. Porter flew back, dazed, and presently beheld the four boys approaching again, closing in on him. He sprung to his feet and ran between the widest opening. He dashed across the meadow, straight toward the nearest farmhouse in the distance. He glanced back and spotted the boys pursuing him and laughing. They were 30 yards back and, despite the fact they were slowed considerably by the effects of their over-indulgence in moonshine, were closing in.

The farmhouse was now only 300 yards ahead, but the boys were only 10 yards back and narrowing the distance. Suddenly a figure of a tall boy loomed in front of them. Porter, exhausted, barely reached this stranger and collapsed for air beside him. The pursuers slowed as they approached the unusually tall juvenile. They stopped and stared up at him.

"Can I join the fun?" said the tall young man.

He was half a head taller than the others and a year younger, but held developing muscles most boys would envy.

They recognized him as the nearby farm boy, Joseph.

"It looks like you're playing with my neighbor, and I'd sure like to play."

They all studied him curiously.

"What do you say the little tyke and I take sides, and we stick-pull you fellas?" said Joseph. "The winner gets that fishing pole." Joseph had spotted Porter numerous times traipsing across his meadow with the unusually straight and stout fishing pole, but now noticed Ezekiel firmly grasping it.

Ezekiel was still breathless and gasping. "I'd say that sounds fair. But this ain't your concern."

"Well seeing as how I'm the nearest neighbor to this boy," said Joseph, "and you're on my property, I'd say it is my concern, and I've got a right to play this game too, so I choose him as my partner. You boys can either leave — and drop that fishing pole of his — or let me join in the fun. The winner gets that pole. Is that all right with you, lad?" said Joseph to Porter.

Porter noticed Joseph give him a confident wink.

"Sure," said Porter.

The other boys backed off a bit, dismayed by Joseph's size and confidence.

"All right," said Ezekiel to his gang. "I think we oughta let him join in the fun." He turned back to Joseph: "It's us five against you two. And we'll use the fishing pole as the stick pole."

In a common contest of the day, the boys faced each other, seated on the ground, and began pulling, hoping to pull the other across a line drawn in the earth. By using such a long pole, this contest practically amounted to "tug-a-war."

Joseph and Porter pulled at one end — Ezekiel and his four friends at the other.

"What's the matter, Zeke?" said Joseph. "You're turning red!"

Indeed, Ezekiel looked ready to explode. All five in fact had the same look.

Porter meanwhile grunted and tugged for all he was worth, but did not hold the strength of any of his opponents, each of whom were several years older.

Ezekiel's team pulled harder and harder — but to no avail. Joseph panted and pulled, now also turning red. Presently he heard little Porter grunting behind him. One minute passed. Then two. Suddenly, Joseph felt the other team getting the best of him. He felt the stick pulling him slowly forward. He let out a roar and yelled, "Enough is enough!" He yanked for all he was worth, and Ezekiel's team went sprawling forward, over the line.

Porter jumped up and cheered.

Joseph stood and extended his hand to each of his opponents. He shook their hands. And said, "Good lads would never gang up five to one on a smaller kid, and you are all good boys, aren't you?"

Ezekiel looked off, embarrassed.

"We did it!" shouted Porter. "Nobody in the world can beat us — nobody!"

Suddenly Porter rushed one of them from behind and, in celebration, tackled him. The older boy was annoyed, but forced a smile.

Joseph broke out laughing. "I've never seen a kid bull with such spunk!"

Ezekiel reached down to pull up his breathless buddy Porter had tackled, when Joseph grabbed Porter and set him on his feet. Among others, Joseph was known for his wrestling and stick-pulling acumen, and county-wide it was rumored he'd never lost a match — even to boys two years above his age, which was the oldest of his age bracket in official contests.

Ezekiel turned and began walking away, and his four friends followed, to retrieve their horses at the creek.

Porter, seeing the boy he had charged now walking away from him, gained renewed confidence and began chasing after him. But he only made two steps, when suddenly he found himself being picked up.

"Whoa, kid bull," said Joseph, setting him feet first on the meadow. "I think that gang is not planning on bothering you again. I think you scared 'em away."

Porter stood with shoulders squared. His little stocky face, with prematurely squared features, smiled at the retreating boys. Panting with the exultation of victory pumping through his veins, his lower lip then protruded, determined and ready for more action. He kept his eyes glued to the five defeated enemy tromping across the tall grassy meadow westward. "Let's catch 'em, neighbor, and whup 'em!"

"I think you already have," said Joseph.

"I reckon you're right."

Three days later Porter carried a bucket of fresh milk into his house when he spotted Joseph and Joseph's father approaching their cabin door. Porter's own father, Orin Rockwell was repairing a gate, and greeted them. Porter was named after his father, except he had two "r"s in his first name, "Orrin," and he went by his middle name, "Porter."

He had pondered the fight scene over and over, at first excited that he had defeated the bullies, but with time he had become cognizant that he had at least in part been assisted by his neighbor somewhat more than that for which he had been giving him credit. The question which consumed him deep down now was simply, 'Why did he help me?'

Joseph Smith Senior and Joseph Junior introduced themselves to Porter's father, announcing they were the nearest neighbors of one mile away. They had recently moved there from Palmyra, New York, while the Rockwells had settled the area just two years earlier in 1817, hailing from Belcher, Massachusetts. Joseph Senior invited the Rockwell family over for dinner the next night.

"I don't know," said the senior Rockwell.

"We gotta go, Pa," said Porter. "Let's go!"

Orin thought it over a moment, glanced at his wife who had just entered, and she smiled approvingly.

"I reckon so," said Orin. "We'd like to bring dessert though."

Joseph Junior extended his hand to Porter. "I'm proud to be the friend of a tough critter like you."

Orin Rockwell had heard the report over and over from young Porter the previous three days. "I want to thank you for helping my boy."

Joseph Junior shook his head. "And I want to thank him for helping me. No telling what those fellows would have done in that stick-pull contest without him on my side." He glanced at the six year old in front of him. "What's your name, boy?"

"Porter Rockwell."

"Well," said Joseph Sr., "in addition to having you over for supper, we just wanted to see if there was anything we could do to help, since we're neighbors."

Orin thought a moment and replied, "We could use help clearing some land, but we'd like to help you as well. And later especially at harvest time. We could take turns."

The Rockwells and Smiths met before sundown the next night. The Smiths had nine children while Orin and Sarah Rockwell had nine eventually, in the following order: Caroline, Porter, Peter, Emily, Electa, Alvira, Merritt, Horace, and Mary.

They all sang several songs and a few older children read poems. Then they feasted on freshly cooked wild turkey and potatoes, warm bread, fresh butter, and apple pie from fruit bottled the previous autumn. The sky turned to twilight when Orin announced they had enjoyed themselves immensely but needed to get home.

Lucy Mack Smith, Joseph Junior's mother, implored the Rockwells to not leave yet, but rather spend time with them into the evening and, at the insistence of the Rockwell children, Porter's parents agreed.

They played games and ate more dessert. Finally Orin announced they truly had to be getting home, and in the warm spring breeze they set out on the narrow dirt road which led to their farmhouse.

Thirteen year old Joseph Junior watched as his new neighbors gathered outside their door and said their last goodbyes. Joseph glanced down at Porter, who was walking away backwards and staring up at him. Joseph realized he had an admirer, and the idea crossed his mind that this friendship with the young fellow might last for more than a short while.

The next week the two families began working together. When certain laborious tasks were limited by a period of time — such as harvest, or where land needed to be cleared, or other synergistic activities needed to be performed — the two families worked closely together.

Six months later, after the last day of harvest when the two families had spent the day harvesting crops on both farms, the Rockwell family sat exhausted at sundown at their own dinner table. Until then, the two tribes had always eaten together on days of mutual labor, but today the Smiths had relatives coming to visit, so they'd departed early. The last crickets of the year chirped outside and an unseasonably warm late autumn breeze cooled their perspiring foreheads. As Sarah fed them, Orin commented, "I really enjoy working with the Smiths. Those boys of theirs are the best workers — along with you boys — I have ever seen. Joseph especially has an honest way about him that lets me trust him more than probably anyone outside my own clan."

Porter beamed, proud to have Joseph as his new big brother.

CHAPTER 2

Eight years later, at age 15, after numerous family labor projects between the two families and many meals and parties, young Porter drove his family buckboard into Manchester, New York for supplies. Accompanying him was his little sister, Electa. As he often visited with Joseph and still looked upon him as his best friend, he had become fascinated with Joseph's recent claims regarding religion. Joseph maintained he had been visited by an angel named Moroni, who had buried golden plates in the nearby Hill Cumorah in 421 A.D.

Under divine inspiration, Joseph then translated them. They purported to be the record of prophets in ancient America and of equal significance as the *Bible*, which was meanwhile the record of prophets in ancient Old World countries. Certainly, these were no small claims and they created a substantial stir in the community which had over the issue become sharply divided.

Joseph within the year would attempt to have the book published as the *Book of Mormon*, named after an ancient prophet in America whom Joseph maintained had compiled and edited the records. That prophet's son was Moroni, he claimed.

Porter, hearing the account numerous times as Joseph related it to neighbors at his fireplace, decided the account was true. He decided to help Joseph raise money for the project. After his farm chores he began picking berries and chopping wood, then selling them in town. On one particular trip to Manchester he decided to haul a load of firewood. Days earlier, Joseph had made the mistake of confiding his activity to a local minister, who soon had told another, and word had spread like wildfire. Numerous fellow farmers in the area looked upon the Smiths as solid, level-headed citizens in all respects, but the religious one, yet Joseph's entire family believed him. Others in the area were also embracing Joseph's claims. Porter, his brother Peter, and two of his sisters — Caroline and Electa — were among them.

As Porter approached the hardware store, three boys on horseback rode up. These fellows were a year older than he.

"What'chu doing with that firewood, Porter? Sellin' it for angel's food?" They chuckled and followed, taunting him all the way to the store.

"It true you just giving it away to Joseph?"

"He your charity now, boy?"

"How can we get on your charity list?" They chortled and taunted.

Porter ignored them, but felt sensitive to his little sister's reception of the verbal barbs. She fought back tears, and Porter noticed it.

"You boys have anything better to do today?" he finally said.

"Or do you just like picking on little girls like this?"

"Little girls? 'You a little girl now?" said one youngster. The other two laughed till they almost fell out of their saddles.

"My sister don't take too kindly to your words, boys," said Porter. "though I find you kind of funny, so why don't you just head on home and tease your own sisters?"

"Cause we like teasing you two sisters instead."

"If you don't know what's good for you," said Porter, changing his tone, "I'd advise you to head away from my wagon."

"Well, now, Joseph takes ribbing pretty good. He don't talk back. He don't get riled. He don't do nothin'. In fact, he's fun to rib. Ain't you like him, boy?"

"Joseph does what he has to. I do what I have to." At that he handed the reins over to Electa, reached under a canvas bag at his feet, and pulled out a shotgun. He quickly whirled the barrel straight at them. "Two of you are close enough for me to take you out with one shot. So you fellows can stop laughing now, long enough to tell me which two want to go out together."

The three boys attempted to smile but their lower lips quivered, and they suddenly galloped off.

Porter took the reins from his sister.

"That the right thing to do?" said Electa.

"I don't know, but it worked."

After supper, Porter headed to the barn with his father. The elder Rockwell's voice was heavier than normal. "I got just one thing to say about all this with you and Joseph," said Orin to Porter. "Even if you're inclined to believe what he's told us — and I know some in our family do — I'd advise you to hold onto your hard-earned silver coins. The day may come you will wish you had saved every cent you had. I've been through tough times myself, and I'd hate to see you suffer the things I have."

"It's something I gotta do, Pa," said Porter.

"You worked for it, son," said Orin. "I'd advise you to keep it for yourself."

"Joseph needs it," said Porter. "Even if I didn't believe him, I'd do it. But I happen to believe him."

Porter's mother made a beeline to them from behind the house, where she had heard them through an open window. "What're you telling your boy?" she shouted to Orin. "He can do with his money what he pleases!"

"You both can believe this nonsense, but — "

"Orin, you know what the Smith's are about. 'Ain't a dishonest one in the bunch."

"I know what they've said. It's just hard to fathom."

"What is?"

"The angel stuff."

"That's your choice," she said. "But you've raised our young 'uns to have their choices. Don't take that away."

"I'm not taking it away."

"I saw you trying."

"I just advised Porter to not give away his hard-earned silver. It's hard to come by."

"He'll do with it as he pleases," she said. "So, let the boy alone."

"But what if it ain't true?"

"What?" said Sarah, incredulously.

"What if Joseph's book ain't true?"

Porter's mother stared at her husband a moment and sighed, then turned away into the house. Orin shook his head and proceeded toward the barn.

Porter walked alone to the chicken coop, frustrated his family was so divided.

CHAPTER 3

T wo years passed. Joseph was instrumental in organizing a new religious body, the Church of Jesus Christ of Latter-day Saints, in which Porter and his mother joined the first official day of its inception, April 6, 1830. Porter was the ninth baptized. Within days, three of his four oldest siblings joined: Peter, Caroline and Electa. Emily was the one older child who did not, simply not interested.

The harassment from neighbors and fellow farmers escalated.

Several months later one of their congregation held a church social, complete with food displayed on a picnic table, and dancing. Over 80 attended.

The Mormons, as they were called because of their companion scripture, the *Book of Mormon*, referred to themselves as "saints," which Joseph explained was short for Latter-day Saints, meaning "church members," as in New Testament times, but not of any particularly saintly status. And for that Porter was grateful. Not that he considered himself a wayward soul, but he had an eye for adventure and thus did as he usually pleased. He was now fully grown, medium in height and stocky, with rugged facial features set in a semi-portly yet handsome face with shimmering blue eyes. He was rather handsome by most women's standards, and fun-loving.

Joseph and Porter were playing a game of chase and wrestle. Porter took out chasing him. The boys were now 24 and 17 respectively, and they ran between the out buildings of their neighbor's farm and through a cornfield. Joseph finally outsmarted him by predicting which row of corn in which Porter would be running. He surprised Porter by lunging at the teenager and tackling him. As they laughed and made their way back to the dance, Lucy Mack Smith sidled up to her son.

"Joseph, some of the folk here aren't used to seeing you romping like little bucks."

"Then they'll have to get used to it, Mama." Joseph was not about to let his position dictate different behavior than that to which came natural. At six feet tall he towered over most men of the day. With a cheery countenance and an amiable air, his charismatic charm was noticed by all whom he met, and his interesting manners and naturalness, coupled with handsome facial features, intrigued even the most otherwise disinterested listeners. His family had more than merely believed him: They had rallied around his cause and supported him with great sacrifices. One brother, Samuel, had gone June 30, 1830 into neighboring states as the first missionary, taking copies of the now published *Book of Mormon* with him. The local printer, Grandin, had published

5,000 leather-bound copies from $3,000 Joseph had obtained, including Porter's hard-earned wood-and-berry money.

The religious adventure had not left Joseph even remotely pretentious, pious, or pompous, according to his neighbors.

Joseph's mother was nevertheless sensitive to the curious glances Joseph was receiving at the picnic. Some even in their fold expected Joseph to act more circumspectly — perhaps somewhat like a minister or priest. Joseph laughed at her and shrugged. "It ain't me." He then played like a teenager with Porter the remainder of the party.

"Joseph, why don't you find Emma and dance," she insisted, hoping to distract him to more acceptable behavior expected of a leader.

Emma, his wife of 2¹/₂ years, was busy in the kitchen pulling pies from their neighbor's oven. She and Joseph had married January 18, 1827 and moved to nearby Harmony, Pennsylvania the summer of 1828. It was now the summer of 1830.

"Emma must be busy," said Joseph. "Cause I don't see her — so why don't you dance with me, Mama?" At that he took his mother and began swinging her through the barnyard, disrupting other people milling about and causing them to break out laughing.

Porter belly-laughed and broke in. He took Joseph's mother away from Joseph and continued the dance. The crowd clapped to the music, and Joseph grabbed a harmonica. He searched the notes as other musicians picked up the beat to a new rendition of "Turkey in the Straw."

Suddenly they heard horse hooves. Porter glanced up and stopped dancing. He walked forward to thirty horsemen slowing down and entering the midst of the gathering. The horsemen all halted, then began prancing through the party, roping the picnic table and turning it over. Food scattered across the ground. Other horsemen roped the fence and pulled it over, snapping whips at cows and pigs to escape into the meadow. Others trampled the garden. Two horseback teenagers threw stones through the window. Suddenly, as quickly as it had begun, all the horsemen took off in a gallop, laughing.

Porter turned red as he watched them leaving. He heard several children crying. He bolted to his horse, jumped horseback, and took off after the horsemen.

Before the band had ridden two hundred yards, he leaped from his horse and grabbed the leader of the band, tackling him. Both fellows crashed to the ground.

Joseph ran out to them. The other attacking horsemen spotted Joseph coming, panicked, and left their leader. As Joseph arrived, he found Porter wrestling the fellow with his face down in the mud. The prisoner was about to lose consciousness when Joseph grabbed Porter and flung him off.

"Get up!" said Joseph to the attacker.

"Keep him off me," said the horseman, about 35, long-haired, and now groggy.

"What'd you want with us?" said Joseph.

"Nothing."

"What'chu mean, nothin'?" piped in Porter. "How come you did this?"

"Just out for fun."

Porter stepped toward him. "I'll show you fun."

Joseph clutched Porter's arm and held him back.

The man's eyes widened as he blurted to Joseph, "What're you going to do with me?"

"What do you think?" said Porter. "I'll turn your face upside down."

The man backed away, "No, please . . ."

Joseph sighed. "Go on home."

"What's that?" said the man.

"You heard me," said Joseph.

The man glanced from Joseph to Porter, then quickly arose and took off running and stumbling.

Porter turned and observed their friends all still back at the gathering. He felt for the first time in his life the need — even the mission — to protect them.

Joseph read his mind. "Maybe you are needed more than you've thought."

Joseph arrived back at the crowd. "All right, let's pick up everything, round up those farm animals, and fix these windows and that fence. Then I want to hear music and see the best dance I've ever seen!"

CHAPTER 4

Several days later, the same group of friends sat outside Joseph's home where he stood before a makeshift pulpit. The sunlight was bright and birds sang softly. "You all knew, when you received witnesses from the Holy Spirit of the truthfulness of this work, that there would be certain sacrifices called of you all." He studied the eyes of the congregation. "We'll presently be leaving here and moving to Ohio."

Porter and his mother glanced at each other, then at Orin, who turned away. He was not a member of their church but was attending most of their meetings and had been for a year, for the sake of his wife and also to please the four of his oldest five children who had joined. Porter had no idea how his father would take this news.

Riding home on their wagon with the children horseback, he learned. Orin and Sarah sat silently atop the buckboard. Porter, walking behind the wagon, finally heard his father speak:

"I spent my whole life building a decent farm."

"And we're not supposed to stay here; it's as simple as that," spoke up Sarah, short and stout with an ever-beaming countenance. Her green eyes contained a constant sparkle behind her Irish-looking face.

"The farm is finally paying off," said Orin.

"I'm proud of you for that," said Sarah.

Orin continued, "What's Joseph and his people going to do in the wilderness? Ohio has nothing."

Sarah blew out a sigh and answered, "The Eerie Canal has taken civilization to Ohio and beyond. We'll do fine."

"We?"

"We," she said.

"We ain't going nowhere."

"We are going to Ohio, Orin."

"You can go. I ain't picking up and leaving something that puts food on the table. I ain't that crazy."

"You expect me and the children to stay here?" she said. "Then you are crazy."

"You stay with your husband."

"Orin, I will. I won't leave. Not you. But as I sit and breathe I know it is the will of the Lord that we follow Joseph away from here."

"But what if Joseph can't make it in Ohio?" said Orin.

"Then you take that up with the Lord."

Orin shook his head and kept driving the team.

Porter was distraught, knowing they would be going nowhere. As stubborn as his mother was, his father was even more so, determined to stay atop the family pecking order, as handed down from generation to Rockwell generation.

———

Sure enough, when Joseph left for Ohio months later, Porter watched him and other families leaving. He felt distraught, feeling left behind and thoroughly disheartened.

The day afterwards, Orin drove the wagon to the feed store to sell a load. As he descended the buckboard he was met by the proprietor, Samuel O'Rourke. "Orin, I can't use your grain today."

"What're you on about? I always deliver on Monday."

"Not this week. Not next. I'm sorry."

"You care to explain this?" said Orin.

"Let's just say I got wind that some of your family have joined up with the Smith lot."

"What's that got to do with you and me?"

"I ain't got nothing against you, Orin. But I'll lose business if I keep buying from you. I am sorry. Now you have a good week." At that Samuel turned his back and strode into his store.

Porter finished his chores early. At four o'clock he rolled out of bed and sauntered through the front cabin room, surprised to find his father beside the fireplace, reading.

Orin slammed shut the book, covered it with another and glanced up. "What're you doing up so early for?"

Porter smiled, "First tell me why you're reading the *Book of Mormon!*"

"How'd you see what I was reading?"

"I didn't, but it was the fear on your face of being discovered."

Orin smiled and sat back. "I still can't find an answer to all this," he said. "I know how much it means to your mama."

"You're feeling the kickback from the community, aren't you?" said Porter.

"O'Rourke's quit buying from me, but I did find a couple other buyers to take up the slack. So we ain't going anyplace."

"Papa," said Porter, sitting across from him. "I know you just want to provide for us. And you do a fine job. A real fine job. But there are other ways to be a provider." That's all he said. Orin watched him curiously as his son walked away, disappearing into another room.

Orin turned his eyes to the fire. He wished more than anything to please this boy, who secretly was the one he wanted to most look up to him. Porter never knew his pa had come to his bedside nearly every night of his life since he was a baby, where he had studied his son with complete adoration. In fact, Porter had slept beside his father — when his pa was home — until he was five years old. Most of the other children half that. Orin gazed upon all of his children with love he had never expected he could have, certainly more so than any non-married man could have for another, and he knew that by experience. He believed in a God simply because of the miracle of having children to raise who meant this much to him. However, he knew it would take another miracle to join their faith. He was that certain it would never happen. Nevertheless, Porter's challenge dug deeply into him. As the dawn's rays crept through the window he realized he would have to be a provider in every sense.

CHAPTER 5

Soon after Joseph left for Ohio, his mother Lucy Mack Smith led the others who had not been able to leave earlier. This was the "Fayette Branch," and with them Orin stood beside Sarah as the barge moved westward and south, down the Eerie Canal. Eighty people surrounded their wagons on the flatboat. Mules along both sides of the canal pulled the barge forward. At Fairport, Ohio Porter jumped off the barge, announcing, "I'm going to visit my uncle."

Porter's father smiled but his mother shouted at him, "Porter, get back on the boat!"

"I will later."

"There will be no later. It's not stopping and waiting for you!"

Porter merely smiled and kept walking.

Sarah, beside herself, ran up to Lucy Mack Smith. "Mother Smith, Porter won't listen to anyone but you. Please get him back."

By the time Joseph's mother got to the gunwale, she noticed six other boys off the barge and following Porter.

"You boys, get back here!"

They stopped and stared at her, torn over continuing with Porter, or remaining with the security of their families. Porter stopped and looked over the coterie of kids following him.

"Boys," said Lucy Mack, you get back on this barge immediately. We will not wait for you!"

The six lads glanced at Porter, who nodded them to go ahead and return, then he simply waved at the folks on the barge who were gathered and watching.

Lucy Mack, who held a soft spot for Porter, held back a smile, then waved back. Sarah Rockwell felt a loss, wondering if their oldest boy would be safe in the "wild western wilderness" of Ohio. Of that, her husband Orin had no doubt.

Several weeks later they arrived at the Ohio drop-off point, when Porter rendezvoused with them, having arrived the day previously.

"Where were you!" shouted his mother.

"Spent a few days with my uncle, then came here."

Orin smiled, glowing and proud of his adventurous son, yet angered over his disobedience. "You get to pull potato-peeling duty the remainder of the journey."

Porter dropped his head and nodded.

Orin noticed his wife shedding tears of joy through her anger that Porter had reunited with them. Porter himself was grateful to be back, but especially to be back in the company of Joseph.

As for the journey, Orin refused to let the boys or himself ride in the wagon and thus strain the animals.

On their wagon south, the Rockwell women rode. Orin was still dismayed at leaving his farm, having sold the land for pennies on the dollar of its potential value merely to comply with his family's "spiritual inclinations," but he tried to maintain a cheery disposition.

At Kirtland, Ohio they arrived May 14, 1831. They set up camp at nearby Thompson, Ohio on the thousand acre ranch of Ezra Thayer and Laman Copley. Six months previously in November 1830, missionaries had baptized about 130 people in Ohio and organized them into three branches; thus, the New York group was arriving into an area of relative strength. As the Rockwells built their cabin they lived in a lean-to, a three-sided structure with an all-important protective roof.

After a few weeks Joseph called another special meeting. He announced a certain number of the fold were now needed to pioneer frontier Missouri, while the others would remain in Kirtland and build a temple for eternal ordinances to solidify their faith.

The Rockwells were chosen with numerous other families to make that move to Missouri. But Porter's two oldest sisters, Caroline and Emily, decided to remain in Hamilton, Ohio with two men they had met — M.C.R. Smith and Christopher Stafford.

Porter felt close to both girls, but his degree of anguish was not as intense as that felt by his parents. Sarah cried as she and her family pulled away in their wagon, knowing she would likely never see her daughters again. She knew both girls had been turning into young women and would, as older teens, want families of their own, but the fact they had chosen to stay behind and not continue with the family — nor that they were even marrying men of their faith — tore at her till she thought her heart would burst. True, Emily had not joined their faith yet herself, and was actually the only older child who had not been baptized — a fact disheartening enough for her mother — but that coupled with her choice to not accompany the family to Missouri caused Sarah a sense of unfathomable hopelessness. The hope to which Sarah had clung for months consisted of Emily "coming around," and certainly staying with the family and settling where their people would settle until she did experience a conversion to their faith. Sarah's hope further consisted of Emily eventually finding a good young man of their flock and settling forever in the same community with them; indeed, she had hoped more than anything to live her entire life with all her children together in the same community where she could help raise all her future grandchildren, a blessing possessed by many grandmothers of the day. Orin's secret hope was the same, yet they had never talked of it, not wanting to set themselves into too vulnerable a situation, knowing they would be heartbroken if any of their children did choose to live elsewhere.

So when they saw their oldest daughter Caroline wishing to stay in Ohio as well, it all but crushed their spirits. This was in Orin's eyes his precious first child.

When Porter observed the anguish of his father being separated from both Caroline and Emily, he decided at that very moment if he ever had a family he would never allow them to live separately from him or from each other: They would travel together, they would settle in the same community, and they would most certainly live out their days as a clan and even be buried in the same cemetery. They were placed on earth together, he figured, by an all-wise Heavenly Father, into the same family, and they would die that way. "It was the right order of things," he now mumbled.

Days earlier, the wedding ceremonies had been equally heart-rending for the two girl's parents, knowing the two young men they were marrying would have nothing to do with their journeys nor their convictions. Orin and Sarah, when alone afterwards, cried quietly together. Porter was the only one of the children to witness his parents' anguish.

So as their wagon rolled over a hill and his two oldest sisters disappeared from view — Porter's only older sibling, Caroline, and the one just younger than him, Emily, the ones with whom he had most played as a child and to whom he best related — he felt tears trickling down his cheeks. He would never do anything, he determined, to place a wedge in his family like what he was witnessing. The stunt he had pulled at the Eerie Canal was a cruel and selfish one. He knew he would never desert his parents again.

As the two girls disappeared behind them, Porter turned back and faced the road ahead. His parents felt the same feelings he was experiencing, only tenfold. No one spoke for hours.

CHAPTER 6

On their journey to Missouri, the oldest boys — Porter and Peter — hunted wild game each day.

The final leg of the expedition came in late July 1831. It was capped with Porter's introduction to the love of his life . . . the Big Blue River and a barge that arrived to take his and all other families across it.

They were headed for the Big Blue district of Missouri outside Independence. Golden leaves turned bronze as Porter's people lined their wagons at the ferry crossing to board the flat-boat. While similar to but smaller than the barges on the Eerie Canal, this ferry held greater interest to him because, compared to the canal, the Missouri River was wide and wild. Porter was captivated by the feel of the barge on the open, thrilling river. And even the apparel and lifestyle of the boatman — with his trademark clothing and St. Louis style hat and boots that held greater interest to him than those of the canal riverboat runners he had seen eastward on the Eerie — captivated him.

Only one old man ran the barge on the Big Blue. Porter could not wait till he could return and study this river vehicle and even ride it again.

As they traversed down a "road" on the other side of the river in their wagon, his sisters and mother rode atop the buckboard as the boys walked. Orin stopped only a hundred yards from the river, and there he staked out a claim to a wooded five acre parcel with a view of the road leading to the city.

Their people settled along both sides of this road leading to Independence, Missouri. Orin decided to settle as far into the rich, thick woodland as possible, near the end of the settlement along the crude road. Their cabin site was 12 miles in fact from the city. Once staked, the land was purchased for the saints by seven appointed high priests at $1.25 per acre. Orin climbed atop the buckboard and scanned the woods of his property. He felt overwhelmed by the challenge of clearing it yet hopeful he could support his family on the new fertile soil.

This would be their home, without a word spoken. The children were not permitted to disagree, and although Porter would have chosen a parcel closer to the river, still, there were some things one does not confront one's elders on, and he was satisfied to have simply arrived. Sarah had promised her husband he could choose to live anywhere, as long as he followed Joseph's admonitions to make the journey. She was somewhat disconcerted by Orin's choice of a lot so far from town, but was merely grateful he had complied with her wishes to go West, so she said nothing.

Joseph arrived shortly afterwards for a short visit. In early August he dedicated a site at "Colesville," a Mormon settlement incorporating part of Independence and points west for the future temple site where certain ordinances, such as "marriage for all eternity," could be performed. He also placed the first log of the future structure into place, but left Independence August 9 to return to Ohio in order to run the headquarters of the church.

During Joseph's several day visit, he managed to visit Porter only twice, as both he and Porter were busy with struggles for survival — Porter with his family farm and Joseph with the new, toddling church spread throughout two communities hundreds of miles apart. Although $7^1/2$ years younger than he, Porter felt an undefinable hollowness consuming him when Joseph rode away to return to Ohio. Joseph turned back and waved at him.

For hours Porter chopped a thick tree and, taking the reins of his horse, finally felled it and hauled it away. The property was being cleared, one monstrous tree at a time. They were clearing it for the cabin, barn and cropland. In the early morning Porter enjoyed the chill. He heard his brothers and father all day long also clearing trees a couple rods away.

As they cut wood and moved logs into place, the November frosts settled in. Porter discovered an inexplicable frustration at cutting wood with only his family day after day, but remained silent.

Each evening as he chewed on cornbread and beef, he stared at the campfire outside their temporary lean-to, wondering when such tediousness would — if ever — end.

Celebrating their graduation to the larger, permanent home, the family cheered as Orin pounded his mallet at the final log of their new cabin. He turned and proudly faced his family. They all gazed silently at the cleared land and the rich forest surrounding their unseeded property. Porter's smile turned to inquisitiveness when he caught sight of someone in the distance. It was a young lady with long blondish hair disappearing between trees on the road 40 yards distant. She was riding on a buckboard with two other people — a man and a woman. He wondered who she was.

The next day he awakened thinking about her.

That morning he walked to the road and gazed pensively down it. Minutes later, a large puppy ambled down the road and arrived at his feet. It stopped, panted, and stared up at him. It decided Porter was a suitable candidate to take care of it the rest of its life. Porter read the creature's mind, and he smiled. The hound was of unusual size — large and gangly — especially for a puppy, yet pliable and full of attention. It also seemed unusually independent for a dog, and Porter liked that. The dog could forge its own way in a wilderness and faithfully be there whenever Porter would return home. It became more or less the family guard animal, but claimed Porter as it's true master. It would remain with him till its dying day; in short, although he greatly loved the animal, Porter would not take that much notice of it, nor would it of him. They were perfect companions. One thing about the creature Porter did not at all mind — it was the ugliest dog he had ever seen. It was not only a true mut, but was a mixture of all the wrong combinations, which gave it the appearance of something almost hideous. He decided to call it "Ugly," and it responded happily, with tail wagging, every time it heard its name. All the family in fact had no problem with its name.

The cabin's interior was now all but finished, yet he chose to sleep in the cool night air with his dog while the family slept inside. Although his face would be chilled and his throat left faintly sore on chillier mornings, he nonetheless felt hearty and, if anything, invigorated by his oneness with the stars and the cold and the wind.

Two weeks passed. One morning as he chopped into a pine log, his mind went to the girl again. He had no idea how to find her. Perhaps she and her parents belonged to their faith, since numerous converts were swelling their ranks and moving to the Big Blue district. Several days passed and he could not shake her from his mind. Clouds gathered and his mother called him to finish chopping firewood before the storm. He approached his father at noon dinner.

"Pa, can I get supplies in town?"

"You know where to find 'em?"

"It's gotta be on the road going east. Everything's east."

His mother smiled. Everyone in the family joked how far west they lived, although no one dare complain.

"I mean," said Porter, trying to correct his subconscious criticism, "I hear Independence has got everything."

"What about the storm?" bellowed Orin, displeased with his wife's smile over Porter's comment.

"It'll blow over."

Orin sighed, and finally nodded.

Porter suddenly felt overwhelmed with thoughts of young ladies, especially that one he had spotted on the road heading east. He could not wait to scout the wild, wooly town of Independence, Missouri — the first town he had ever had a chance to explore since sprouting such a fondness for the fair ladies of America.

He exuberantly whistled, preparing the horse and wagon to invade the place.

CHAPTER 7

The whole family gathered about, and waved as Porter disappeared down the road. Although it was spring, snow had fallen the previous night. On the road he was dazzled by the sight of snow-covered woods and meadows. He passed dozens of cabins and, as he did so, he scanned the doorways and fields. No young ladies were in sight whom he did not already know — and none of those particularly interested him — most were silly young women who incessantly giggled when around others their age.

He rode several miles. Soon he would be in the city proper, he figured. Around a bend in the woodland road he picked up his pace.

The woods seemed quieter, he mused. Perhaps people were working nearby, so the forest animals and birds were hushed. Porter drove his wagon under a bough heavily weighted with snow. Just at that moment a slight breeze swayed the limb and snow crashed behind him. He whirled to the side and saw a stretch of blonde hair swaying in the same swurry of wind. Twenty yards through the winter brush he discovered the outline of a young woman — or at least so he thought — but as he glanced again the figure was gone. It was possibly the same girl he had seen days earlier, he surmised. Perhaps she lived nearby.

He continued on the woodland road. Suddenly his wagon horse reared and whinnied. Startled, he noticed three people just in front of him — all gathering firewood . . . a middle-aged man, his wife and the young lady, the same who had days earlier captured his imagination. She appeared to be in her late teens.

Porter gazed at the girl and heard the vocal welcome from her mother, but he did not reply. He simply sat atop the buckboard, looking the girl over.

The young woman seemed flattered by his attention, but her mother was embarrassed for him: He found himself floundering through some conversation, something about why he was on the road, getting supplies in town.

"Come in and join us for supper," her mother haltingly said. "We want to know our new neighbors."

"Actually I live twelve miles from here," said Porter.

The mother looked down, curious. "Then why did you come this far alone?" It was unusual to travel without one's parents or other family members for so great a distance.

Porter realized his traveling this far alone might seem strange, perhaps even obvious.

"Hoping to find young ladies in town, are you?" said the girl's father.

Porter gulped. He knew they could see right through him. "Reckon I better be goin'," he said. He was not used to social morays and realized how few he possessed. "I need them supplies."

The girl spoke up, "And I need help getting this firewood inside." She glanced at her mother who smiled.

Porter's heart jumped and he looked straight at the girl, holding back his smile, but not taking the hint.

The girl realized he was not comprehending her comment so she made herself clearer: "So," she continued, "do you feel up for that?"

He beamed. He nodded. He helped.

They talked of farm chores and birthdays at dinner. He was 15 months older than she: His birthday was June 28, 1813 while she was born October 3, 1814 in rural, New York. Porter had been born in Belcher, Massachusetts and at the age of four his family had moved to Manchester, New York, he explained.

Over noon dinner Porter listened to the young lady. He was surprised to learn she and her brother were also active members of his faith but attended a different branch in Independence. The parents had joined recently in New York where Porter had never seen them, and had come straight to Missouri, barely stopping in Ohio. They had arrived days before Porter's group. They were impressed by their new neighbors but, due to commitments on the farm, admitted to rarely attending church. Porter was so absorbed by the young lady's beauty that when he heard her name it passed him. Soon the family seemed anxious to return to work; the awkwardness of his quietness began to bother them, and the conversation seemed to dry out.

How he was going to get her name again without coming across as an actual idiot, he felt, was beyond him but, after finally realizing there was no smooth way into it, he simply climbed atop his wagon, looked down at her and blurted out, "Now what was your name again?"

"Luana. What's yours again?"

Her sparkling green eyes penetrated. She was flirting with him and he liked it.

He knew he would see her again. He wiped cold sweat from his forehead as he answered, "Porter Rockwell."

She nodded. He re-entered the road and drove the wagon toward town. Olive Beebe darted her eyes at her daughter, who was still studying the young man as he disappeared. Luana then looked at her mother. And both women smiled.

CHAPTER 8

Porter's twelve miles home went quickly. He had fantasized of courting a girl in Manchester, New York, until one day he met her and quickly lost interest when she could not hold a coherent conversation. And then he had met two other interesting young ladies at Kirtland, Ohio — interesting until they opened their mouths and bored him to extinction with their talk of mundane farm chores *ad nauseam*. Since then, of course, he had spent all his hours — with absolutely no free time to "hunt" or socialize — consumed by farm chores. His urges and his loneliness were escalating.

At the cabin Porter returned with supplies. His mother greeted him first. "Did you find what you were looking for?"

He blushed.

Sarah studied him. "Well?"

"I reckon."

The next day he resumed plowing land, his mind wandering farther and farther from his tasks. Orin and Sarah commented on his problem and, though neither would state their feelings, they suspected his preoccupation.

The next 48 hours passed as weeks. Porter felt imprisoned.

Upon finishing his chores, his father gave him cash to buy more supplies in town. "But the horse is a bit overworked from plowing; you don't mind walking, do you?"

Porter jumped at the chance. He prepared a bath for himself, took a sharpened knife to his face, then set out in shined boots at high noon.

Across the ice-hardened rode of dirt he trod. He found himself facing feelings he had never before experienced. He knew he was very much smitten by this young lady — although he hardly knew her. He discovered an exhilaration to his walk which he swore even the earth beneath him seemed to feel.

Suddenly he was short of breath . . .

He realized he was afraid of rejection.

He arrived near the woods which housed the young lady's cabin. He ambled up to it with a withered wild flower he had plucked nearby.

Smoke drifted from the fireplace yet not a soul was in sight. He stood at the Beebe's front door and knocked. He felt his throat tighten. The door cracked open and there stood young, beautiful Luana.

"Greetings," she sang. She possessed cultivated social tones, those which he were lacking, and though that bothered him, it also attracted him like a magnet. He held out the flower.

"That's a pretty miserable excuse for a flower," flirted Luana with a wink, "but it's the only one I've received today, so it'll have to do, huh?"

He was taken back by her openness.

She smiled and took his hand, then led him inside.

There, he discovered Isaac Beebe accounting his finances beside the fireplace. The man was prematurely gray, gaunt and pale, consumed by farmwork.

Standing by the mantel, three sets of eyes were glued on the young man. He wasn't sure he had ever felt this awkward. It was even worse than their first conversation because now he was about to ask her out, to be alone with her.

"Won't you sit down?" said Luana.

Porter wasn't sure who said it, such was his nervousness, but he acted on the request.

He gathered his wits and searched her eyes.

"Why don't you ask the boy for some stew," said Mrs. Beebe to Luana.

"Ain't hungry."

"Well, what can I do for you?" Luana finally said after they studied each others' eyes another moment.

"Well, uh, I was just wonderin' . . . I'm going to town about some business, and maybe thought you wanted to tag along." He corrected himself, "Come along."

Luana glanced at her father. He obviously did not want her away from the chores. "I don't know . . . ," she said. " . . . I guess I'm kind of busy cleaning."

"Yeah, well," Porter offered, "I guess I'm gonna be late." He peered into her eyes. He felt mesmerized by the eyes.

Outside, she strolled with him to the road. "I'm sorry," she offered, looking down. "Don't take it as a rejection."

"What do you mean?" he said.

"I guess Papa just likes me around here till sundown."

He thought a moment and spoke up. He tried to speak up. It sounded like a frog trying to speak up and he cleared his throat. He tried again.

"Then I could be back at sundown."

"Sundown?"

"And I'll take you fishing." He was very pleased with his sudden surge of confidence and especially that he had actually asked her out.

"In the dark?"

"There's lots of moonlight lately," he said, feeling better with each passing second.

"Can you be trusted?" she smiled.

He cleared his throat. He never thought of himself as untrustworthy. "I reckon," he said. "Can you?"

She grinned. She liked his cheekiness. She could not hold back blurting out a giggle.

He said, "Better stop while you're ahead. I hate girls that giggle."

"Oh," she said, suddenly drawing a straight face.

He looked at her seriously and both burst out laughing like old friends.

"You know something?" he said. "I like blonde hair."

"Uh, oh," she said, suddenly getting serious. "Better stop while you're ahead. I hate boys that say they like blonde hair."

"Then let's just say I can't stand it," he said, "but I'm willing to see how much I can tolerate it. So I'll be by at sundown." Reading her grin, he felt increasingly relaxed.

"Are you asking or telling me?" she laughed.

"Take it either way you want," he mumbled with a smile, then walked away. He was proud of his sudden confidence. When he was out of her sight, he clenched his fist and swung it in the air.

CHAPTER 9

The crickets chirped loudly. Porter spotted the ferry barge dead ahead through thick trees. A bag of supplies he had just purchased hung over his shoulder. Sundown was still hours away. He had not forgotten the ferry since first feasting his eyes upon it, and wished to spend the remainder of his day fishing from the ferry and daydreaming.

He heard a voice ahead, swearing. As he approached the barge he found Cecil Pritsimmons untying a rope with difficulty. The old boatman was pushing 70, with greying, long locks of hair and a droopy moustache. His black eyes possessed a nervous twitch but his barrel-chested muscular frame gave him a certain confidence when he spoke to others. Porter approached cautiously.

"You still selling it?" said Porter.

Pritsimmons looked him over. "Yeah, so you know somebody who wants to buy it?"

"Maybe."

Pritsimmons resumed untying the rope. "How'd you know it was for sale?"

"Overheard in town," said Porter, clearing his throat. "I could work it off."

"You?" said Pritsimmons, laughing. "I guess you could, but I won't let you."

"You've got nothing to lose," said Porter.

"Only the ferry. I can't give it away when I got a man interested with cash."

"You wouldn't be giving it away," said Porter. "I'll get you paid."

"Well, he's supposed to buy it any day."

"Who?"

"One of my neighbors. He's been eyeing this thing for weeks."

"And if he doesn't?"

"I need cash, boy."

"So," said Porter, suddenly curious, "why are you selling it?"

Ferryman Cecil Pritsimmons confessed of coming into an inheritance from his sister in St. Louis, so he wanted to sell the ferry right away.

Porter had walked right into this; he could hardly contain himself. "How much?"

"Fifty dollars."

"Fifty dollars?" Porter hadn't a penny to his name, and his father's funds were allotted for farm supplies to get them through the first winter and then spring planting.

The proprietor felt it ludicrous that a lad — and a non-established resident at that — could make a turn with the business.

"You ain't serious, lad, what with knowing nothing how to run things?"

"I am."

"Well I'm heading east any week now and your working it off just won't help."

"Mister," said Porter. "I know you'll get your money if you let me work it off . . . I'll give you—"

"Never mind, boy," said Pritsimmons. "I'm not interested."

Porter studied him a moment, and finally looked at the barge. He wasn't in the mood to gaze at something he couldn't have anyway, so he turned and walked away.

Luana Beebe trod from the wood shed towards her cabin, making her way across pine needles reflecting in the moonlight. A figure loomed in front of her. Startled, she slowed.

"It's been an hour since sunset," said Porter to the young lady. "Do you like working in the dark?"

"Papa said I didn't finish my chores. I can't leave with you till I finish. He said it's a busy month. Maybe next month."

Porter felt the wind knocked out of him. She would not look at him. He wondered if she were merely making an excuse. He strode away, mumbling, "Yeah, well, see ya."

At his cabin, questions drifted from his parents. From his disinterested answers, they knew something was amiss, something beyond the mere frustration he had recently displayed from tedious farm life. He sat at the fireplace warming his feet. He did not even hear their "Good night."

The next morning he awoke to an almost hopeless day. But by noon as he chopped firewood a thought eased in and would not let go.

He chopped harder.

That evening, just after sunset, he set out for Luana's cabin once again.

He spotted her carrying firewood. He approached her from the side. She was startled. When she beheld his face, she was simultaneously relieved and annoyed.

He was curious at her disturbance. "I don't bite little girls in the dark," he informed her.

"You do have some cheek, don't you?" She strode past him. "Didn't you hear what I said last night?"

"I'll help with your chores," he said. "That's the ticket." He wondered if his idea would work.

Luana noticed for the first time, from the wet shirt tight on his skin, his extraordinarily muscular shoulders. She attempted to cover her attraction:

"I'm busy, but all right."

CHAPTER 10

At the ferry station Cecil Pritsimmons gathered firewood. Porter strode up to him.

"Persistent plucker, ain't ya?" said Pritsimmons.

"I can make it work. And you'll get your cash, I promise."

"You keep dreamin', boy."

"I don't need to," said Porter. "I know you need something out of this ferry . . . And I bet it ain't sellin', is it?"

"Well, if you come up with forty dollars and split profits for the rest, we could talk."

"I'll split from the first dollar, 'cause I don't have forty dollars," said Porter.

"No, I can't do that."

"I know you want to move soon, so let's strike a deal," said Porter.

The man turned on him, his voice graveling and harsh. "And just how do you plan on running this rig — you know anything about riverboating?"

"That's why I'm back."

"Expect me to teach you?"

"Darn right."

Pritsimmons leaned on his ax and with a stern eye pierced Porter's. He couldn't help but like this lad. He'd have to think about it.

The next day, Luana Beebe and her brother, George, ambled down the muddy road to Independence, dressed in their finest attire. George was large-eyed and sober-faced. In the mud behind Luana came sloshing feet. Luana was impatient with her brother constantly lagging behind, driven by some interminable habit of always arriving late for church. And, somehow, always muddy. He was two years her senior but, for a twenty year old, remarkably scatter-brained and dirty.

George was light-skinned, green-eyed, tall and lanky. His wife of seven months was also of their faith, but she was visiting relatives in Ohio for the month. His new home was less than a mile from his parents and sister.

She assumed her usual, impatient eyes of ice, and turned to glare. "Watch how you're walking and don't get mud all over my dress!"

She then noticed she was barking at someone other than her brother. She turned red. It was Porter.

He slowed beside her. "But this mud would make a pretty good pattern on that white dress, don't you think?"

She tried to act unamused.

"How far is it to the church?" he added.

"Just around the bend. How come you didn't go to your own branch?" said Luana.

"Felt like something different. I like a lot of things different. I'm getting out of farming into a new line of work soon — and it's more exciting than a bucking mule ride."

"Oh," is all she managed.

Porter did not know it, but Luana was beginning to feel smothered. He had seen her two consecutive nights and, though she had appreciated his efforts — taking the three hour walk each way from his home after his own chores just to help her — she had discovered by the end of the second evening that she was already becoming annoyed by his over-attentiveness. Every time she would glance at him she would catch him staring admiringly. It was disconcerting.

At church they eventually arrived. The building was a neighbor's large cabin just west of Independence. Porter opened the door. Luana entered and took a seat. He followed her in and sat beside her. Her brother finally wandered in late and sat with friends.

The service began with opening remarks from the bishop's counselor conducting the meeting. Soon they sang a hymn. Whether Porter's loud, boisterous, off-key singing was meant to simply draw attention to himself or to embarrass her, she was not certain, but it was successfully accomplishing both tasks at once, she decided.

After the opening prayer Porter whispered to her, "Took years of practice to do that. I could break the bishop's glasses if I wanted."

For the first time in several hours she found him amusing. And though she still felt somewhat bothered by his constant attention, she realized for the first time ever that with this boy she could feel, at least, comfortable. There was no need to try to impress him. Not with the way she dressed. Not with the way she spoke. She was surprised at herself for taking his hand.

He felt his stomach fly upward — much like the feeling of jumping off a high bluff into a lake. He had never felt a young woman's hand. He'd only fantasized sitting like this with a girl he knew deep down probably didn't exist. But now, with actual, physical touch, he was sailing through the sky. This was the girl of his dreams, he decided.

She glanced at him out the side of her eye, and caught a twinkle as he stared ahead at the first speaker of the church meeting. She had to admit . . . she was somewhat intrigued by this ruffian.

The speakers in Sacrament Meeting gave stirring messages. He didn't hear a word, until mention was made of Joseph:

Joseph would remain in Ohio, but he and the church there were enduring hardships — financial hardships. The Ohio bank was faltering and some of the saints were even blaming Joseph, who had admitted from the beginning he was no businessman. Indeed not just Kirtland, Ohio but all the nation was in a depression. Some however chose to blame Joseph.

Another piece of salient news was announced from the pulpit: The Lieutenant Governor of Missouri, Lilburn W. Boggs, had just requested their people to not vote at the polls if they wished to avoid trouble. After the report on Joseph, and through the remainder of the meeting, Porter whispered comments to Luana, some profound, some amusing, some inane. But he kept her curious as to why he possessed that strange twinkle, and she was certain by the closing hymn, when again he would bellow out his version of the melody, that he had no intention of impressing her — at least in any conventional way. She liked the fact he was different from her other young admirers which, he was to soon learn, were numerous, if not voluminous.

After the meeting, a small group of hopeful beaus surrounded her. Porter had not been expecting this, and felt for the first time in his life, straight-out jealousy. "Where did all these dog-breaths come from?" he mumbled to himself.

CHAPTER 11

As he studied the faces of other young men "waiting in line" as it were to flirt with her, he realized they were all jealous — and all very competitive — for her. He had thought he had "discovered" her like a child in the forest — and an enchanting one at that — but now he was facing grim reality. He realized he would have to position himself differently than these other young hustlers. While they gathered about Luana in a circle he simply leaned against the doorway several yards away and began whistling. Noticing his antics did not command her attention, he then began softly singing the lyrics of some beer song to the tune of "God Be With You Till We Meet Again."

Several of the young chaps glared. While talking to the other young men, she overheard Porter's singing and began to smile, but caught herself. Porter saw it and grinned.

Finally he swaggered up to her, took her arm, and proceeded out of the building. "Sorry, boys," he announced, "but the lady feels faint, and I gotta be ready to catch her."

They watched her leave with him, mouths agape.

She was curious at her growing realization that she really did like his off-beat charm.

On the road home Porter kept her arm in his and joked of the lads seeking her favor. "If that tall fellow—" he said.

"The handsome, exciting one?" she interjected.

"The handsome, exciting one — if he tried lifting that big ax your daddy owns, to chop a log, I'm afraid he'd take off his foot with it."

"He is a bit uncoordinated," she added with a chuckle.

"But then, who knows," he resumed, "maybe you like fellows with no feet."

By the time they reached her cabin, she was finding him even more entertaining, at least more so than the lads she knew from church with their incessant hunting and fishing tales, bragging how big the game was they bagged in order to impress her. She discovered she was disappointed when Porter announced he had to leave.

As she walked with him to the edge of her property in the thick of the woods near the road, she stopped and stared into his face. "And just what was this work you claim is more fun than a horse to ride?" she said, referring to his earlier claim.

"I'm still working on it," he said, "but it will be mine. I'm just learning the ropes."

"The ropes?"

"I'll give you another clue when I return."

"I'll hold you to it," she said. Then he drew her close and, despite the rules and mores of civilized society for young, unbetrothed couples, he moved his mouth next to hers. She felt an excitement tingling through her soul, but before kissing him, she proceeded to pull herself away. She knew she was too attracted to this ruffian for her own good and, as she quickly said goodbye and headed home on the road alone in a fast gait, not 10 feet away she muttered aloud to herself, "Oh, why not?" She turned back and ran up to him and was about to fall into his face for a gigantic kiss when she again stopped, and said, "Why? Because I'm still sane." With that she pulled herself away again before kissing him and ran off, afraid of her self-discovered, increasing vulnerability.

'Someday . . . ' he thought, 'I'm going to give her a kiss she'll never forget.' And with that he came up with the plan of a lifetime.

The sun set over the river. Beside the sloshing waters was a large meadow where all local members of their faith gathered to dance and eat. It was a Saturday evening church social.

Beside the muddy river bank sat numerous picnic tables, at one end of which the pie table attracted several teenage boys like bees to pollen as they hovered over the delectable pastries. Several boys used the pies as an excuse to approach Luana who was sitting nearby. She invited them to sit. Soon, seven of them were surrounding her, all sitting, flirting and laughing.

Presently Porter strode up. Luana glanced at him askance: He was the only one not "dressed up."

He scowled at the other boys, observed them all in Sunday

best, and analyzed Luana's fine attire. All he could think to say was:

"Wanna dance?"

"I will later." She was busy soaking up the attention from the coterie of past and potential, future beaus.

As Porter turned, one of the boys blurted out, "You can take a good boy off the farm but you can't take the farm off a good boy."

Porter whirled back, grabbing the fellow's lapel, then caught himself and patted the young man on the shoulder. "Nice suit." He turned away. "You boys have a good time." He knew their families all worked the land as well, but mostly prided themselves on specific crafts which had been in their families for generations. Additionally, their parents were better educated than his, so the term they applied was meant to pigeon-hole him as nothing but a farmer, an easy label for him since he had showed up to the gathering in work clothes.

"Oh, we will have a good time," responded one as they all laughed.

"And so will I," mumbled Porter.

With Luana leaving her seat to dance with the tallest boy, Porter moved behind several tables and slipped a rope around a leg of her now-empty chair.

He then snuck away. From behind all the picnic tables he waited and watched, feeling that gnawing jealousy again as Luana continued holding hands with the one particular tall boy after she had danced with him. Then she sat again in her chair, with the tall fellow sticking to her like a fly to flypaper.

Presently, Porter's horse began moving forward with Porter leading it.

The rope sprung tight.

Suddenly, across the dance a scream was heard. Luana's chair flipped over and she went flying. She landed face down in the muddy river bank. She tried standing but fell again into the soupy mess. Now knee deep in glop, she glanced up and spotted all seven admirers at the pie table standing safely on the grassy knoll, staring down at her, fearful of ruining their own Sunday clothes and incurring the wrath of their mothers if they dare attempt a rescue. The tallest boy gazed at her and shrugged.

Casually, Porter came striding across the knoll. He glanced at her down in the mud, took a deep breath, and dove in.

Three hundred people were now gathered and ogling from the river bank meadow above. When they beheld young Porter emerging from the mud, carrying Luana safely onto the grass, both of them now drenched in brown, they let out a cheer and broke into spontaneous applause. Luana did not know how she had fallen into the mud but, despite her red face, was extremely grateful for her rescuer, the only "man" in the lot. Arriving atop the river bank, she caught sight of each of the seven beaus, and gave all a sharp, scornful scowl.

CHAPTER 12

Beads of sweat dropped from Luana as she milked the family cow. Suddenly the wide door swung open and the September cool air refreshed her forehead. Dawn was 30 minutes away and the lantern lit the barn's interior.

Porter burst through the open door. Luana was startled. He reached down, grabbed her milk bucket, and took a swig. As he set it back under the cow, he wiped his mouth with his tongue to erase the milk moustache.

With a sly look on her face Luana stood and sashayed to a different bucket across the barn.

"I heard," she said, "something from a girlfriend. She saw 'someone' at the dance tie a rope around my chair." Suddenly Luana, revealing a wicked smile, grabbed the bucket, ran to Porter and dunked it over his head. Fresh, loose, green cow manure oozed down his face and flowed all about his head. Then she caught a gleam in his eye. She shuddered at the prospects, screamed, and took out running. He chased her up the loft ladder.

Arriving atop the loft she looked back. Porter was climbing after her, still wearing the bucket like a helmet. Within seconds he reached the loft.

Backed against a wall in the loft, Luana screamed and laughed simultaneously, hopelessly watching him come forward.

Standing suddenly, Porter did not see a roof beam directly above his head. With the bucket still on his head, he clonked the beam with a resounding thud and his eyes floated upward.

This time she screamed in fear. She watched as Porter, obviously out cold, fell over backwards, crashing down from the barn loft to the floor below into a foot of hay.

Luana fearfully approached the edge of the loft and peered over it. She beheld Porter lying with all fours spread out, the bucket still helmeted on his head.

She scampered down the loft ladder and knelt beside him. Lifting the bucket from his head, she wiped the cow mud from his face.

"Porter? . . ." She panted heavily, fearing the worst. "Porter!" She discerned his lifeless look.

Suddenly, he grabbed her, and she shouted. He clutched her in a wrestler's hold and rolled with her toward a cow pie 10 feet away. She spotted it and screamed:

"No!"

But he kept rolling with her, over and over, straight towards it.

Three feet from it he stopped.

"Please, Porter," she laughed.

"You really don't know how badly I want to do this," he said.

"Porter, my good friend, wasn't the mud thing last night enough?"

He chuckled, "You think only a mud bath is equal to a bucket of manure over my clean-bathed head? You're dreamin', honey!"

He rolled over once more.

She stared at the pile, now two feet from her face. "Porter, please!"

"Think of this as Russian roulette," he muttered. "We're not sure whose head is going to have the honors of rolling through this."

"No, please," she implored in more serious tones.

They rolled towards it one more time and . . . squish — his head landed in it.

She screeched with laughter.

Then she noticed another pie four feet beyond.

He saw what she saw.

"No, Porter . . . ! "

It was his turn to laugh.

Then he began rolling towards it — three quick times — and stopped. She stared at the new pile and merely shook her head. "Don't you dare!"

"I do dare!" he said — and, grabbing her firmly, he rolled one more time and SPLAT.

Her left cheek was covered with it. She felt like crying but inexplicably broke out laughing. Then he completed the roll-over and her entire head mushed through it.

Porter sat up while she simply lay there. However, in what he considered a gentlemanly gesture, he began pulling blobs of the gunk out of her hair.

She was now laughing and crying at the same time.

He announced loudly, "I can do that, too." Then he lunged forward, face down beside her, his mouth and nose "sploshing" into the pile.

She shrieked.

He lifted himself up and wiped the brown-green mess away with his hand, spitting out manure, then also broke out laughing.

"You," she shouted, "are the most disgusting young man I have ever met! Dirty, filthy, sweaty, smelly — nay — stinking... creature I have ever beheld... in all my days!"

He stared at her and lost his smile. She studied his eyes and gradually lost hers. Their faces moved toward each other... and suddenly their lips met. With manure dripping off her hands she wrapped her arms around his back and held him tightly, then proceeded to kiss him harder than she had ever imagined. Immediately, she found herself wondering aloud, "What the devil am I doing?"

CHAPTER 13

Porter's parents could hear him outside singing as he bounced the last hundred yards to his home but not quite so much off-key as usual, yet louder than they had ever heard him.

"What's this all about?" his father asked upon Porter practically pouncing through the portal.

"Nothing."

Porter's gait was equally alive as he bounded along the dirt road to Luana's the next day. Actually he had every right to be exhausted after a full day's labor on the farm, but the long walk, rather than tiring, invigorated him.

"I think you're lucky I have errands this way so much lately," he said tongue-in-cheek as they strolled through the woods toward the ferry.

"So what is this wonderful contraption you wish to show

me? It better be nothing less than wonderful: This is more than a stroll we're taking."

He excitedly pulled her along, his hand firmly gripping hers. She could scarcely keep up. They fought through thick brush and arrived at the ferry landing. When he pointed ahead to the barge shimmering in the water, her eyes widened.

"Why didn't we take the road here?" she said.

"Shortcuts are better. 'Saves time."

"My clothes are in shreds, so this better be good. What am I supposed to be seeing?"

"That."

"Pritsimmons' old barge?"

"Soon to be mine."

She forced a smile. "That's your dream?"

He nodded.

She said, "You learned how it all works — even in bad weather?"

"He's got to decide to sell first, but I know he will — and then he'll learn me the business.

She cleared her throat.

"I've never ridden one," she muttered, "since we crossed the river to get here, but I'm sure you know what you're doing."

Her question had to do with its capability of making money, but she did not clarify her concerns.

Pritsimmons was not in the best of moods, but acquiesced to Porter's requests: Soon he and Luana were on the ferry in the moonlight, talking of their feelings about life, laced with a kiss or two. She reigned in her reservations about the barge and simply enjoyed his companionship.

Two hours later they were walking towards her cabin. Somewhere between the garden and the door she said something she had never before uttered to a boy. "When can we get together again?"

He smiled in her eyes.

Upon entering her cabin and watching him stride away, she kicked herself for being so forward. Genteel society just doesn't do such things, she thought, and that was one of the things on which she had prided herself. Then again, she mused, the rough-hewn farm boy was anything but genteel. Her mother was the only one in the cabin still awake. She had warned Luana that if you show too much interest in a boy he will no longer feel challenged and will lose interest.

"Luana," her mother whispered so as not to awaken her husband, "are you feeling safe with this boy?"

"I don't know."

Porter entered his own cabin at two A.M.

His father noticed, but pretended to sleep.

Next day while clearing land, Porter rested on his ax handle. He did not know how to answer his father's sudden question:

"How well do you know her?"

"What her?"

"I was your age once, son. This is four nights in a row you're home late. Real late. And it ain't affecting the chores yet but soon will. I' been there."

Porter blushed. He studied his dad's face and finally decided to let it out.

"I'm getting married."

His father coughed. "Come again?"

"I think you heard me, Pa."

"Who to?"

"Some girl."

"What girl?"

"Met her outside Independence — she goes to the branch there."

"What do her parents think of this?"

"They don't know about it."

"You plan to tell them?"

"Eventually."

"Son, you've got to get her pa's hand for this."

"Maybe."

"Well, we've talked about the rules of life . . . and the right thing," said Orin authoritatively, proud of his firm family instructions over the years. "And you've got to get his permission to marry this daughter of his."

"I don't believe in it."

Orin sighed with exasperation. "Tradition is tradition. And we don't change it." He calmed somewhat. "So how're you gonna support her? We don't even know what kind of crops will turn out this year."

"I'll hunt if I have to — I can keep us alive."

"Somebody'll have to."

"Don't worry."

"That's easily said, son. Now, when is this wedding?"

"Soon as she agrees to it." Porter picked up his ax and resumed chopping.

His father stared at him and shook his head. "You mean she don't even know about it yet?"

"She don't need to."

Orin Rockwell smiled and walked away. The thought crossed his mind how much mockery his son could bring on the family by these half-baked plans, but he couldn't really care less about such things, and then he could not help but chuckle. He recalled how it took five tries before a young lady finally said yes to his own proposal, and that fifth girl was his wife Sarah.

Porter watched his father trudge up a ravine, and he could hear him belly-laughing now. Eyes wide with indignation, he wondered what was so all-fired funny.

CHAPTER 14

Over the next week Porter became extremely familiar with the road to Independence.

Luana would await his visit each evening, counting on his characteristic door knock three hours after sundown. She would discover herself growing less and less patient until the moment he would actually arrive. She also felt alternately charmed and uncertain by his assertive nature, but little did she realize its basis: As his familiarity with her grew, so did his confidence.

Luana's parents demanded he be gone by midnight. With their church's precepts in mind, and Porter's staunch determination to not disappoint Joseph in any way, he nevertheless felt tempted by her physical attraction, yet remained in possession of his wits.

But when he finally brought up the subject of marriage, she balked.

"I thought you liked me just as much," he said.

"We've only been courting two weeks."

He returned home that night frustrated and anguished.

His feelings evolved into a new phase. Confusion coupled with exhaustion. His lack of sleep began wearing on him. His father said nothing, seeing his prediction fulfilled. Porter would arrive home by three each morning and awaken by five. Moreover, his father was not gracing his social life by awarding him the extra hours for sleep needed for farm survival.

Some nights after visiting Luana, Porter felt tempted to simply crawl under brush by the roadside to sleep, but never did; he always made the twelve mile walk.

Then influenza hit him. He did not know what it was since disease was considered a curse to most people of the Missouri territory; however, he sensed it had something to do with the exhausting courtship.

He continued visiting Luana, not missing a day. In the back of his mind he feared other beaus were waiting like vultures at the very first sign of problems.

Soon she, too, became ill, as did her entire family, but she insisted on seeing him.

After a week of such struggle with the illness it finally dissipated and, though still frustrated with unfulfilled infatuation gnawing at him, Porter could at least travel with new, renewed health.

Yet she still remained noncommittal about marriage, and one night so told him.

The next day he decided to not see her; instead, he stopped at the ferry to see if Cecil Pritsimmons had decided to help him master the craft of business and boating. This old river pilot, though he liked Porter, still felt impatient with the lad, fearing the long-term payment enterprise futile yet somehow strangely fulfilling, being able to pass on his knowledge to one so passionately persistent in learning. He stared at Porter a long moment, thinking.

Young Rockwell could earn his training, Pritsimmons finally decided, by his chores. The young man was elated.

Beginning the next night, Porter would arrive shortly after dark and work an hour for the proprietor, then receive an hour or two's instruction. He did not see Luana that entire night, nor any night that week for two reasons: First, his pride was still hurt over her noncommittal attitude and second, he had to convince Pritsimmons he could effectively run the operation in order to even be considered a serious buyer on terms only.

A week after not seeing Luana, there was a knock at the door. His parents were surprised to discover in the threshold a stunningly attractive, well-dressed young lady with cultivated tones. It was their first time to meet her.

"May I see Porter?"

Mrs. Rockwell merely nodded her inside. She wondered how such a lady of class and flair could be interested in her rugged son.

Porter gulped and glanced at each of his siblings and parents, all with mouths ajar.

"Well," said Luana to Porter, "it's a lovely sunset. Shall we saunter off into it?"

He glanced at his parents and smiled like a drunk frog.

CHAPTER 15

As Porter and Luana walked moments later to the river, they gazed at the silhouetted woods across the shore. It was twilight. Luana broke the silence.

"Your parents seem very nice."

"They are," he responded.

"I guess you wonder why I'm here."

He said nothing.

"Did I surprise you showing up here and all?"

He nodded.

"Well I suppose you've surprised me not coming over the past week," she said.

"And?"

She considered not answering but blurted it out anyway:

"I've missed you."

"Same here."

"So where were you?"

"Learning the ropes."

"The barge?"

He nodded. "I'll own it in a week. Sort of. I'm getting it on terms."

"Mama would strangle me if she knew I was telling you this but I've more than missed you," she said.

He merely smiled, but inside felt wild buffaloes stampeding. She reached over and kissed him a second, then turned and left. "I'll see you tomorrow?" she called over her shoulder.

"If I was a betting man," he said, "yeah, I think I'd bet on it."

The next night and all that week Porter would finish his family farm chores early, work and train under Pritsimmons three hours, then finally slip away to see Luana. All those nights he would arrive at her cabin just before midnight. They would visit only a short while before he would again launch the long trek home.

A week later he approached her again with the topic of marriage — in a jesting manner to test the waters.

"I'll think about it," is all she offered.

"Wait a minute. Wasn't it you that tracked me down to my place and woke me up 'cause you couldn't stay away?"

"Oh, did I inconvenience you?" she teased.

"You know what I mean. You went all-out to get me back when I wasn't over here for a week, and now — "

"Now, what?" she said with anger entering her voice.

"Stringing me along is what it looks like."

"Stringing? Look, Porter, I don't want to lose you, but marriage is a long way from where we are at the moment, and I just need to think about it longer, and you should, too."

"Are you serious?"

"I am serious," she said.

"How much longer?"

"Who knows how long it takes to figure something like this out?" she said.

"Yeah, I reckon," he mumbled, seeing that pressuring her was only causing her to retreat.

"Son," said Orin, "five tries was the magic number for me. And I figure you're twice as good-looking and smart as I was, so maybe it'll take you two and a half."

Porter's mind was elsewhere. "Two and a half what?" he said grumpily.

"Two and a half tries — girls — before you get hitched to the right one."

"Two and a half? How can I propose to two and a half girls?"

Orin rubbed his chin. "Well, I reckon the girl after the second one could be a dwarf."

"Real funny, Pa."

Orin could see his son not being consoled very easily. "You'll live through this, son."

"Thanks, Pa," said Porter, a mite miffed as he jumped from the kitchen table on which he was sitting when he noticed his ma approaching from the back pasture. He immediately headed out the door to work, wanting to avoid a lecture about sitting on the kitchen table. Orin, left alone in the cabin, watched his boy with concern: He stared at Porter's hasty departure with knitted brows.

When Sarah entered she noticed Orin's concern.

"He going to ever be the same again?" she said, trying for a smile from her husband.

Orin seemed weighted with worry. "I think I remember how much he's hurting inside."

CHAPTER 16

Independence, Missouri was a rough and tumble, mud-soaked frontier town. On a wooden city downtown sidewalk, Porter strolled hand-in-hand with Luana. They spotted several children gathered ahead outside the general store. As they approached the children they came upon a traveling puppet show where the puppet-master's wagon was parked parallel to the store while a small, portable stage faced the sidewalk, protruding from the puppet-show wagon.

Sunset was an hour away so Porter needed to obtain his mother's sewing supplies at the store quickly. After he did, he and Luana stopped amidst the laughing children.

Behind them Porter noticed a group of parents who had paid a penny each to the puppeteer for a half hour's entertainment. Most of the adults seemed as enthralled by the theatre story as their children. The puppet master's wife meanwhile sat atop the buckboard counting the pennies and adding them to a sack of coins. She would join him for the second act and manipulate some of the puppets.

Porter smiled. One puppet baited another to go with him for a walk, then tripped him, which flew the puppet into the air with a somersault. All children and adults roared. Amidst their peels of laughter Porter suddenly discerned other, derisive laughter a block away. He glanced downstreet and discovered an unexpected scene: His neighbor David Patten was surrounded by four locals, all shoving him over and over, backing him toward a horse trough. Once they had him backed up to it, the gang's leader threatened to punch him. Patten winced and ducked, but his main tormentor merely extended his hand to shake it. Surprised, Patten forgave the ruse and smiled, then offered his own hand to shake when the fellow pushed David backwards. He fell into the horse trough with a loud splash and more laughter. The four men turned to walk away, when they beheld Porter standing before them, arms folded, gazing at them confidently. The four men stopped.

"What do you want, stranger?" said the gang's leader.

Porter sighed, "I had the same question for you."

"What's it too you, boy?"

"That's my neighbor there," said Porter.

"You know," said the biggest among them, "I've often wondered what kind of contest we could have — to see who could drink the most horse trough water in one sitting. I think you have just been recruited."

At that they charged at Porter.

Sizing up their positions as they ran at him, Porter stepped to the side, tripped one local, twirled, and elbowed another in the face. Knocking him cold, he spun and punched another in the neck, de-winding him, and grabbed the fourth. He shoved that fellow head first into the first one he had tripped, and both men's heads collided: They collapsed unconscious into the muddy street.

Porter turned and spotted Luana standing on the sidewalk, staring at the scene aghast. He then noticed the small crowd of the puppet show, including all the children, gazing at him rather than at the show.

Porter called out, "I'd charge admission, but I didn't bring any change."

Several chuckled and a couple applauded, disgusted by the bullies' treatment of the immigrants. But another group across the street came from a saloon and one of them barked at him:

"If you immigrant folk think you're going to vote, you think twice. Our neighbors have settled long before you people, and got a right to the say of things here abouts."

A dozen others outside the saloon applauded the spokesman.

Porter helped David Patten onto his horse and suggested quietly that he stay away from town a few days till the storm blows over.

Patten looked down at Porter from his saddle, "I reckon you be the one to stay away from here awhile. They seem to like me. I'm someone they can play with."

Porter smiled and headed to the sidewalk. He was surprised by something and stopped. Luana was gone. Nowhere at all to be seen.

A glance to the end of Main Street revealed her riding away, driving the buckboard alone.

CHAPTER 17

Two miles and 20 minutes later Porter knocked at her door. Luana would not answer it. Her mother came to the threshold and said, "She told me what happened. She doesn't take to violence like you people."

"My people?"

"Certainly not ours, I'm pleased to say."

"Pleased?"

"We're befriending the long-time settlers here, Porter, and when our new friends began pointing their fingers and laughing, we could see the handwriting on the wall: We have to live with these folk; they are our true friends, and they're good people. Religious enough for us. We think Joseph is fine, and support Luana and George in whatever path they wish to follow. But you and your friend created a spectacle on the street today from what Luana said."

"My friend David created a spectacle? All he did was get pushed around."

"Then just you were the spectacle?"

"I reckon so, ma'am, and I apologize. But I just don't take to — "

Olive Beebe cut in, "You had your own little show out there, from what Luana tells me."

"Maybe I shouldn't apologize," said Porter. "Don't you stand up for your friends?"

"We're a city here," said Olive. "And our family hails from the East where it's civilized."

"I'm from New York as well."

"So you should remember that we set examples of civilization here, young man. We don't further the cause of savages by acting like them, no matter how others may act."

Porter blew out a silent sigh.

"And it seems to me like not just you but several of your friends here are talking violence. I've overheard some of our neighbors on the west road."

Porter did not have a problem with Luana's folks not being active with their people, figuring they could choose whatever path suited them, but he was concerned over their accusation that his friends promoted violence.

"I'm sorry I lost my head a little," said Porter. "But don't judge your neighbors on what I do or what a few others say. The last thing anybody wants is a row. I've just always had a little temper when I see bullies, that's all."

Luana appeared behind her mother. "I have never been so embarrassed, Porter. I knew all four of those men — they gave us planting seeds when we first arrived. True, they're rough sorts, but they have good hearts and extending hands to help others in need as.much as any people I've known."

"David Patten looked about as much in need as anyone I've known," said Porter, feeling his neck heating. "And I didn't exactly see the hand extended to him a helping one." At that Porter turned and marched away, leaving Luana and her mother standing on the porch staring at him as he disappeared downroad.

The river's waves rippled onto the shore. A campfire flickered beside the waters. Two men sat upon river rocks. Porter sat across the fire from his father and focused beyond his face at the barge across the water, shimmering in the moonlight.

"I've always dreamed of a land of peace," said Orin.

"Why can't it be more than a dream?" said his son.

"It can be. People don't have to greet us with prejudice everywhere."

"I'm not sure they are here, Papa."

"You don't see the signs?"

"I just see good folk trying to get by," said Porter.

"They're not like us."

"Wait a minute — did you say, 'us?'" said Porter.

Orin darted his eyes about.

"Is that a slip of the tongue or what?"

"I don't know what you're talking about," said Orin.

"Yeah you know what I'm talking about."

"All right," said Orin, "maybe I do know what you're talking about." He began walking away.

Porter stood. "So . . . what are you talking about?"

"I think you know."

"I don't or I wouldn't be asking!" Porter followed behind him, "Papa, what have you got up your sleeve?"

"I think it's obvious, son."

"Maybe to you."

"And you," said Orin.

"O.K.," said his son smiling, "if you want me to guess, I'll take a stab at it."

"No, I'll just 'fess up right here and now," said Orin. "If that's what you really want," he added with a smile.

Porter gazed wide-eyed and expectantly at him.

"All right," said Orin, "all right. I'll tell you everything." He then paused . . . And pondered.

"So tell me!"

"All right. I have gone and done it. I have gained religion. I've been baptized."

"Really!" exclaimed Porter.

"Yeah, I went and joined the Baptist Church."

Porter stared, speechless.

"And the very next day," Orin continued, "I said to myself, 'What have I gone and done? What'll my family think of this?' So I went to Brother Pettegrew next door and told him to tell the bishop to go ahead and baptize me."

Porter beamed, and gave him a hug.

The next morning they made preparations for Orin Rockwell's baptism. His family excitedly welcomed the bishop,

David Partridge, into their home for a private interview, then planned a service at the river with friends and neighbors. Porter's dog ambled in and slobbered on the bishop's hand. Pretending to pet the animal, he wiped his hand across the dog's fur . . . only to find the beast had rolled in the ripe carcass of a dead woodland creature.

Shaking hands with each of the Rockwells, the bishop left, his appetite ajar.

The Rockwells, sniffing their own hands, walked quietly to a narrow stream leading to the river and washed their hands thoroughly. Sarah had possessed the foresight to bring a bar of homespun soap. There, they discovered the bishop, and all laughed heartily. They also lent him the soap. Porter then called his dog:

"Ugly, come over here."

Ugly simply stared, sensing what was on his master's mind, afraid to lose the glorious perfume he had within the hour gleefully applied to his heretofore monotonous, lifeless, plain, black fur.

"I said, come here!"

The big black dog ambled over to Porter's side.

Porter glanced away, then suddenly surprised his pet by charging it. The dog got no more than a yard when Porter tackled it to the ground.

Amidst cheers from his family, Porter picked up Ugly and carried him to the creek. Into the water they both splashed, and Porter wrestled with him a full minute while applying Sarah's rugged soap.

He scrubbed the dog thoroughly and the dog finally scampered out of the stream wagging his tail. Feeling invigorated, he headed into the barn for a good, solid nap. Porter, covered with perfume, now had to bathe head to toe in the stream, applying soap generously, while his mother retrieved a clean set of clothes.

After that ordeal, Orin called Porter into the front room. "I want to thank you, Porter, for your example. I've read the *Book of Mormon* on the sly. Twice even. I know this is the right thing. You and Sarah and the others have been real patient. And I guess I couldn't fight it any longer. The Spirit of the Lord has testified it's all true. I know it is. Every word."

Sarah hugged her husband and retired with him outside for a walk.

Later, Porter sat alone with his father at the fireplace when everyone else had gone to bed.

"Well," said Porter. "I guess I'm all right in someone's eyes — even if it is only my pa's."

"What's that, boy?"

Porter merely glanced at him, then down.

Orin understood, knowing his son must be having more problems with Luana. "I'm sorry, boy."

"Papa, I don't want to take away from your day, but have you got any idea what I can do to not lose this chance?"

"There will be other chances," said Orin. "I promise you."

"This one chance," said Porter. "Is the one I want."

"Maybe your mother is right. She sees problems ahead. Mamas are good at that."

Porter cut him off. "I said I know what I want. And that I don't want to lose her."

Orin sighed and pondered a moment. "You want to know a secret?"

Porter studied him.

"Flowers. Moonlight. Dinner. The right place. A romantic setting. And then as the gypsies used to say with their traveling show, 'Presto.'"

"Magic?"

Orin looked at him and nodded.

CHAPTER 18

Moonlight beaming on them and flowers resting on a dinner table in front of her is not what Luana had ever expected... on a barge.

There on the deck she sat across Porter, holding back a smile. 'This is ridiculous,' she thought but, taking a bite of his fresh-roasted chicken, suddenly reversed herself and exclaimed:

"This is great!" Followed by a bite of his northern-style, moist cornbread, laced with corn kernels, butter, cream and buttermilk, the meal truly surprised her.

"And this cornbread is wonderful!" she sang.

Porter smiled. "Now try the potato stew and green beans and sweet potato pie."

"This is the best pie I've ever had!"

"Thank you."

"You're deceiving me," she shouted.

"Come again?"

"You're taking credit — you're deceiving me," she reiterated, loudly now and with a broad smile.

He smiled and looked down.

She spoke softly. "You can't tell me you made this."

"All right."

"See, I told you!"

He smiled again.

"So!" she laughed. "What's the truth? Did you really make this or not?"

"Believe what you want," he smiled.

"O.K. All right. I believe you really made this. Am I correct?"

He nodded. Then shook his head no. "Maybe."

She stared at his face.

He broke into a smile.

She realized the truth. "You're hired."

Porter had learned it all from his mother and sisters, who prided themselves on kitchen fare. Only, he rarely cooked, not particularly enjoying the task.

After dessert she leaned back. "I'm stuffed. I've never had such a meal."

He arose and ambled to the rope railing at the edge of the barge.

Back at her chair she gazed at him. "You borrowed this boat, I suppose?"

"Rented it."

"My, you do know how to treat the ladies."

"I look at you like that moonlight looks at you," he said turning and facing her, his back leaning against the rope. "I see golden colors on your forehead, and a rose on your left cheek."

She glanced down, embarrassed but flattered. "And my right cheek?"

"It's covered in shadows. But I can remember what's in the shadows."

She gazed at him seriously, actually feeling his words. "You really are a poet, Porter."

"Not really. My sister read that in a book and told me to tell it to you."

She laughed and he joined in.

"But I'll tell you what is in my heart," he said. "Come here."

She studied him a moment, liking what she saw. She arose from her chair and glided to him.

He took her hand. "Your beauty to me is like this river." He turned and glanced down at it, still leaning against the rope railing. She leaned forward against the ropes as well.

"The river," he said, "flows from the soul of the land, as the beauty of your face comes from your soul."

She melted and stared at the river.

"No matter which way the moonlight moves over your face, or how you look at me," he said, then paused.

"Go on!" she said. "What's the rest?"

"You're just as beautiful . . . I'm sorry I'm not a poet."

"Your heart is full of poetry," she said. "I've never heard such poetry!" Her heart now beat faster.

"Maybe I'm like the river after a storm," he said. "Its waves splash high and out of control at times, and you've seen me at its worst — like at the puppet show — but what I feel, like these waters, runs very, very deep."

She gazed into his eyes. "Your heart is wonderfully pure."

"Luana," he said, "fate made this river flow here — it was an act of nature and God. And what I feel flowing between us is . . . well . . . as strong as any river."

"That positively is," she said, "the most beautiful thing I have ever heard. I don't want to ever forget this evening."

"I don't think you will," he said. "I'm sure I won't."

And with that he turned to face her, both of them still leaning against the ropes. They slowly moved their faces toward each other. He kissed her on the left cheek, then studied the shadows dappling her face. He kissed her chin, then moved toward her lips. She trembled.

She felt a thrill she had never before felt. She felt feelings she could not comprehend. She felt a love she had always craved. She felt ropes zipping across her dress. The rope railing was disappearing . . . And then she felt nothing. Nothing between her and the edge of the barge . . . except air.

Porter tumbled overboard first, and on his way down grabbed her dress. Then she, too, fell — rather flew — face forward into the freezing water.

Treading the Big Blue River she gasped and spit out water. She turned and glared at Porter, treading beside her with a face as red as a beet.

She knew it was a deeper red than that merely caused by the cold water. She had never seen a man so embarrassed, so defeated-looking and so downright humiliated from trying so hard and failing so miserably. "All right," she shouted at him. "All right! I'll marry you!"

CHAPTER 19

T he wedding date was set four weeks away.

She felt torn, but made herself determined. That night, soaking head to toe, she announced to her parents the engagement with hesitancy:

"Hello, Papa, Mama. I have something unusual to tell you."

Whether she felt a certain possessiveness mixed with a growing fondness for him — or whether it was genuine love — she was not certain, but she knew she feared losing him. Particularly in light of her noticing other women flirting with him at church. True, she had envisioned a different sort of mate — a gentleman, in fact — but she was beginning to accept reality: They were both attracted to each other, he seemed stalwart enough in the faith, and he had potential as a provider.

"Are you serious?" her mother demanded. "This is the young man you've waited for?"

She said nothing.

As Porter journeyed home, he seemed as if he were floating on air, but when he crashed open the cabin door and awakened the entire family with the news, they were more than a little surprised.

"Is it the same girl?" Porter's younger sister Electa quietly asked.

"Yeah, why wouldn't it be the same girl?" said Porter.

"She just seemed so . . . nice."

"She means refined," explained Porter's mother.

"Electa isn't used to such people 'gracing' our cabin," said Sarah dryly.

The next morning they discussed it over breakfast. While Orin Rockwell was quiet on his son's choice, Sarah was cautious.

"Such women sometimes need to be pampered," she mumbled to her son.

Porter foresaw potential conflict with the two queen bees on the same property. It was at this point he decided to build a separate cabin for him and Luana rather than to add a wing to his family log house which he had been planning.

He began construction on it the next day, a hundred yards from his parents' house through the woods, which would also be a hundred yards this side of his next closest neighbor, David Pettegrew, and a hundred yards from the river.

That weekend, the Rockwells sponsored a cabin-raising party for their son: Sarah rounded up several neighboring women to cook wild fowl and fish, while Orin organized two dozen men to help the Rockwell males cut and place logs for Porter's new home.

The Rockwells had aided numerous neighbors over the months with cabin-raising parties, and now it was their time to cash in on the labor harvest.

After one day's construction, Porter assessed the shell of his cabin. He still had weeks of finishing touches to add, yet refused his father's offer to clear his son's land for farming. All the elder Rockwell cleared with Porter's permission was a small plot for a garden. For major income, Porter counted on the ferry soon being his.

Life before the wedding went smoothly enough, yet making time to court his fiance while finishing his cabin and training on the barge after family chores seemed triply exhausting. Nonetheless, he managed to never miss a night of seeing Luana. He knew that the six hours of walking each evening plus one hour visiting, in addition to his barge training and chores for both Pritsimmons and his parents, would all soon come to an end. The wedding was now only two weeks away.

One evening he arrived at the ferry for his usual chores but Pritsimmons was not willing to talk. And then he felt sickened: After he pressured him for an explanation, the old man finally replied, "I've found a cash buyer."

Porter shook his head disbelievingly. As the old man explained about the new buyer, he turned his back on him. Porter trudged away to Luana's, uncertain if he should reveal his business matters to her.

She wasn't home.

"Where is she?" he said.

Her mother was the only one home. "Off with her aunt."

"Why?"

"You'll have to talk to her."

At that his heart and mind raced. "Where's her aunt?"

"Across the county . . . "

He banged his hand once on the door frame. "Where across the county?"

"Porter, she's thinking about things."

"I said where!"

On his way westward, Porter realized that Olive Beebe, mother of Luana, was as stubborn as himself, and when a mother is in the death throes of protecting her daughter, a man has a real fight on his hands. Since she had refused to tell him where Luana's aunt lived, he was determined to search her out himself.

As he strode the last two miles to his cabin he was not exactly sure of the dominant feeling seizing him, but what eventually surfaced was anger.

He arrived home eleven P.M. and went directly to bed.

"For once," Sarah muttered to Orin in their bed, "Porter's

going to get a decent night's sleep. His first in months. It should be a good night for him."

About 2 A.M. a knock awakened the family.

Porter laid in his blankets, his ears dead to the noise. His father answered the door.

Standing in the framework was Luana. "Can I see him?"

Orin, without a word, nodded toward his son's bed.

Luana stepped inside the cabin. Orin awakened him and retreated to the back sleeping room to allow the couple privacy.

She and Porter sat beside the fireplace, but did not talk, knowing every word could be heard throughout the cabin. She scanned the room and realized his brothers and sisters were all hard asleep, yet she was fearful of an eavesdropping mama bear.

Porter was half asleep when she leaned forward and whispered: "Porter, I can't do it."

CHAPTER 20

His look was as curious as it was pained.

"You're not what I've been looking for," she began. "You know how you always dream of someone . . . You are wonderful, but rough, and . . . unsteady," she whispered harshly.

"Unsteady?"

"Father says there's nothing steady in the ferry."

"He doesn't have to worry — I think it's sold," Porter whispered. "I have a week to come up with the money before another buyer does. So the deal is dead."

She gazed at him, feeling somewhat relieved.

"I can support you anyway," Porter said harshly.

"But you don't like farming," she whispered louder.

"I could do that," then he beamed with an idea. "But now that I know the barge business, I could build my own ferry."

She looked away. "That's what Papa's afraid of — the whole ferry idea."

He continued, "More people will come — I know Joseph.

He'll get more people here. The ferry business will boom."

"Father said most who are coming from Ohio and New York have already come . . . and the ferry has had its day."

"He's wrong . . . the whole nation is spreading west."

"It's a wilderness there. No one will ever move further west."

"Even so," he said, "I'll keep us fed, don't worry." His little brother Horace piped in, "He was the best shot in Manchester and never lost a contest. And he can track game better than anybody."

She smiled, "You want to get rid of him that badly, huh?"

"Darn right," said Horace with a laugh.

She melted and smiled.

"I guess we'll make it work, huh?" She then announced she had to leave.

Porter offered to walk her home.

She declined. "Papa's waiting for me around the bend at a friend's."

He accompanied her outside and watched her ride away, disappearing into the moonless but bright, starry, chilled night.

Shivering, Porter climbed under his quilt and collapsed for another two hours' sleep.

As he hauled logs from the day's cutting, his mind burned from the unsettled question of the ferry. He realized deep down he could not build a competing barge — even if a second one could be profitable. He simply hadn't the time . . .

It was now three days before the wedding. Luana rode out one afternoon to help prepare the new cabin. Social protocol demanded a betrothed couple first visit with family before spending time alone; however, it was not too many minutes into her conversation with them that she found it, at best, forced.

Sarah Rockwell felt protective of her son and discerned every conceivable weakness a woman could decipher in a potential daughter-in-law.

Porter suspected such analysis, and after his mother's report to him that day, he quickly dismissed it, realizing they simply did not know one another well enough. After all, he figured, "When good folk get to know other good folk, they get along."

The next evening Sarah made another attempt to counsel him — this time with a bit more brass: She outright warned him of marrying her.

"Why?"

"I can just tell."

"Tell what?" he said.

"You're not ready for this."

Certainly life is a compromise, she felt, and working together with her own husband on the farm had taught her that. She feared her son's future off the farm. What would life away from a simple family farm produce for a marriage? It would take an exceptional woman to understand. She feared Porter would not grasp the principles of compromise if he were engaged in other work situations away from the farm, away from one's spouse all day where life does not teach compromise so fully. One gets one's way entirely twelve hours a day when self-employed away from the spouse and children.

Then there was Luana. What would she become with independence from her husband? Especially with Porter's already decided nature to do as he darn well pleased? And the biggest question was — did her son really grasp all this and —

Porter cut her short: He was in love with this woman — she fit his dreams — she's what he wanted — and that was that.

The day of the wedding was fraught with mixed feelings. Porter awakened early. He assured his parents that even on this day he was committed to his daily farm chores. By mid-morning he had bathed and shaved for the final time as a single man. He nervously nicked himself with the razor knife and his father awkwardly paced around pretending to straighten up the family cabin.

Orin Rockwell never did get out what he wished to say, but when he left the cabin with a mumble about less hands on the property to do all the work, the inference was clear: The underlying resentment Orin felt was the realization that his son was not following the multi-generational family tradition.

Porter was hurt by the complaint and went outside to discuss it with his father. The family patriarch shoveled manure as he listened to his son but pretended not to.

"You want me to keep shoveling this the rest of my life, too?" said Porter.

His father said nothing and just kept working. Finally he looked up: "So you think you're better than me? And my pa and his?"

Porter walked away. The expectation of adhering to the

family tradition of farming held an imprisoning effect on him. He could not wait to escape it.

Inside as he dusted off his suit one final time, his father re-entered the cabin, shoved a hand inside a cut in the mattress and pulled out some bills. He strode up to Porter and placed them in his left hand. He mumbled something about buying the ferry.

"You *are* better than me," said Orin. "And I made you to be," he smiled. He had fought internally over the issue, and outside had taken out his frustration on his son, but now had it resolved.

Porter knew this money was meant to buy a larger plot of farming land to increase their cash crops and save for their retirement. The young man was touched by his sacrifice. For the first time in 11 years he hugged his father. Then thanked him with tears in his eyes.

He set out immediately to visit Cecil Pritsimmons, and took with him neighbor David Patten as a witness. Patten was tall and broad-shouldered. He looked as one imagines a Roman gladiator — rugged and noble-looking with black eyes and curly hair. Arriving at the ferry landing the two men beheld the old proprietor cleaning the barge. Pritsimmons glanced up at Porter, then back down, feeling guilty over the reneged agreement.

"Mr. Pritsimmons," said Porter as he strutted up to the old fellow, "I'm back."

Pritsimmons mumbled something about the other cash buyer still planning on paying with cash.

"How much is he paying?" said Porter.

"Forty-five. He's supposed to pay next week," said Pritsimmons.

"Well I've got 42 cash. You can take it now or hope he comes through next week," said Porter, flashing gold coins in front of Pritsimmons. "And I'll send you four more when I get it."

The man's eyes fairly dilated. "Where'd you get all this?"

"Never mind, is it a deal?"

Pritsimmons smiled at Porter and nodded. "I wanted you to run this ferry, lad. You were born for it. I can see it in your eyes."

"I brought my neighbor along as a witness," said Porter. "He can read, and drew up this sales paper for us to sign."

Pritsimmons glanced it over, asked Patten a couple questions about the wording, primarily just to act difficult, Porter figured, then signed the hand-written document and also signed a copy for himself. Porter signed both documents with an 'X.' Patten witnessed them with his own signature.

Pritsimmons presently placed personal items in a large leather bag, took one last look at his ferry-landing that had served him faithfully over the years, then turned to the young man, thanked him, and smiled. Twas the first smile Porter had ever seen on the old gent's face. He turned and set out for St. Louis with an old horse to await the settling of his sister's inheritance.

The ferry was all Porter's. He swung his fist in the air once again.

CHAPTER 21

Dozens of buggies arrived for the wedding. Orin spotted Luana's carriage coming to a halt. As he approached the closed door, he heard Luana inside being addressed by her mother.

"It is never too late, dear."

"You think I can back out now?" shouted Luana. "Look at this! Everything is set!"

"I'm saying . . . if you want to!"

"You're assuming I want to!"

"I just read your eyes this morning, that's all."

"Maybe I just need encouragement," said Luana.

"Maybe you need to reconsider."

Orin Rockwell shook his head and quickly opened the carriage door. "Welcome, Luana!" He extended his hand to help her out. Luana considered taking his hand and proceeding with the ceremony. Then she glanced at her mother, torn over whether to follow her counsel and simply return home. She took Orin's hand.

Porter's father helped her down from the carriage and shot a forced smile at Olive. She gazed at him aghast, realizing suddenly that he had not only overheard the conversation but had achieved victory.

The wedding was festive. As the first ceremony among the saints in Missouri, it took place on the riverbank under tall, seasoned oaks at sunset February 16, 1832. The young Rockwell stood before Luana like an oat-fed stallion with 400 people surrounding him as he faced his dream-come-true straight square in the eyes with only one "yes" separating his current state from the next.

That single word from him was softly uttered — the same as had been seconds earlier more hesitantly whispered from her lips, and soon the smiling couple retreated from the ferry to their cabin down the road . . . or so Luana thought . . . when suddenly she noticed her husband comfortably disappearing into the crowd and soaking up accolades of what a fine and handsome woman he had landed.

Luana's mother watched impatiently as Porter made a near spectacle of himself, bellylaughing with his comrades and requesting they all remain for a "community dance," dedicated, of course, to his wife. All they needed was whiskey — and quickly a keg arrived. This was still decades before abstinence was a commandment to Latter-day Saints.

The improvised hoe-down, with Brother Conrad Peterson providing harmonica music, was completely Porter's idea. Luana stared in amazement at the crowd. She had pictured a formal ceremony followed by a quiet retreat to their cabin for an intimate, romantic wedding night. 'Surprise!' she thought to herself. She stared in disbelief as the mob got drunker and louder. She was amazed by how quickly the party degenerated into a full-blown whiskey-fest.

A dazzling, raucous dance developed, lit by torches along the riverbank, with half a dozen fast fiddlers and three wild harmonicas blazing. A tambourine appeared on the scene, with which Porter found occasion to beat upon with his hand as he stomped his foot to the noisesome music when he wasn't dancing with every woman 14 and older — and it was all reflected off the river's surface — the same spectacle Luana's mother saw reflecting in her daughter's eyes as Luana gazed at her groom flirting with every woman in sight.

Olive Beebe was furious.

Porter's mother meanwhile attempted an embarrassed apology but Luana's mother ignored her. She simply glared at the scene, mortified.

Luana turned to her mother and offered an excuse for Porter's impassioned exuberance, adding, "He's usually not like this."

"You don't even know him, child." Olive and her equally offended husband, Isaac, climbed atop their carriage and left in a huff.

Luana watched with intolerable loneliness, including, for the first time in her life, the emotion of stranded isolation. The proverbial apron strings had been jarringly and completely severed, as her parents rode away. She turned a glare at Porter, who came barrelling over to her and began their "wedding dance" — a clumsy, boot-stomping foot movement accompanied by loud clapping and yells, the harmonicas, fiddles, and tambourine still piercing the still, night air.

PART II

Awakening

CHAPTER 22

T heir honeymoon lasted a day. They exchanged gifts after breakfast, in which Porter gave her a necklace that was handed down from his grandmother, and Luana gave him a pocket watch that her parents had bought which included a small painting of her that fit inside the top locket of the watch. He promised to always carry it. But the very next night he developed a fondness for another.

Luana's unfolding awareness of the curious affair began immediately. At first she fought the inexplicable mistrust overwhelming her, but it became increasingly obvious to her.

Porter's morning began with a knock at the door.

"Mister Rockwell, we got a party of folk comin' later this mornin' wanting to get across. 'Think you could help us?"

Porter was alive with excitement. Luana's suspicion at that point began to rise, and when her husband did not return home until late that evening and again spent all the next day at the river, all doubts fled.

On the third evening of their marriage, Porter set out alone to spend another night away from her. About midnight she decided to visit the river herself to see just what was stealing his attention.

As she approached the river she trod on the muddy road, wondering what her husband was up to. And there, in the frigid winter wind, Luana beheld a sight that would for weeks haunt her. A sight she would have to come to grips with, but which now infuriated her: Porter's idolatrous attentiveness to his ferry barge.

Everything about it sparkled in his soul. When he was not busy ferrying and laughing with his passengers, he was gazing into the water fishing for catfish. He was downright in love with this river.

Even at their cabin when he arrived at dawn, he spoke only of his passengers, of his barge, of his river.

Finally, Luana could conceal her feelings no longer. She had prepared simple but tasteful dishes each morning and evening, and they had satisfied him. This particular morning would be no exception. But as he sat to a plate of catfish he had caught and hushpuppies she had fried, the conversation turned unexpectedly:

"Upwards of thirty folk came across last night — you know what I decided's gotta happen?" he said.

"What?"

"Gotta put in a little extra time on the barge. The dock needs repairing today."

She seethed. "You haven't put in enough?"

He was quick to catch the emotion in her voice. He did not know what could so concern her. She then confronted him about his occupation. He retorted that it kept her as well fed as most women on the Big Blue.

"My folks came up to the river last night," he added, quickly changing the subject, not used to confrontations in the solid, orderly Rockwell household in which he'd been raised. "They said some of the local Missourians are getting riled over all the new saints moving in."

"Mother and Father think it's changing things too much," said Luana, deciding to follow his lead into the new conversation, yet unable to hold back her confrontational emotions.

"I'd say it's helping the economy." He could not believe his own wife would parrot the argument of a few cantankerous Missourians which he knew were a tiny minority. He caught himself, realizing he had needlessly argued, and changed the subject. "Why don't you invite your folks over this Sunday? My family's coming and maybe yours could join us."

"You didn't say anything about your family coming over."

"Well, now I am. And now you know about it."

Luana was not about to release her feelings about his boring family or silently critical mother. "I'm still decorating the dining area."

"Then we'll eat over at my folks'," he said.

"Again?"

"What do you mean 'again?' It's only been two days since we ate with them."

That's all either of them said that morning.

That night when Porter returned from the barge, Luana was ice. He could not understand her animosity towards his family or his ferry. His pa was the most generous man on earth, and at the rate the boat was producing, he'd have him reimbursed by the third autumn. Luana's ingratitude grated at him.

The next morning she could not understand his coldness. After all, she felt refreshened after having disclosed her concerns, and certain that after a night of sleeping on it, he would finally be sympathetic.

Within two days, his lack of romantic interest was even more apparent, and she was distraught. It was obviously due to his new lady, she mused. She was blind to the fact her criticalness of his river work had cut back on his romantic interst, but he said nothing. Still, deep down he knew he had launched the problem by choosing to spend too much time on the river and away from her, causing her to feel neglected, but he pushed the thought from his mind. On this day, her contempt for the ferry operation escalated. It happened at noon, when she took his noon dinner to him at the river. There, she witnessed firsthand the thrill he received at meeting new folks, displaying verbal and physical antics that made people delighted with him and in love with their river barge ride — while he treated her differently, without so much enthusiasm. She did not realize he had the capacity of feeling excitement over his work *and* her, and therefore she felt in competition.

Porter meanwhile was discovering within himself somewhat of a showman. Even the straight-laced Catholic missionaries passing through to the frontier chuckled at his off-beat humor. His demeanor became even jollier when he took on the roll of self-appointed "greeter" to Jackson County Mormon immigrants, welcoming worn, weary faces entering the territory each week.

At home, although he and Luana displayed feelings rarely, his resentment towards her earlier coolness was slowly dissipating. It would not evaporate entirely, but he did file it away as far as possible since he still did not know what to make of her or how to deal with it. Despite her resentment of his work, she encouraged him to report his daily activities each night at supper.

But greeting him at the cabin each night, Luana did not smile at him like she did with neighbors and family.

That concerned him, and he practically ceased displaying his humor to her. That bothered her, so she began listening to his daily reports of the river business with even less enthusiasm. Sensing her lessening interest, he quit reporting to her altogether. That actually pained her. Their relationship became consistently sober and distant.

She occasionally sauntered to the dock and peered at him through the trees as he "performed" for his passengers. Had someone asked, she would've told them her husband never tried to charm her like he did the rest of the world. His rare attempts at humor with her would fall flat without his charm behind it. Perhaps he was too tired from his day's ordeal of greeting and entertaining, she felt, for him to be charming.

Despite these frustrations, she was growing increasingly dependent on his daily return from work, and was not unaware of the irony.

Porter also looked forward each night to returning to his wife for companionship. He caressed her gently, but rarely gazed into her eyes as before. At times, however, the feelings soared.

At the ferry one afternoon he saw Bishop David Partridge and invited him and other local church leaders to his house for meetings. Partridge accepted graciously. He was extroverted and kindly, with dark deep-set eyes and broad shoulders. The first thing he asked Porter was if his dog was around.

Porter smiled, "I think he's off in the woods doing what he likes to do best."

"That's what I'm afraid of," said Partridge, chuckling, then muttering, "Perhaps you could get me across the river fairly fast, before he shows up."

After Partridge crossed the water, Porter took advantage of the moment and confided in him of his not-so-perfect marriage. Partridge listened with a small smile. He advised the young man of the fact few marriages match the story-book romances. But if they simply cared about each other, he said, that was probably enough, which was far beyond fairy-tale romanticism.

"But why can't she be more interested in what I do?"

Partridge had heard the complaint before. "You work it out with her, Porter. But also see where your own heart is."

Porter wondered what the devil that meant as he watched his bishop ride away. He was only trying to make ends meet, to do the best job he could. Surely Luana could be satisfied with that and with what he did, yet he always came home to her same, dour expression. Maybe the bishop had a point: They did deep down care for each other, and maybe that's all that mattered.

Nevertheless, it gnawed at him. His own folks had maintained a happy relationship — not particularly romantic — but satisfying. Joseph also. Other folks he'd seen at church meetings through the years had, as well.

He wanted theirs to be one of them. But what he really wanted, deep deep down, was a story-book romance . . .

Maybe his mother was right: If he stayed on the farm — with no glimpse of outside society on a daily basis, and if he lived each day with the company of only his wife — he'd be closer to her, and she to him.

But the tedium of farm life was out of the question. He should be able to leave and return, he felt, from the river life he loved to a woman he loved.

He thought of pursuing the problem with his father, but realized he was too proud for that. He figured life would take care of it in time.

Four months later, by the summer of 1832, nearly 900 saints had moved into the area. And Porter's business was booming.

Ten months later David Patten asked him to help get feed sacks in town. He needed help lifting them once they reached the feed store, and he perceived in Porter the additional benefit of protection.

They were now on their way into Independence on Patten's buckboard. Porter scanned the crowd for potential problems: He studied pedestrians, vagabonds, wagon drivers and horsemen on the muddy road. Patten scrutinized them also.

Half way down Main Street they observed two men outside the saloon taking notice of them. One dozen farm hands were soon outside, strolling parallel to Patten's wagon, staring at them.

Porter glimpsed at Patten beside him, then down at his shotgun by his feet. Soon he halted the wagon. As both men strode inside the feed store, Porter glanced over his shoulder to see if the men were still following.

He regarded them stopping at a barber shop across the street, gawking at Patten's wagon.

Patten quickly paid for the sacks of feed, then he and Porter slung them over their shoulders and hauled them to the back of his wagon. They sighted a dozen more men now across the street, leaning against store walls and leering at them.

Porter caught Patten's nervousness and smiled, "David, you remember a few months back I told you what Bishop Partridge said about me and Luana? Well, I've decided Luana's a fine woman after all."

"I could've told you that — I'm glad you're just now figuring it out," he said, eyes riveted on the crowd.

Porter tried diverting Patten's concern of the townspeople: "But I wonder why sometimes."

"Why what?" said Patten.

"She doesn't take to the river."

"She doesn't like it?"

"Doesn't dislike it. Doesn't like it."

"Doesn't sound like much of a problem," said Patten.

"Only one thing is a problem."

Patten glanced at him.

"To me, the river is life itself."

Patten blew out a sigh, then spoke:

"I think you've got a problem."

Placing the last sack of feed in the back of the wagon,

Porter surveyed the street and discovered even more towns-men adding to the crowd's numbers. Many were now on their side of the street. Porter did not discern hostile intentions among these new-comers, but the first crowd across the street seemed more ominous.

Suddenly one walked behind Porter and called out, "Get everything you need, boys?"

Porter felt a bitter tone in the voice and did not turn to face him.

"Yeah," said Porter, "thanks for caring." He then whipped himself up on the buckboard and in one motion jerked from the floorboard the shotgun and set the stock on his knee with the barrel pointed up. He moved his eyes toward the spokes-man on the wooden sidewalk, forced a steely little smile at him, then tipped his hat with his free hand. "Have a nice day," he muttered through gritted teeth.

Patten, taking the reins, saw the man's lower lip quiver.

Patten yelled at the horses, his own voice cracking with nervousness. In silence they rode to the other end of Main Street, Porter carefully surveying the three dozen townspeople glaring at them. As they turned a corner, Porter mumbled to Patten:

"I don't think they'll be inviting us to the town picnic this summer, David."

CHAPTER 23

With darkness setting in, Porter rushed through dinner, grabbed his coat, thanked Luana and shot out the door.

"Again?" she muttered.

"I gotta earn money to make payments."

"What if nobody comes across the river tonight?"

"What if somebody does?"

"You want to leave me for the gamble somebody might?" she said.

"They came last night."

"For the first time in three nights."

"So I've gotta take the chance." He reached forward to kiss her on the cheek but she withdrew. He blew out a disconcerted sigh. "Luana, my folks need me on the farm every morning now, and I've gotta help. That leaves only afternoons and evenings to run the barge."

"So make changes," she said.

"What changes?"

"We could leave."

He squinted at her.

"The county," she explained. "We could leave the county." Hope gleamed in her eyes. "We could leave the whole area and work our own farm, living alone with just each other."

"You know how I take to farming."

"I know your dreams. But the barge doesn't pay for dreams."

"That's why I work the folks' farm — that keeps us in food. And the barge gives us cash. Between the two we do fine."

"You told me the farm work was to only help them."

"But if I wasn't helping them I'd be working our own land to get the same food."

"So why don't you just work our own land then?" she said.

"Because they need our help and I need time to work the barge."

"You've got brothers and sisters to work for your folks."

"Why shouldn't I work it," said Porter, "and feed us at the same time?"

"Cause you have your own farm you could be working!"

"Don't you see?" he said. "My working their farm feeds them and us."

"Where's the future in that?"

Exasperated, he blew out a sigh. "I get to build a future with the barge."

"You really see a future in that thing?"

"That's why I bought it."

"No, you bought it for your crazy love of the river."

He stared at her, thoroughly frustrated.

"Your love for the river is everything," she said. "You'd do anything to stay on the river, even if it didn't make money. But your river has to take second fiddle to real life, dear one. Especially with a growing family."

He studied her, taken back. "Growing?"

"Honey," she said, "we're growing." She patted her tummy. "As if that's what we need now."

Porter felt, for the first time in his life, panic. He felt confident in providing for himself and his wife — but the dependency of children on him — for food, attention, emotional support and training — was an element of life to which he felt less predisposed.

He lay beside Luana all night without a second of sleep.

Four days later he returned to his cabin at midnight. Inside he heard Olive Beebe lecturing her daughter:

"You have a place to stay if he is unable to support you in the manner to which you're accustomed."

"I have no intention of leaving my husband," said Luana. "And we eat quite well — better than most, in fact."

"You're still wearing the same clothes?"

"Because I want to."

"You heard my offer."

Porter entered and ignored Luana's mother. "I'm as hungry as a horse, girl. Got any supper left?"

"You ate it all, speaking of horses," teased Luana.

"You didn't feel like having more grub ready when I'd get home tonight, huh?" he said with the cheer suddenly gone from his voice.

"The smell of food nauseates me."

He looked her over. "I guess that comes with the territory, huh?"

"So," she said, "why don't you make your own for a change?"

Porter was stunned. There must be something he could eat that didn't smell up the cabin. "How about bottled tomatoes and stale bread — food that won't smell? I could use anything right now."

Olive spoke up, "I think you heard her, Porter."

"You talking to me?" he said to Olive.

"I most certainly did," said Olive. "My daughter is in no condition to be your slave."

"Where I was raised, the woman keeps her man fed."

"Well from what I surmise," spoke Olive, "that has become quite a challenge."

"What do you mean by that?" said Porter.

"All you do at home is eat," said Olive. "Which means all she does is cook — and clean after you."

"I think we're doing OK," said Porter, miffed at Olive's intrusion.

"And what about her?" said Olive.

"Mama," said Luana, smiling over the fact someone was taking up for her but on the other hand realizing her allegiance must remain with her husband, "I think we'll work things out just fine on our own."

"That's the way it's supposed to be," said Olive, "but a lot of things are supposed to be a certain way. And chasing an elusive butterfly certainly isn't going to put bread on the table — or cash in your pockets, pockets of new, decent clothing. I've said my peace, dear. Goodbye."

Olive sashayed out the door, leaving Porter in the wake of her bad perfume.

Porter sighed and glanced down at Luana, then walked without another word to the cupboard and took out a jar of bottled tomatoes and yesterday's bread, now stale but edible. He began eating without even looking at Luana. She was surprised he would even eat in front of her, given her nausea. So she gave a disgusted little snort at his negligence and arose, then strode briskly to their bedroom and slammed the door behind her.

CHAPTER 24

Porter sat outside in the dark beside his father. It was January 31, 1833. Their chairs were tilted back and their heads rested against the pine of the cabin logs.

"Porter, you will know no greater excitement or happiness, and that's a promise."

"That's what they said about marriage."

His father smiled and looked down. "Well, when the baby's born, Luana should settle down from some of her anger. Women go through a lot for these babies, and their feelings go through a lot. She'll be happier, believe me."

"I hope she will be toward me."

His father was hurt for him but extended a smile. "The miracle of all this is the child. You are about to be so happy at this little miracle that you won't know what to do with yourself."

In silence they sat for an hour. Porter looked upon the birth as a mystery, and doubted he would feel that close to the newborn, feeling no excitement whatsoever for the coming child. Nor could he get Luana's increasingly difficult disposition out of his mind.

He could not comprehend — although his pa had once told him — how men could so differ from women: Whereas women as a rule could forget a row to the point of holding hands with another woman during a country walk together immediately after a fight, men on the other hand more often could not let go. That's why, perhaps, menfolk usually sought perfect harmony in their working relationships, knowing if a temper or any piece of tactlessness were displayed among other men, that could be a permanent ax in the face of a relationship. Oh, they'd be polite enough in the future with each other, but never again would many men truly trust each other after a row. Therefore, Porter thought, men sought ever so cautiously to get along — at work, church, and everywhere among themselves — while women could often explode any number of times and almost immediately, completely, make up. Despite knowing that basic difference, Porter could not so quickly adjust from the tight feelings he felt resulting from her occasional, albeit regular, verbal attacks on him recently.

Porter knew he would forget them in time. He knew he loved her. He knew he always would.

He had glanced in her eyes that very morning — and told her he loved her. She could tell he meant it, but she could not tell he was still hurt.

Presently in the early morning darkness a baby's cry pierced the air. Porter's mother and sister Electa cleaned the newborn and brought the child outside to him as he still waited on the porch beside his father.

Electa had the honors of presenting him with his first child:

"Behold, the next generation of Rockwells!" she smiled, handing the baby to her brother. "She's your very own daughter, Porter!"

He gazed upon the infant, surprised to see it was so doggone ugly. He awkwardly took the little creature and noticed that it flopped worse than a fish. He wondered if he would ever get used to this whole fatherhood thing. Despite his pa's counsel to the contrary, he doubted he would ever get that much attached to this little urchin.

CHAPTER 25

One hour later, seeing the baby stare at him and cry, he felt an unearthly compassion for her, and suddenly — inexplicably — fell madly in love with her.

Not many weeks passed before he announced he was taking his daughter — Emily Amanda Rockwell — on the barge that day to cross the river. Passengers knew from a sign he had posted — which Luana wrote — that operating hours were "after noon till sundown" and "after supper till midnight," and that he was especially proud of the name he had christened the barge, which Luana had painted on it: "The Emily." As he steered the ferry, several women surrounded him, talking to and holding the child.

"She's a special little girl, Porter," said David Patten's wife, traveling with others to a "craft fair" across the river.

Porter grinned and took back his daughter.

Luana awakened in the middle of the night. The baby was not beside her. She rolled over. Porter was also gone. She heard loud singing from somewhere.

Outside she peered, and in the moonlight she caught a glimpse of Porter holding up his child, twirling her around in circles, humming a lively little tune, and dancing.

A tear trickled down Luana's cheek.

Three days later Bishop Pettegrew crossed the river and told Porter he would accept his earlier invitation to hold meetings at his home since it was strategically located.

The following Thursday they arrived at Porter's cabin. Porter greeted them at the door and turned to face Luana with a sheepish grin. He had forgotten to tell her. She felt peculiar inviting them into her not-immaculately-cleaned house, but made them feel welcome. The bishops found in her a gracious hostess. She was ungenuinely grateful to see them yet enjoyed the cheery atmosphere they brought. As they left she glared at her husband. One of the bishops walking away turned and faced them:

"You realize you've got the most popular business in the county."

"Luana might argue with you about the money in our pockets," said Porter smiling, "but I do hope to get it paid off someday."

"It's the talk of the territory," continued the bishop. "You put on quite a show for strangers, and make them feel at home."

Porter beamed.

"I do what I can to support him on the river," she explained. "We're sacrificing for what needs to be done."

The thought crossed Porter's mind she was playing a martyr, at best; at worst, a prevaricator. Luana felt, meanwhile, Porter's invitation to the men without informing her was downright disrespectful if not thoroughly insulting.

As the men left, another bishop commented about the approaching church conference and where it should be held.

Porter's eyes flashed. "How about the ferry?"

"Pardon?"

"The ferry — you can hold it on my ferry."

And so it was planned — the first such church gathering ever held on a ferry — in a river — his river — and he was proud as punch.

Several days later under the spring breeze of April 6, 1833 the meeting began. It was the third anniversary of the "restoration" of the Church of Jesus Christ on earth. Over two hundred families were seated on both the large flatbed and on shore listening to speakers who spoke from the barge.

The gurgling and sloshing of gentle waves added to the mesmerizing effect of the meeting. Indeed, to many gathered, time seemed to stand still. The talks by congregational members on the atonement of Jesus Christ, coupled with the passing of bread and wine, brought tears to the eyes of several, including Orin and Sarah Rockwell. They were especially proud of Porter's participation, not only offering his property for the gathering but even providing many refreshments.

After the closing hymn and prayer, they all congregated to shore, ate, and fellowshipped with cheer and laughter. Porter, Luana and several neighbors served fried chicken from a table to a line of hungry saints. Neighbor Pettegrew suddenly spoke up. "Why don't we get our non-member neighbors out here next time?"

Orin Rockwell laughed, "I've tried to invite a couple, but they said it's too early in the morning for them."

Added Sarah, "I think that's a polite way of saying they're not interested."

At which Porter broke in, "Well, why don't we just go fire up some branding irons, and herd the lazy pigs out here where they belong?"

While several politely chuckled, the comment was met by many with somewhat of a collective gasp.

Luana blushed from embarrassment.

"Joking," said Porter into the silence.

David Pettegrew politely smiled and resumed with another topic: There was growing talk in town of certain citizens critical of their society.

"They're just jealous," offered Orin, but Pettegrew quieted him with reports of what some of their ministers were saying about the saints. An air of concern captured the group, and Pettegrew cautioned them that they were, for all practical purposes, still outsiders who should tread softly and not engage in loud or boisterous claims to which some were prone, bragging that they would convert the whole countryside, etc. Pettegrew urged them to tolerance.

Orin Rockwell agreed vocally. Porter, meanwhile, had grown bored of their conversation and drifted to a group of children where he was entertaining them.

He put two gloves on backwards, drew a quick face on each glove, and pretended they were puppets. Using two different voices, he improvised a scene: The first puppet told the other to jump in the river. The second one shrieked, "But I can't swim!"

The first one yelled, "I can't either, but we need a bath!" It yelped and jumped into the river, taking the other puppet with it — and at that Porter pulled off both gloves and threw them into the water beside him.

The dozen kids around him laughed heartily. Porter reached into the river to grab the still-floating gloves when he yelled, "Help me!" Then acted as though the puppets were grabbing and pulling him into the water. The children laughed heartily. Suddenly he threw himself into the river. The kids shrieked with laughter. Several adults looked over, wondering what the commotion was all about. Porter now stood waist deep in the water and donned the two puppets again. "Look what you've done!" screamed one puppet to the other. "You've got the human soaked!"

The other shouted, "You call this thing human?"

The kids laughed even harder, and a few adults surrounding them now joined in. Although an official church gathering, the group was dispersing to food tables, where gaity and laughter abounded. Suddenly Porter looked up. The county sheriff and three deputies stood over the river's edge, wearing sardonic smiles.

"Well, look what we've got here: A clown in the county," said Sheriff David Isaacs to his deputies. "But you know what?

Even clowns gotta pay their dues. 'This your ferry, boy?"

Porter nodded.

Sheriff Isaacs pulled from his pocket a paper. He was medium, square-faced, and had eyes and lips that resembled a bulldog.

He muttered to his deputies, "Think they can just move in without paying their dues, don't they?" He turned to Porter:

"I'm issuing a warrant for your arrest, son."

Porter stared, surprised. The saints surrounding him quieted.

"I'll make it a conditional arrest — it means jail if you don't get licensed within twenty-four hours."

"Whose idea is it to get licensed to work?" said Porter.

The sheriff glanced with a smile at his deputies, then his eyes settled on Porter with a smirk. He began walking away but said one thing more before mounting his horse:

"You got a lot to learn about living with civilized Christian society, don't you, boy?"

"Like what?" muttered Porter.

Porter's talking back surprised the sheriff, who decided a short lecture was fitting:

"Like getting licensed. Don't you folk know you can't just move in somewhere and disregard the law?"

Neither Pritsimmons nor anyone else had thought of informing the young proprietor that his business had to be renewed with a license.

The sheriff regarded his deputies, and chuckled. "Now good ole local Missouri boys would've found out you need a license for a business."

A deputy piped in, "Cause he'd have enough sense to ask."

The sheriff and all three deputies laughed. They turned their horses to leave.

Porter felt the heat under his collar rising. "Well, sir," he said to his back, "at least I work for a living."

The sheriff's smirk turned to a glare. He turned his horse and faced him:

"You care to explain that, son?"

"No, sir, I think it's obvious, even to good ole local Missouri boys."

The sheriff turned green. "You want a warrant for contempt, boy?"

Porter glowered at him. The rest of the church gathering felt a mixture of intimidation and contempt for the lawman.

"You tell me what you meant by that," said the sheriff louder, placing his hand on his pistol.

"Nothing, sir," said Porter, "that anybody who knows real work would have trouble figuring out."

"All right, young man," said the sheriff. "You are fined. I was going to let it go till you got licensed tomorrow, but you need a little lesson in respect for the law. Bring three dollars to the court tomorrow." As the four horsemen turned, they gave one last scowl at the staring saints, then spurred their animals.

Porter watched them gallop away. Luana gazed across the group of silent saints. The crowd's happiness, excitement and celebration was dead. The neighbors quickly dispersed, leaving Porter and Luana alone. Orin and Sarah Rockwell felt it best to not rub salt in the wound with any words, so they also left. Porter's wife felt thoroughly humiliated, watching the wagons pulling away. To her this was even more distressful than their wedding party. Suddenly she pulled out of her self-absorption and discovered Porter's plight. His face was splotched as red and white as a radish from embarrassment, and he was trembling with anger and humiliation. She consolingly took his hand, and quietly accompanied him into their cabin.

CHAPTER 26

Ugly, the dog, led the life of an emperor. He laid about with meals brought to him by Luana, yet could still hunt with the best of them when he felt like it. One afternoon in late October 1833 when he returned from the woods, Luana smiled and brought him dinner. She adored the dog. He ignored her but wagged his tail appreciatively.

"Just like your master," she mused aloud. She petted him while he ate. "This is the only time you've even let me touch you — when you're eating."

A couple hours later he was again hungry, and sauntered off to Porter's parents for another meal, somewhat tired of Luana's over-attentiveness yet once again hungry.

Luana came later with Emily to his parents' cabin. She found Ugly asleep on the porch with a bowl of food beside him.

"I don't believe you, Ugly. Do you go through the whole neighborhood when you're hungry?"

Ugly awakened but pretended to still be asleep.

"Actually," said Orin, "he's a loyal family dog and wouldn't be caught dead begging from neighbors."

"Especially," said Luana, "when he's got begging from us down to an art."

They both laughed. Orin went inside, stepping over a newspaper that had been delivered minutes earlier by a paper-boy.

Luana watched the following scene from Porter's parents' porch: Porter held Emily, now nine months old and strapped to his back in a homemade leather carrier, as he worked in his parents' field.

Luana glanced now at Ugly and smiled — catching him looking at her and pretending to go back to sleep — and then she caught sight of the newspaper on the porch. She picked it up to take inside for his parents. On the way in she immediately noticed the article, "Free People of Color."

As the morning melted away, a lazy, sun-drenched afternoon bathed the river in heat and buzzing river flies. Wearing a straw hat, Porter sat at the water's edge and listlessly waved mosquitos from his ears. He gazed across the river and spotted a piece of frayed rope. True, he had nothing to do, as no one had utilized his services on the barge in days, but he suddenly realized how much he loved this river. His friend David Patten came along with two baited fishing poles, and plopped down beside him.

"Joseph wrote me a letter. Said things are still tough in Ohio. He also says hello."

"I miss him," said Porter. "Growing up in New York was prob'ly the best days of my life."

Patten thought a moment.

"You're a lucky man with this barge.

Porter flashed him a smile. "That I am." He knew what Patten meant. He had to be grateful for the good things he had anywhere he lived. Soon both moved to the barge deck and re-baited their poles. They didn't have to talk the rest of the after-noon — they merely enjoyed each others' company.

Patten had been fishing with him every day that week af-ter mid-day dinner to digest a while. Soon he departed and Por-ter was left alone to his thoughts. His listlessness began both-ering him, so he decided to leave an hour early.

Walking from the ferry to his cabin, he felt an urgent need to head to Independence to get away. Although he would offer Luana to go with him, he hoped she would decline.

At his cabin he was relieved to learn she was too busy with chores to accept.

"I'll bring home some geese," he said heading out the door. "So I'll be gone a couple days." He turned to baby Emily, "Next time, I'll take you," then he was off, horseback.

He rode into the city to obtain new rope and other sup-plies, then smiled at the prospects of a couple days freedom — sleeping under stars, hunting, and relishing the wilderness miles upstream from civilization.

He might even try it for a week, he mused, but he knew he could not stay away from baby Emily that long and in fact was missing her already. Being away from the tension between him and Luana however was refreshing. Luana had mentioned she'd check the ferry twice a day for possible passengers. It was common for passengers to wait for hours until the operator arrived. He had taught her over the weeks how to operate it — using Pritsimmons' mule that came with the barge to walk along shore with a rope which, fastened to a set of pulleys, pulled it across the river.

He had not been horseback much in recent months, not like he'd been in New York when he'd ride the farm several times a day and breed fine horses for the county fair. He missed riding and working with horses. He recalled the birth of this very colt, now a sizeable, respectable roan.

Saddle leather once again grated at his thighs and it felt good. He knew he'd be sore when he'd return, yet the rocking and rolling on horseback felt comforting to his system, and this particular animal had a rhythm he especially appreciated. It felt invigorating to feel at one with another creature again. He could tell the horse enjoyed him, as well. Their energies suited one another. He sensed it wished to be subservient to him.

He had sensed that in every animal he'd ever ridden — but especially this one. It was in fact the horse he loved more than any he had known, and was the only one he'd ever been able to actually call his own. He smiled as he realized how badly Luana and he did not get along: His horse respected him more than his own wife. One advantage, however, to married life over living at home with his parents: it felt satisfying having silver in his pockets — for the first time in his life in fact — to buy whatever he wanted, though most revenues from the ferry had to be saved for his pa's loan.

Arriving into Independence at dusk, he found large sway-ing oak trees overshadowing large homesteads in the heart of the city.

He came upon the merchandising district. A hotel or two, a barbershop, all the advantages of civilization were here, he observed, and he felt he'd enjoy them a few hours before part-ing society.

Several saloons were open and he heard peels of laughter drifting from one. He was tempted to enter before buying his supplies, but knew the stores were about to close, so he kept riding. The first general store was closing as he approached it. He dismounted, tied the horse, and entered just in time.

Gathering rope and several boxes of ammunition in his arms, he approached the proprietor, Ebeneezer Goodson.

"How much you sell this for?" said Porter.

The man looked him over carefully. "Two dollars for the rope. Fifty cents for each box of ammo."

Porter set down the supplies and stared into Goodson's firmly set eyes. "Is that what you normally charge?"

"I reckon," said Goodson, annoyed.

The door flapped a moment after Porter left the premises.

Down the street he entered another general store. Out-side, his horse seemed restless and whinnied. Inside the pre-mises Porter glanced back at his horse through oiled, wax-pa-pered windows, and decided to ignore its nervousness. He gazed directly at the proprietor. "How much is this rope?" Then, pointing to certain boxes of rifle balls, "and these?"

"Twenty-five cents for the rope, five cents for the ammo."

"I'll take it." As Porter pulled out cash and paid the man,

"How can your competition stay in business?"

"Which one?"

"Goodson's."

The man's eyes winced and he commented on the Indian summer they were having.

Porter read the proprietor's meaning: He was a proud Missourian, not wanting to admit some townspeople treat outsiders unfairly. Porter accepted the man's dodging the question. He tipped his hat and left.

Downstreet he passed the loud saloon with intentions of entering, when he saw upwards of thirty farmhands gathered across the road and a minister preaching to them — about rights. Their rights. To arise as one and shake off the intruders.

Porter was stunned. He'd witnessed problems in New York, he had seen the teasing of his friend Patten right here on Main Street — and the stares since — but this was the first sizeable gathering of organized opposition he had seen on the frontier. He slowed his horse to listen to the pastor.

CHAPTER 27

As the minister preached, bottles of cheap whiskey were passed around. At the climax of the sermon, calling upon the crowd to exercise their "Christian duty" to arm themselves and move out that very night on Mormon farms, one of the gentlemen in the back called for a toast to the preacher, while others began applauding and shouting. Soon a half dozen men began pouring whiskey over each other.

Porter smiled at the debacle.

He figured these were just a handful of prejudiced roughnecks, unlike most of the folks he'd ferried across the river, and that this group would be harmlessly drunk before they'd ever gather arms for the reverend's emotional outburst. It was also obvious that the reverend himself was a bit high on firewater and probably the next day would feel embarrassed for his rantings. As Porter rode downstreet, the mob began staggering away.

Porter smiled.

On his way out of town he decided to take the supplies

home first, then go hunting.

At his cabin, he loaded a sack full of beef jerky and bread for the hunt, recounting to Luana his interesting trip to Independence.

Luana was seated at the fireplace. "Why are you going out again?"

"We could use the meat, couldn't we?"

"Can't you hunt around here and be back in a few hours?"

"Not if you want good-sized game. They fled the area when we built up the village."

"But do you have to do that now?"

"If you want to eat meat anytime soon."

She grumbled, "I suppose you can go."

Porter was amazed how his wife wanted to keep him imprisoned close by, just to have him around, when she treated him like he she didn't want him around. He had seen that "clutching on" trait by a few other spouses — men and women, as well. He smiled as he thought of walking out the door any second. Momentarily, Luana held up the *Evening and Morning Star* she had borrowed from his parents:

"Brother Phelps doesn't have a right to say this," she said.

"Say what?"

"'Free People of Color.' That's the name of his article."

"What's wrong with that?"

"The original settlers here don't heed much to abolitionists," she said.

"Maybe they ought to."

"Folks in these parts don't take to newcomers like us looking down their noses at established customs."

Porter didn't say anything. He began whistling, looking forward even more to the hunting trip. He had learned another reason women don't act like horses — it doesn't do any good to attempt re-training them: Trying to straighten out his wife's opinions was like teaching a spirited mare a different way of galloping, and she probably found him equally stubborn. He was looking forward with even more relish to his impending journey.

"How could Phelps write such trash!" she said louder.

Porter wished he had bought a fifth of whiskey to take with him.

On the marshes near the river he heard geese squawking. He approached with his shotgun. A storm was coming and the birds were excited. As they landed, their honking seemed louder than he could remember. Thunder roared in the background and lightning crashed a hundred yards away.

The geese fluttered in panic. Porter fired and missed. The birds lit into the sky. He reloaded but it was too late. They were gone. Presently, he felt raindrops. He rambled to his gear and placed a poncho over himself. The rain poured furiously. He wondered why Luana could not see that local church leaders held the mantle to inspired leadership. They probably supported the newspaper's position and the fact Editor Phelps was outspoken about the truth, as well he should be. But arguing such matters with Luana only created contention, he had learned, so he tried whenever possible to bite his tongue in frustration.

Hoping the autumn storm would pass, he waited patiently. If anything, the torrents sheeted the forest even more ferociously. Then he smelled odors off the rich forest wind.

Lightning flashes came in a series — like artillery on a battlefield — and Porter packed his gear. He began the long hike to his ferry. He wondered why he had missed his shot at the flocks. Rarely did he miss. He noticed his hands shaking. He was angry.

He arrived at the barge. There, he noticed it tied securely, nonetheless vulnerably, several yards offshore. Luana's comments had dug into him.

Lightning bolts hit several hundred yards away, and he felt it best to move the craft as close to shore as possible, not leaving it an isolated target for lightning. He tied the ropes, using his mule to pull the barge tightly to shore.

In his hut he slept . . . or tried to sleep. The lightning would not cease. The wind set up a howl which haunted him. More thoughts of Luana. More frustration.

The hut window was perpetually open and the wet wind penetrated his blankets, which relieved him only slightly from the shiver he felt. He decided he had no alternative but to return to the cabin.

Luana was not home, and he felt disappointed not seeing Emily. His wife had mentioned earlier she might visit her parents in Independence. He was rather surprised to find himself actually missing her as well.

Flames leaped in the fireplace. He changed into dry wear. He ate bread crusts and milk, a favorite dish of his, then laid on the bed.

The rain outside would not cease.
Nor the lightning.

Later that morning, Porter awakened to distant thunder. He noticed outside a carriage passing with a man and woman, grim looks possessing them, and soon another carriage. They were old-time settlers living in the country heading home. He thought it odd they were returning so early in the morning. They must've spent the entire night in town, he mused.

As he rose to tend the fire, the door opened.

Luana entered with Emily and they began doffing their wet wraps. "I went to my folks' place for the evening," she said. "And you should've seen the courthouse."

"What're you talking about?"

"Independence courthouse," said Luana.

"What?"

"I'm talking about the townspeople — what do you think? And they're just like I said they'd be."

"That's nice. But what're you saying?" he said, slicing bread with a butcher knife and handing her a piece.

She placed it on the table. Her words were slower and more deliberate. "It's that article — I told you it'd do it."

"Guess you're a prophetess in your own right," he mumbled with a smile. "But I still don't know what the devil you're talking about."

"They're serious. I saw four, maybe five hundred people at the courthouse all night going on about the article Phelps wrote.

That small mob you saw with the preacher were just low-life rabble out for excitement. But Phelps has succeeded in stirring up the rank and file — the respectable citizenry."

Porter doubted her assessment but nodded politely and headed to a nearby meadow to bag small, wild game. He had no idea how accurate her intuition was, and how quickly it would soon affect their lives.

CHAPTER 28

At the ferry the next day, through the mist of the falling rain, Porter noticed the autumn's colors on the opposite shore fading.

On the trek back to his cabin he caught himself worrying. A depression set in and he could neither define its reason nor conquer it, despite his mental efforts.

At midnight Luana was awakened by a door rap. Porter was still awake, eating beef and cornbread, when he answered it.

"Porter, can I come in?"

A bit surprised at Mary Pettegrew's unaccustomed assertiveness, he allowed her inside.

"Luana," announced their neighbor, still somewhat breathless from a quick hundred yard journey, "I think David and I are going to another county."

"What're you doing that for?" said Porter.

"Haven't you seen them in their carriages? And that look in their faces when they ride past? 'You find it natural?"

"What are you saying?" said Porter.

"The folks here. They're going to their meetings every night at the court house. And the women look just as hateful as their menfolk."

"Prob'ly just upset over the weather," said Porter.

"What with them lightning storms and all, you'd think they'd see it as a warning to 'em from the heavens to stop their meetings. 'Ever notice how the storms don't start till their meetings begin? Folks all over say it's the loudest, meanest lightning they can remember. You'd think they'd stop."

"Oh," said Porter, "They're prob'ly just having big poker games in the courthouse."

"I've seen resentments grow for weeks, ever since their ministers started losing some of their flock to us."

"That's what I was telling you!" shouted Luana.

Continued Mary Pettegrew, "And if you was wise to it you'd be packing up."

"Wise to what?" said Porter.

"The courthouse mob had 500 folks. After they got mad at Brother Phelp's article on abolition, they wrote up a document. A dozen of 'em took it to Bishop Partridge and tried to get him to sign it."

Porter was surprised Mary's story was not only corroborating Luana's but was adding more detail. He said nothing, shocked at his sudden realization.

"What document did they write?" said Luana.

"Demanding our newspaper close," said Mary. "And all our businesses. They say it's competing with their businesses — ones that were established before we got here."

"I don't blame them," said Luana.

Porter whipped out of his reverie. "Are you loco? Having us here means more business for everybody!"

"Not for some of the businesses," said Luana. "It's too much competition. You know that."

"I . . . also know what I see — and they're the ones that're loco." Porter, however, knew Luana was right on this issue, but did not want to back down. He turned to Mary, "Well, what did Bishop Partridge tell the mob?"

"That we're not leaving."

"Myself, I'd tell them where to go," said Porter.

Luana raised her voice, "So what did Bishop Partridge tell them?"

Mary turned to her. "He said he'd have to get permission from Joseph in Ohio before he could make a promise to leave, and that it would take weeks to get word to him and then an answer. Then he told the mob to just give us some time."

"I'm sure with time they'll calm down," said Porter. "Most I've met are reasonable folk. It's just a misunderstanding." That's all he truly considered it. Certainly if the locals merely understood what Phelps was editorializing in the newspaper, they'd not be so antagonistic. Phelps had simply wanted a legal means, using Missouri's existing laws, to get "people of color" who were non-slave saints to move safely into their community to live, but the local Missourians were afraid such freemen would inspire an uprising among the local slaves and, with Phelps' closing admonition to "shun the very appearance of evil," might inspire some sort of widespread abolitionist activism.

Porter supported the abolitionists. In fact, he figured, if folks were educated to the evils of involuntary servitude, they'd think just like everyone else he had known in New York and Ohio who were opposed to the system. The good folks here seemed just as reasonable as New York and Ohio citizens with the exception of a few roughnecks and jealous pastors he'd run across, but that was to be expected anywhere — certainly no entire community would resort to bloodshed over differences on slavery. These were folks who did business with each other daily. He liked them. Still, he was disconcerted over the mob's demand that their newspaper close. He quickly came to the conclusion they could not be blamed; they were undoubtedly led by a few pastors who were riling them up with false information. In a few days, he figured, the false information would be exposed and everyone would settle back to their normal ways.

The next night at Independence Courthouse 500 people again gathered. These were the "old settlers" once again — regular Missouri folk. They angrily cheered as a preacher shouted, "Will we allow these immigrants dictating their beliefs to us?"

"No!" shouted the crowd.

"And will we allow their newspaper writings for abolitionism to go unchallenged?"

"No!" they screamed.

On the following night, Porter steered his barge after sunset. Twelve riders across the river waited, holding torches.

CHAPTER 29

Porter arrived at the shore of the horsemen and hailed the 12 riders. 'Bit warm for Halloween, eh boys?"

They muttered to one another and a couple chuckled, taking final swigs from a whiskey bottle and tossing it into the river. Then rode onto Porter's barge.

Half way across the river, Porter said, "That'll be 50 cents each."

One burped, "We're looking for charity tonight, son."

Porter was amused. "Sorry, boys, 'can't do that."

The same horseman pulled his rifle and pointed it at him. Porter lost his smile.

"Charity never faileth, boy, and neither does my aim."

Porter could perceive the fellow was so drunk he'd miss by a foot if he pulled the trigger. Porter held his composure and spoke again, "I don't know, boys. Maybe we oughta turn back."

Another horseman bellowed, "You take us the rest of the way if you value your barge." He held his torch higher.

Porter muttered, "What're you gonna do, burn the barge down with you on it?"

All the others chuckled.

One mumbled, "He ain't dumb. I like this boy."

Another, to the one with the torch, "At least not as dumb as you! You woulda' burned us clear down into the river!"

The others laughed. Another piped in, pulling up his pistol to Porter's head, "Just get us across and make good time. But forget about pay."

Porter shook his head, not fearing them. Were it not for the weapon now being lowered from his head, he would have fully grinned at their drunken conversation. As it was, he still thought them comical. He figured them merely drunken old sots — good old boys — out having a good time, so he said softly to their leader, "Tell your buddies they can pay up later when they return sobered up."

As they arrived at the opposite shore one turned to face Porter:

"You're one of 'em, ain't you?"

Porter was silent, but knew what he meant.

"You know what hot tar and feathers feel like on bare skin, son?"

The man was a couple years Porter's junior. He frowned in contempt at the backwoods designation of him as "son."

"Then promise you won't help other immigrants come across the river," said the roughneck. "And don't never visit your meeting-place again to worship whatever the devil you people worship. Is that clear, son?"

Porter was suddenly too angry to utter a sound. As he watched them lead their horses off his barge he heard:

"Why don't we just burn up his barge now?"

"He can build another one — but if we tar and feather him, his pores will give him something to think about," said another.

"You got your choice, son," said their leader. "Which'll it be?" They all stopped, turned and faced him. They were off the barge and now cornered him.

Porter glared into each of their eyes. Then he surprised them with:

"That's five cents a head."

"Come again?" said their leader, taken back by his brazenness.

They glowered at him, and more than one felt like shooting him on the spot. "You got a fast lip, boy," said the youngest. "I could take off them lips with my bowie knife, then maybe they wouldn't be so fast to talk back."

"You try it," said Porter, "and I'll take your whole rotten face off."

They all fell into silence, finally turned their horses, and left. They knew they'd get their revenge, but first had other things to do.

The same 12 horsemen rode into Independence and joined 30 others at the courthouse.

A mile west of town, the same horsemen arrived with the other 30 at the farmhouse of W.W. Phelps, editor of the *Evening and Morning Star* newspaper, printer of the infamous "abolition-ist article." The horsemen threatened him so he would divulge the whereabouts of the printing press but Phelps would not tell them. In retaliation, they swarmed into his cabin, smashed his furniture, then lit into the woods searching for the press. They discovered it at an outbuilding and proceeded to demolish it with clubs. Phelps' wife sobbed: The press, used mostly for commer-cial work, was their chief means of livelihood.

Meanwhile, Porter tied down the barge for the night, then swabbed the deck with water and soap, brushing mud and manure from the surface with a broom. Suddenly, David Patten galloped up and reined to a halt.

"Bring your rifle!" yelled Patten. "There's trouble!"

Porter jumped from the deck and ran the hundred yards across the woodland trail to his cabin. From there he emerged with his rifle, quickly saddled his roan, and joined Patten and neighbor David Pettegrew on the road, riding briskly.

They arrived at the public square where several saints watched with dismay at the "old settlers" now rendezvoused at the public square. These local citizens suddenly turned their horses and galloped away, howling like wolves.

Porter, Patten and Pettegrew rode to a home across the street from the square, and this is the scene they discovered: The wolf-hunters had dragged Porter's bishop, Edward Par-tridge, from his home into the square and tied him beside an-other, Charles Allen. Both had hot tar poured on them, followed by a bag of feathers, while their families watched.

Porter and his two neighbors stood stunned as they saw both the victims moaning in excruciating pain from the hot tar.

Allen was taken back to his home by family members and friends, while Porter, Patten and Pettegrew picked up David Partridge and carried him into his home where he would undergo the even more distressful experience of having the tar scraped, necessitating pulling off large pieces of skin. There, his wife cried as all three men removed the tar. Porter meanwhile held Partridge's hand.

Several hours later they were all exhausted. Porter helped lay Partridge on his bed, where he groaned. A tincture of herbs was applied across his body to help with the healing and the pain.

Porter went to the doorway and gazed at the moon, angry that his friends and fellow immigrants had been the target of both religious and political prejudice. He recalled the threats of the 12 horsemen directed toward him and his barge. His heart sank as he suddenly pictured his ferry as a target.

He shouted for Patten and Pettegrew to join him. All three ran to their horses tied in the town square. He would have to save the ferry.

CHAPTER 30

Porter and his two neighbors rode to the dock and discovered the barge missing.

When he gazed across the river he was relieved to find it tied at the opposite bank. The twelve horsemen had evidently used it at their leisure and left it unharmed, possibly too drunk to even remember to carry out their threat.

Porter immediately climbed into a small boat with David Patten and together they rowed across the river to retrieve the ferry.

Neighbor David Pettegrew meanwhile sat at the hut to guard it. He feared the large mob might take out their frustration on the ferry hut. He cradled his shotgun in his arms. He heard a horseman approach. He cocked his weapon. The horse hooves grew closer. He discerned the outline of a man on horseback. He aimed at him, then tightened his finger to the trigger.

"David?" said the voice.

Pettegrew, peering through the mist, recognized the oncoming rider Orin Rockwell.

An hour later Orin and his son sat alone at the hut, cradling weapons and guarding the barge. Pettegrew and Patten had returned to their own homes.

Porter's father fought a nagging cough; he had come to merely visit his son, not knowing all the trouble until Porter told him. Presently they heard eerie noises in the dark. As they sat in silence, the younger Rockwell brought up a topic even he was surprised to hear himself say:

"Pa, when I was a kid, how come I didn't get much time from you?"

"Well I don't rightly remember it, but I was awful busy trying to make ends meet on our farm back in New Hampshire and New York."

"I'd come to you a lot, just to get picked up and held, and usually got turned down."

"I better get back to my cabin now, boy. I'm not feeling the best today." He coughed again and arose.

Porter watched him disappear in the dark. He glanced back at his barge sitting in the moonlit waters, wondering how well he really knew his father.

In the cabin at breakfast, Porter sat across from Luana.

"I read the article," she said. "Brother Phelps had it coming to him."

"To actually destroy his press?" said Porter.

"The settlers already have their ways about slavery, I told you that."

"So any viewpoint different from theirs can be destroyed?"

"We must be more sensitive around our neighbors," she said.

"Whose side are you on?"

"Both sides are at fault."

"How can a side that wants former slaves living with us be at fault?" he said.

"For publishing about it."

"And making our views known?" he said.

"That can be destructive."

"I'd say," he said, "after what I saw at the Phelps.'"

"So hopefully we've learned to keep our views to ourselves."

"How can you support something without making your views known? If we're for free people of color living with us, should we just think it and not say nothin'? How're things ever going to get changed?"

Luana held a dish and smacked it on the table without breaking it:

"You don't get it. These people had a claim to this land before we came. We should come here, keep quiet and be respectful of the old ways. They see us as Northerners tromping in and saying anything we please and too loudly while we're at it, and it all flies in the face of their traditions. It really smells badly to them. It stinks."

Porter studied her a moment. "You really have a ways to go to learn how to defend the truth."

"I think you have twice as far to go."

Porter arose to walk outside for fresh air. He slammed the door behind him, angry at not only her for justifying their enemies' outrageous attacks but at himself for contending with her. Outside, he reflected on his deepest theological discoveries; he now realized Joseph's teachings were correct even on the issue of enemies: Whereas Porter had thought others around them were reasonable folk who mainly differed on doctrines which they for the most part did not understand, he was beginning to realize there was a bit more to their opposition than he had at first accepted. It seemed clearer to him there was indeed a Prince of Darkness who influenced men to oppose the Kingdom of God, which Joseph maintained had been restored by Divine personages and angels. The witness of the Lord's Spirit to Porter was undeniable on these tenets; he merely had his own weaknesses to deal with, a particularly disconcerting problem since he was tossed into a spirited cockfight with his wife almost daily; thus, he felt he had experienced on a first-hand basis the matter of opposition, and had found it more distressing than he'd ever imagined. Additionally, his frustration with himself increased whenever he realized he gave daily service to the Adversary with his contentious nature. He further felt, as Joseph had enlightened their people, that all disputations, especially the spirit of fighting, gave not only homeage — but an actual, increased power — to the Adversary, a being, Joseph taught, who had been cast out with a third of the hosts of heaven in their pre-mortal life and who was now the author of all wars, inhumanity, anger, and contention. While it was becoming increasingly apparent to Porter that the Adversary inspired men to fight the church which Porter felt deeply to have the authority of God, he also saw the role of this King of Darkness as one who inspired mediocrity, neutrality, and apathy toward spiritual matters. His frustration with himself remained, but his anger evaporated as he thought through these issues.

Luana came to the door and blew out a silent sigh. She gazed at his back, her demeanor also softening. He turned around to face her.

She calmly announced, "Sister Pettegrew overheard 'wolfhunters' in town bragging that it hasn't come to an end."

"Then," said Porter in a new voice trembling with determination, "we'll have to make it end."

The next day Porter stood inside his favorite general store at Independence with Mr. Ellison waiting on him. Two women in the store spoke in hushed tones . . . yet Porter overheard them — talk in the community had it that local Mormon leaders were refusing the demands of the mob leaders, and would pay.

One of the women, whose husband was among the mob committee, whispered what she had heard. Her husband had admitted to her that most of them would probably not take any legal action against the outsiders, as there wasn't a lot they could do. "So they would figure out something else."

Mr. Ellison, the proprietor, seemed embarrassed once again for his community, and acted almost apologetic to Porter; he seemed especially uncomfortable that the two women had acted with such indiscretion in speaking in front of him, despite their whispers.

"Ladies," said Ellison, "Mr. Rockwell here is our ferry operator, one of our guests in the area."

The two women laughed nervously and shook his hand.

"Ladies," nodded Porter, then he thanked Mr. Ellison for the goods, paid him and walked to the door. He turned and smiled back at the three. "I ain't what you'd call a guest. Guests are temporary." He strode out the door. The two women gaped as he left.

In the town square he discovered a teenager holding a large red flag. Shouts from people on the street gathering indicated it was a token of blood. From his ponderings the day previously, Porter was now not so surprised that an entire community could be polarized against a society which possessed different political and religious ideologies.

He rode home sickened. He just wanted a peaceful community to raise his coming child and to operate the ferry — a profession in which all the family funds were now tied up. He had repaid his father only $12 of the loan, and it would obviously take even longer than he had planned, the way business was suddenly slowing, to pay the balance.

Three official-looking Missourians wearing suits and carrying papers arrived at the W. W. Phelps' cabin where the front broken window had been patched with boards. Chiefest among them was Lieutenant Governor Lilburn W. Boggs, a stocky, surly soul whose goatee reminded one of a distinguished-looking, well-fed billygoat.

Phelps, Porter, his father Orin, David Patten, David Pettegrew and several other Mormons greeted the Missouri officials, hopeful something would be done to put a stop to the escalating threats. Phelps showed them the ransacked interior of his cabin. He then led them through a woodland path across crackling red autumn leaves sparkling from the dew-covered ground, and finally arrived at the wrecked newspaper press.

Boggs and the other officials stood over the smashed printing apparatus and gazed at them sympathetically.

"Well?" said Phelps.

"Well," muttered Boggs after a long, assessing silence, "it looks like it'd be best if you and your people simply left."

"What're you talking about?" said Orin Rockwell, aghast.

"I believe you heard me," said Boggs.

"Leave what?" said Orin.

"The county. Just leave Jackson County. Obviously the people don't want you here."

"The devil if we care what they want!" said Porter. "This is our land, too!"

"Wait a minute, wait a minute," added Orin. "It's not all the folks that are doing this."

"But most folks would if they could," said Patten. "I've studied 'em."

"I believe he's right," said Boggs.

"Well, we ain't leaving," said Porter.

"Porter's right!" added Patten. "This is our community! We can't leave!"

"Well, you're gonna face the consequences then," said Boggs. "Good day, gentlemen."

Rockwell, Phelps, and the other immigrants glanced at each other, stunned, as the three Missouri officials strode back to their horses.

Patten rushed ahead to catch up. "Can't state militia protect us — and can't the governor arrest any of the mobs doing this?"

Boggs mumbled without breaking stride. "And put 500 men in Independence jail?"

Presently, Porter and the others studied the three officials as they rode down the road and disappeared around a woodland bend.

Orin muttered, "What's next?"

CHAPTER 31

What's next was William Phelps coming to Porter's ferry. He wanted to cross the river and visit several saints in order to collect money.

"What for?" said Porter.

"We need a thousand dollars to pay for four attorneys I talked with."

"What good will that do?"

"Governor Dunklin said he'd personally guarantee the law will be enforced, and that we'll be protected by the state militia. But first we need the attornies to begin the fight in court. I think the Missourians will come to their senses when they see the law is on our side, so they'll settle down." Phelps was enthusiastic. "I want my press replaced so badly it itches."

Porter donated three dollars — considerably more than he could spare — and he was relieved to find Luana supportive of the donation when he informed her of it back at the cabin.

At first he hoped she was coming to grips with the fact they needed to oppose their enemies; within moments, however he realized she was merely optimistic that successful attorney intervention would placate the restless locals, while forcing the Saints to admit they were wrong.

Porter broiled when he heard her assessment. But he kept his mouth shut.

When the local ministry learned the saints were not only staying but were actually retaliating with a lawsuit — they were livid. Then the inevitable happened.

Hundreds of Missourians descended on the courthouse the last day of October, 1833. After a short meeting, "wolf-hunters," as they called themselves, swarmed horseback into the 12 mile long cluster of Mormon villages. Ten riders attacked a lone cabin a mile from Porter's home — they entered the cabin, drove out the family, tore up the furniture, ran across the street to the next cabin, and repeated the adventure.

A second group of wolf-hunters arrived, spotted the horses of their comrades, and joined in, ripping the place apart and breaking windows.

Meanwhile at Porter's parents' home, a dozen wolf-hunters dressed in war paint crashed in, whooping, yelling and chopping up furniture with axes. Sarah Rockwell and her oldest daughter still living with them, 17 year old Electa, watched in horror as the men cut open beds and scattered thousands of feathers in the air. They finally threw chairs out the windows. One man grabbed Sarah and shouted, "Where's your husband?"

"Gone."

Orin was in fact searching for Porter, having heard the wolf-hunters attacking another cabin two hundred yards through the woods. Porter's younger sisters and brothers meanwhile were playing with friends at the Pettegrew property. The rain now began pouring in torrents.

The wolf-hunter who held Sarah pushed her out the door. She fell outside and Electa ran to help. They watched in the rain as seven other wolf-hunters arrived horseback.

One shouted to the others, "This is Rockwell's parent's place!"

"Who's that!" said one.

"The barge boy!"

The man at the doorway yelled, "Tie the roof!"

The seven newly arrived horsemen screamed with glee and tied ropes to the roof, then with their horses they began pulling.

The roof roared and groaned, and finally jerked forward and crashed to the ground.

The men cheered.

Sarah and her daughter burst out crying.

The rain poured into their roofless home, soaking furniture and destroying heirlooms.

"You womenfolk tell 'barge boy' his place is next, and so is his barge!"

The men galloped away cheering, laughing and whooping, joining other horsemen on the road who were breaking up other cabins.

Porter stood guard at his barge, having left his dinner half eaten. He did not know of the attacks on his parents' farm or at his neighbors, and was concerned primarily over the safety of his ferry.

He chewed beef jerky as he sat outside the hut by the river. He cradled his shotgun and two pistols, when his wife ran up. She breathlessly announced:

"Your pa's at our cabin. He says the neighbors are being attacked!"

"Take the horse!" cried Porter. He began to run the hundred yards towards his cabin, carrying his weapons, when he stopped and glanced back at his barge, wondering if the vehicle he so treasured would be safe.

He resumed running towards his home, knowing his father must be feeling weak since he had not made the trip to the ferry himself.

Arriving at his own cabin, Porter noticed his father handing little Emily back to Luana. She had just returned on horseback ahead of Porter, and had earlier rounded up Porter's brothers and sisters, who were now all standing around them and listening.

"Son," said Orin, eyes wide with fear, "The wolf-hunters are moving on the whole settlement!"

Porter stared in amazement. His dog, Ugly, was barking with excitement. "You can't bark anymore, boy," said Porter. "Not if you wanna give away our whereabouts."

Ugly seemed to understand, and ceased barking.

"I've gotta get back to Sarah and Electa!" cried Orin.

"You stay here!" said Porter. "I'll get Ma and Electa out of your cabin. Luana — you take these kids and some food and follow Papa. Pa, take them to our old lean-to in the woods."

Porter noticed the older man shivering. He grabbed a blanket and put it over Orin's shoulders. "Luana, get all the blankets and bring them!"

At that, Porter mounted his horse and began galloping toward his parents' home.

On the road he noticed other cabins in the distance being unroofed. Then, as he arrived at his parents' property, he spotted his mother and Electa crying beside the small barn. He beheld the roofless house that he had helped to build, which held their most precious possessions. His stomach turned.

"Mama, Electa, I'll help you get to the lean-to in the woods. They'll be back to burn the barn, but they don't know about the lean-to."

"What about the cow!" yelled Electa.

"Bring her!" said Porter. "She's all that's left."

CHAPTER 32

Within the hour, all were safely at the woodland lean-to, not visible from any cabin or road. Ugly was quiet and the place was peaceful. All were lost in thought, re-living the last few hours, and wondering what would happen next. Mary Pettegrew ran up and told Porter her husband had found eighty year old David Bennett ill in his cabin where the mob had grabbed his gun from his hands, beaten him with it, then broken it over his head and left. One Missourian had returned to the cabin to finish him off by shooting him in the head, but Pettegrew had found old Bennett still alive, then had run to find a doctor. After David had returned to his wife Mary, he told her what he'd seen. At that point Mary had gone searching for Porter. She now requested both Porter and Orin to join her husband in a rendezvous with a small army of Mormons on the road to Independence.

"I thought," said Porter, "you wanted to flee from the violence."

"I did!" said Mary. "But I hate bullies."

"Know how you feel," he mumbled. He mounted his horse and asked Mary to stay with his wife, mother, brothers and sisters.

Porter's younger brothers demanded they ride with them, but Porter refused.

"The womenfolk need your protection," he said. While partially true, he also wanted them free from the impending warfare.

He and Orin loaded their weapons and launched their ride toward Independence. Three neighbors galloped up next to them. Soon came five others led by David Pettegrew.

Still other Mormons came from cabins along the road, all armed with rifles. They joined forces with his band, and soon Porter, Pettegrew, Orin and a dozen others were riding toward Independence to face the mobbers. Moments later they came upon a messenger who told them the Missourians had retreated for the night.

Porter's band decided to stop at Phelp's cabin. There, another dozen Mormons were arriving, and they held a quick meeting. Porter listened to heated proposals and counterproposals. Pettegrew suggested all the villagers move into one small area for protection. Another argued they hadn't any central place to gather since they were scattered twelve miles along the road. Nor did they have food or stock in any one place in case the enemy decided to lay siege against them. "We could bring our animals, but have to leave our cropland," argued another.

Finally Porter spoke:

"Why not just meet them head on? We've all got guns."

At that there was silence.

David Whitmer and William Phelps argued the proposal — they volunteered to seek peace warrants against some of the mob leaders, and their charismatic presence swayed the gathering to one more attempt at peace.

Porter figured most of them were afraid of battle. Indeed, the saints were vastly outnumbered, and the mob members all owned guns, too. Porter returned with his father in the silent night air to their original Missouri home — the lean-to concealed in the woods near the river.

The next day Porter accompanied Whitmer, Phelps and Pettegrew to the home of a magistrate, and there they explained their case. Whitmer voiced his fear the mobs would return that very night.

The question was where.

The magistrate, Danton Andrews, confirmed the mob indeed did have a plan. Porter discerned Danton's sincere desire to help, but he also perceived his fear. Apologetically the judge declined to issue warrants.

On their return home, the four Mormons turned their horses onto the main road leading to the Whitmer Settlement. Nightfall had set in and they discovered wolf-hunters with torches passing from the opposite direction. It was dark and the enemy did not recognize the other riders as immigrants. Whitmer overheard comments from one of the riders — something about Colesville, one of the Mormon villages. Whitmer, in order to not be heard by the riders, whispered to Phelps, and the latter took off in a gallop. Phelps rode ahead to Colesville to advise Parley P. Pratt of the invasion.

And the warning proved timely.

Later in the evening, after Pratt had been warned, two Missouri spies were sent ahead of the main Missouri force to ascertain if the Colesville community were asleep. Pratt caught sight of the two men, and yelled a warning back to the others. The two Missouri spies — in a panic — jumped Pratt. They began clubbing him, when Pratt's neighbors galloped up, grabbed the two spies, and dragged them into Colesville, to jail.

By midnight the two spies confessed of a main force waiting downroad to attack the village. However, since the two spies did not return to the mob, it became apparent the mob had become fearful and abandoned its plans. The two spies were then released by the Mormons.

Frustrated by the Colesville events, the Missouri mob decided to move on another community which had already proven itself vulnerable.

Meanwhile, Porter rode at the forefront of 10 neighbors horseback. All carried rifles and shotguns to avenge the destruction of 15 cabins. Porter figured his family was still safely gathered at the lean-to in the woods. He also guessed his full-sized cabin was still probably untouched by the wolf-hunters, as they had all retreated hours earlier when they had seen several parties of Mormons mounting up to come after them.

Most wolf-hunters were now beating a hasty retreat into Independence. One group of a dozen, however, was looking to celebrate at a nearby tavern, not knowing the Mormons were out in full force.

Porter was the first to spot this party. He broke into a gallop, feeling exhilerated. The growing anxiety which had gnawed at him for days suddenly gave way to a thrill he had not felt since he had faced bullies in his younger days in New York.

He noticed the Missourians were accompanied by the same 16 year old boy he had seen earlier sporting the red flag as a token of blood, and he observed that the boy was again carrying it.

The dozen wolf-hunters were about to dismount and enter the tavern, when Porter and his neighbors arrived. The leading wolf-hunter spotted him, and immediately assumed them to be fellow riders of another wolf-hunting group.

"Come join us, boys!" he yelled. "Time to get soused a little and celebrate!"

"Just one question!" yelled back Porter. "You want us to shoot you all now or wait till it's easier after you're drunk as skunks?"

The wolf-hunter gasped. He shouted at his men, "Turn your rifles on 'em, boys!"

The wolf-hunters whirled their weapons and opened fire.

CHAPTER 33

A rifle ball zinged past Porter's ear. A glance behind him revealed none of his fellows had dropped.

Then all his men opened fire on the Missourians.

Most shots missed. But Porter aimed straight at the dismounted leader and fired. The ball whistled past the man's head and hit someone behind him — the 16 year old boy — right in the thigh. He grasped his leg and screamed. His horse whinnied. It frightened the other horses and they bucked.

One Missourian fired at Orin and missed. Not giving up, the same Missourian charged Porter's father and reared back to fist him. But Orin met the Missourian's chin with a rifle swing and the fellow flew off his horse.

Another fired at Porter's chest yet managed to hit only his rifle butt. The ball ricocheted away and hit another Missourian in the big toe. The man screamed and galloped away. Porter then charged their leader. The Missourian froze with fear, and Porter recognized him as the most obnoxious of the mobbers who had threatened him on his ferry. Porter smiled and clobbered the fellow with his rifle stock across the chest, knocking him off his horse. The man sprang to his feet and took off running.

David Pettegrew defended himself from a blow by one of the Missourians, then fisted him in the mouth.

Another Missourian grabbed his wounded sixteen-year old comrade's reins and retreated toward Independence. The other locals broke into a gallop.

Porter and the others, seeing the retreat, slowed their horses. A quick check among them found none of the immigrants even wounded. Eleven of them had repelled twice as many Missourians. They sent up a victorious cheer.

From 30 yards away, while still retreating, the wounded boy's big brother halted his horse and turned back to shout at Porter:

"I know you, boy, and where your ferry's at!" He and the other wolf-hunters galloped away foaming with anger.

Porter's band rode back surveying the damage: They traveled on the main road leading to the Whitmer Settlement. There they discovered the biggest mistake they'd yet made: Every hundred yards they found a pillaged cabin. If they had known, they would never have left the village.

His band dispersed to their cabins.

David Pettegrew and Orin Rockwell were the last to part from his side. The former commented he was coming down with the ague. Porter returned with his father to the family lean-to. Seeing all were safe and asleep, he rode toward the river. The cold night air revealed the steam from his horse's breath, and the low-horizoned moonlight cast a blue pallor across the woodland path. Wearily, he made his way to the ferry.

There, he waited with four weapons loaded, again standing guard. He found the cooling air forcing him to build a fire. As he sat before the snapping flames, he heard horse hooves approaching. The now moonless sky filled him with a mild apprehension; he could see practically nothing. Then a dozen horsemen appeared. They slowly came forward. The flames from his campfire bounced a wavering orange light off several heavily whiskered faces. They stopped 10 yards from him and stared. He heard a gun click.

He blew out a sigh and stood, waiting for their first move.

CHAPTER 34

Watching the horsemen scatter to the sides, Porter moved into his hut for cover. When he noticed them take positions behind trees he yelled:

"Halt there!"

"You know why we've come, boy!" yelled their leader.

"I know you're trespassing!"

"We just want your services!" shouted another, laughing. Several others chuckled.

"I service who I please, and I don't please to serve you, so you can turn around!"

"Then we'll just have to borrow the ferry," yelled their leader. "Unfortunately," he mumbled, "we don't have anyplace to go on it."

The others laughed harder. Suddenly they heard Porter laughing. Curious, they stopped laughing.

Porter aimed out the doorway. They caught sight of his rifle barrel gleaming in the campfire light.

"That's no way to treat customers, son," said their leader nervously.

Porter cocked the rifle, aiming right at him. Immediately the men opened fire. One shot cracked a window, the others harmlessly hit the outside log walls.

Porter fired but the ball hit a tree. All his weapons were single-shooters, so when he fired, he had to go to his next weapon, not having time to reload. He picked up a shotgun off the table beside him. "Come out here and face me!" he shouted.

He heard more laughter. Their leader called out, "You out of ammo, boy?"

Porter fired toward the voice — his shotgun boomed.

The fellow bellowed, "Whoa! That was close!"

Porter grabbed a pistol from the table. He pointed it toward the sound of footsteps running towards him. He pulled the trigger.

"Sorry, boy!" said a voice. "Missed again."

He picked up his last pistol.

Someone threw a stone to the roof of his hut. It hit and Porter whirled his weapon to the sound and fired.

Disgusted with himself for falling for the trick and wasting shots, he decided as a last resort to pick up the rifle and use it as a club.

He ran into the mist where, 20 feet from the hut, he came directly into a semi-circle of men now on foot, moving towards him. He dashed toward the leader to strike him with his rifle stock . . . when he was clubbed from behind.

Lying on the ground, Porter beheld all the men, each now holding an ax, moving past him toward the barge. His eyes were tilted skyward, dazed, as he heard the sound of chopping from a dozen axes — and then a peel of laughter.

Porter awakened, what seemed to be one second later, to observe the men on horseback all disappearing into the mist. He moved his dazed head slowly toward the river and beheld his barge sinking, one end tilting up like the bow of a great ship and then, without warning, suddenly diving below surface with a mass of loud, gurgling bubbles.

He passed out.

CHAPTER 35

The next morning Porter awakened to the sun's red ball beaming through tall trees, the dawn light melting the November frost.

He crunched across stiffened leaves carpeting the woodland floor, and with a few breaths of fresh air he found his horse feeding. He mounted it.

Stopping at the woodland family lean-to, he found all were safe, but learned they had worried themselves sick over him. He reported the barge incident, then decided to do something about it. He quickly ate fried eggs and wheat mush over a campfire, then rode off alone to the William Phelp's cabin.

There, he discovered four church leaders plus five other men mounting up to ride into town. Without hesitation he joined them.

On the road they split into two groups to visit circuit judges.

Arriving at the home of Judge Samuel Weston, Porter's group appealed for arrest warrants for mobbers they had recognized.

Weston's response was similar to their last attempt. "You'll have a grand time of it," he said, "trying to get the constable to use these warrants."

"Why?"

"The whole county's up in arms." He handed the five men two signed warrants.

As they rode into Independence to visit the constable, they were silent. Porter knew what each of the others was thinking, and was the first to stop his horse and turn around.

From the corner of his eyes he noticed the others also stop and turn around.

The whole scheme seemed futile. Without a word said, they agreed the warrants would act as empty tin buckets under a waterfall. Porter noticed three Missouri horsemen passing from the other direction and stopping. They were neighbors to Phelps — non-Mormons, but friendly.

Phelps greeted them cordially and the three expressed dismay at the recent turn of events. One had recent news:

"Last night three Mormons caught our neighbor pillaging a store. Everyone recognized him — Richard McCarty. Seven folks testified against him, but he was acquitted. Then he decided to counterfile, and the three Mormons who had caught him were jailed!"

"Where are those three?"

"I doubt the sheriff will let you see them — but we'll get a message to them if you like."

"Tell them," said Phelps, "we'll get them freed."

One of the Missourians glared at him. "I'll do that, but if I was you I'd worry about my own hide. Things are going farther than you think."

Porter snorted.

"I'm telling you this for your own good," the Missourian blurted. He felt genuine empathy for the Mormons, but discerned Porter's warlike spirit. "Whoever wounded that sixteen-year old at the skirmish Halloween night shouldn't have even got up that day."

Porter glanced to the side.

Another Missourian added, "Most of the folks around here are saying this Monday'll be a bloody day."

Monday was three days away, November 4th.

The Mormons thanked them for their support, then dispersed to each of their cabins. It began to rain. Porter went to his property, figuring his family safe at the woodland lean-to.

At noon he arrived at his full-sized cabin. He knew it was vulnerable to the mobs, but the last time he'd seen the structure it was still untouched. Now, however, he discovered a sight that sickened him. The door had been left wide open. He walked inside and found his furnishings vandalized. The feather bed was cut open, Luana's books were ripped, clothes were in shreds, windows were smashed and furniture was chopped into firewood. One chest of drawers that Porter's mother had given them — which had been handed down from her grandmother — was destroyed beyond repair. And the roof lay beside the cabin.

Still dazed from the sight, he staggered to his woodland lean-to. To his relief he found his wife and child, parents, brothers and sisters all still safe. Luana greeted him with a hug.

Porter smiled, "Our guests back at the house don't treat the furniture like they used to."

Luana smiled through her tears. "It happened today."

Porter's mother asked, "Has anyone seen Luana's parents?"

Porter shook his head, still dazed. He had seen none of his in-laws. He stared into the pouring rain, teeth clenched, seething.

CHAPTER 36

The Missourians also seethed. Three days passed and Monday arrived, November 4, 1833. On this dew-covered morning, 19 Mormons rode forward to attack any Missourian wolf-hunters they might discover. Soon, the Mormon band was spotted by two children. The youngsters ran to Wilson's grocery where three groups of Missouri riders were gathered, eating. The two kids told them what they had just seen.

From Wilson's store, a combined army of fifty Missourians charged off to ambush the 19 Mormons.

When the 19 spotted the coming Missourians they slipped into a cornfield. Suddenly 11 other Mormons appeared, creating a force of 30.

The 50 Missourians saw them and opened fire. All 30 Mormons charged the 50. Attacking each other through rows of corn, 17 of the Mormons had guns while all 50 locals were armed. They converged on each other in all-out war. One Mormon was shot — the first to ever die in battle — Andrew Barber. But the Mormons killed two Missourians — Thomas Linville and an attorney, Hugh Brazeale — and wounded six others.

Several Missourians were knocked unconscious when they had horses shot out from under them and they crashed onto fallen trees. Within minutes the Missourians were overrun and suddenly consumed with confusion. Hearing the Mormons whoop and holler, they looked back at their leader and saw him deserting the battle. Overwhelmed by panic, they turned their horses and galloped away.

The Mormons chased them a few rods, then stopped. They watched them retreat from their far smaller force, and howled with laughter, joy, and relief.

Back at Wilson's grocery, additional Missourians were gathering and, having now heard the report of the battle, glanced silently at one another. Several mumbled and others swore. They knew the men who had been killed — brothers, cousins, friends — and were as angry as hornets. But they felt — for the first time ever — afraid of the Mormons, who were now fighting back — and successfully: first, four days ago at the tavern skirmish in which Porter had participated, and now this one.

"What the devil do we do now?" said one wolf-hunter.

At the Rockwell lean-to in the woods, Porter and his brothers Peter, Horace and Merritt arrived with David Pettegrew and four others. They animatedly announced to Porter's parents details of the cornfield battle. Sarah Rockwell had considered her three youngest sons too young for such fighting, and heretofore had kept them, with Porter's assistance, sheltered from the fray, but today the boys had managed with Orin's blessing to convince her they were not only old enough, but were in fact needed to defend their village. They were mere teenagers, she argued, but the boys got their way. As they recounted their adventure, they leaped in the air, punching it with excitement.

Their father, Orin, demanded they should all continue the offensive and rescue the three Mormons jailed by Judge Weston.

Excitedly, they shouted in agreement.

Another dozen neighbors arrived before the Rockwell band left the lean-to and, by the time they were mounted up and riding towards Independence, they were joined by yet another, larger band under the direction of Lyman Wight.

Now, the Mormon force of over 200 strong were riding towards Independence. Porter looked over at his father and brothers and sensed their consternation. He said softly, "Pa, Horace, Merritt, Peter . . . "

They looked at him curiously.

He smiled.

They relaxed and also smiled.

He then let out a war cry. His brothers shouted in return and, with a thrill in the air, they broke into a gallop. The entire force began to gallop behind the Rockwells. Any fears the force had were now dissipated as the band whooped, hollered, and shouted.

They were all ready for war.

With the sun lowering into a greying sky, their official leader, Lyman Wight, caught up beside Porter. Both looked back at their force and realized the power of their band. Before, the Mormons had been reticent. Now, after a key victory at the cornfield, they were confident. And more importantly, they had had enough.

Unknown to them, however, were several hundred armed mobbers waiting in the streets of Independence.

Further unknown to them, a mile up the road and riding directly towards them, an armed Missouri state militia was ready for them with twice their number.

CHAPTER 37

Porter's band was determined to make its revenge.

Thundering horse hooves were heard all the way into town as both armies converged on each other. Porter glanced up, noting a full moon, a good sign for armies of ancient days.

At the forefront of the Missouri militia was Colonel Thomas Pitcher, commander of the state force. He slowed his horse and trotted alone toward the halted Mormon troops. Porter glanced at his own commander, Lyman Wight, who now rode forward to greet Pitcher. Troops from both the rag-tag Mormon band and the uniformed militia glared at each other.

"Sir," announced Colonel Pitcher, "the governor has sent me, but not for the purpose of war. I hereby confess that we citizens are to be blamed for grievous injustices to your people, mostly from a certain unrestrained prejudice. However, as an act of good faith, I request you to give us your arms, and we will all feel better about one another."

Porter shouted, "What!"

Colonel Pitcher piped in, "As a gesture of reconciliation, of course."

"Of course not," echoed Porter's lone voice.

"No," mumbled Porter's father. "My son is right."

But Lyman Wight looked relieved to hear the commander's offer.

Pitcher continued unruffled, "The state militia will be at your service for protection as well as at the service of the local Missourians in case any warfare re-emerges. You will all be protected."

Porter rode forward to his commander, Lyman Wight, and mumbled, "It's a trick."

"I'm not sure we have any alternatives," muttered Wight.

"We've always got 'alternatives' when we keep our weapons," said Porter.

Wight thought a moment, then turned to face his men:

"You all gave me authority to lead you, and now we are at a crossroads. As your leader I feel we should follow the road of peace. The state is offering peace."

"Don't do it!" shouted Porter and his father Orin, as well as their neighbor David Pettegrew.

Porter's neighbor Patten shook his head. "We can prove to these people we are seeking peace at any cost. And by surrendering our weapons we will prove our point. I say we give them our weapons."

Porter glared at his friend Patten.

The Mormon horsemen mumbled among themselves, and nearly all agreed with the peace proposal.

Lyman Wight finally turned to Porter and Orin. "We're

farmers, not soldiers. Let's have these soldiers do the fighting for us."

The Mormon horsemen cheered.

Porter whirled his horse around and faced them: "I say we control our own destiny!"

But he was shouted down by a dozen men directly behind him.

Orin shouted, "How do we know whose side these soldiers will take?"

Colonel Pitcher yelled, "You have my word, gentlemen. We shall be neutral and fair!"

Another dozen Mormons bellowed, "Give them our guns! Let's give them up!"

Colonel Pitcher, seeing the flow of opinion, jumped in again:

"Excellent, gentlemen. Such overtures of peace will prove most convincing to the populace as a whole. And now, if you will simply throw down your weapons."

Lyman Wight turned to Colonel Pitcher, "We will on one condition."

Pitcher assessed him curiously.

"That you take arms," said Wight, "from the mobbers as well."

"The colonel thought a moment, smiled and nodded. "Again, you have my word, gentlemen."

Lyman Wight nodded in agreement to the peace proposal.

Pitcher turned to a non-commissioned officer beside him. "Sergeant, have the weapons gathered."

Wight called out to his men, "All right, men, show your faith and throw down your weapons."

The 200 Mormons dropped their rifles. Most of the men were relieved from the burden of fighting, but Porter held onto his.

Wight gazed at him. "We have made our decision, Porter. We need to act as one to show our intentions of peace."

Porter glared at him, then glanced at the militia colonel, who held a poker face, and finally back at his father, who nodded for him to join in.

Porter dropped his rifle.

That night he surveyed the damage to his barge. In the moonlight he found it difficult to assess anything beneath the murky water. He poked long sticks onto the submerged barge deck and found it riddled with ax holes. It seemed hopelessly damaged.

He glanced at the moon and noticed smoke drifting in front of it. His eyes widened. He realized the moment it had come . . . He jumped onto his horse and raced down the woodland path. Turning onto the main road, he galloped toward Independence. The torrential rain blurred both sights and sounds of the following scenes as Porter rode toward the center of their community: Hundreds of Missouri settlers attacked cabins, tossing torches. He realized every home was being hit. It seemed as if on cue that when the Mormon army had surrendered its weapons, the Missouri populace launched its rampage.

Mormon refugees poured onto the road, huddled in blankets.

The Missourians meanwhile stole all horses and farm animals they could find, herding them toward Independence, led by Reverend Isaac McCoy.

Porter grabbed a stick for a weapon. He spotted a Missourian riding towards him, and wanted his rifle. At 30 yards from him, Porter broke into a gallop. The Missourian panicked and pulled out his rifle — but was too late. Porter reared back with the stick and — like a knight with a lance — whacked the fellow from his horse and, in one motion, grabbed the rifle whirling in the air. He found it depleted of ammo. Another horseman spotted his comrade flat on the ground and shouted threats at Porter, then took out after him with a band of others.

Porter galloped toward the woods, mud flinging behind his horse's hooves. He had to get back to his family, but first lose his pursuers. While riding, he strapped the rifle to his saddle bag, hoping to load it later. With a half-dozen Missourians behind him now, he glanced to the sides and caught sight of 20 families running from burning cabins. The families joined hundreds of other immigrants being herded from the settlement. Porter glimpsed back and saw two riders opening fire. The gunshots whistled past as he turned a corner. He galloped off the woodland road. While passing a cabin 30 yards to his right, he noticed a man in his nineties being forced from his home — Jones was his name — and he was suddenly pushed into the mud. A young woman jumped to his aid. As she helped him up she scolded the Missourians surrounding them: "Grandpa was a life guard to General Washington himself. Do you call yourselves citizens?"

A Missourian scoffed, "He should have died at Valley Forge, little lady, and saved us the trouble."

The others laughed, then three threw torches into his cabin and galloped away. Porter dismounted and helped the old fellow to safety. Across the road he spotted two other old veterans who had been driven from their sickbeds. As their wives helped them, Porter grabbed the shoulders of both old fellows and got them to their wagons. Before a horse could be hitched to the wagon, a mobber fired his rifle and the wagon's horse fled. The mobber faced Porter and threatened him to stay away from helping "the old folk," so Porter dove under the mobber's horse to frighten it, and the horse reared up.

The horseman fell off the back. Porter grabbed the fellow's pistol and whirled it up towards him. Disconcertedly, the Missourian watched minutes later as his horse disappeared, pulling the two old Mormon families away in a wagon. Porter smiled, pointing his pistol at the man. He finally placed it in his own coat pocket, tipped his hat to the mobber, mounted his own horse, and galloped away. The Missourian stood in the road, stunned, stripped of his horse and gun. "What about my pistol?" he yelled.

"The spoils of war," mumbled Porter.

Riding further, Porter noticed the sky lit from cabins burning.

He glanced back and spotted three other Missourians aiming at him. He instinctively ducked and rode in jagged lines. They stayed behind him horseback for two more minutes, shooting and missing. He finally out-maneuvered them, dodging trees and disappearing into the forest. His pursuers tried keeping up, but quickly realized they were no match. They stopped and stared at him disappearing into the thick woods.

Porter, sick with worry, rode took off deeper into the forest. He had to find his family. He wondered if the lean-to had been discovered. He hoped his parents and Luana possessed the wherewithal to douse any campfire they might have built, as the Missourians would most certainly by now have discovered it. Even without a fire they may have been found. He felt most fearful for little Emily.

He doubled his speed, galloping more recklessly into the woods. His head approached an overhanging tree limb, but at the last moment he ducked and barely missed it. He rode hard.

CHAPTER 38

Galloping through thick trees Porter finally laid eyes on his lean-to ahead. His heart pounding, he reined in and jumped off his steed.

"Luana! Emily! Pa! Ma!"

No reply. No sounds.

He glimpsed inside and noticed most things left behind, including a half-eaten meal. He went to a spot where he had buried one of his pistols in a safe, leather bag. He uncovered it and checked to see if it were loaded, then re-mounted his horse, taking a blanket. He rode at a slower pace through the woods, checking for signs of passersby and simultaneously resting his roan, calling out for his family. He was now armed with two pistols and the unloaded rifle.

He discovered the early morning rays of sun barely brightening the sky. Emerging from the woods he arrived at the edge of a prairie — a burned prairie. He discovered on the ground a doll. He rode harder. He now discerned, in the low light, sparkles of bloody footprints on the sleet-covered ground. Thousands of footprints.

He trotted faster. Soon he spotted moving figures. He galloped to them and halted. One hundred and ninety souls trudged along — all women and children — most of them barefoot. They trekked toward the nearby woods where they would find relief to their feet from the burnt stubble. He rode through them, searching desperately for his daughter, mother, wife, and sisters. He agonized over Emily, but in the early light caught sight of her and Luana, then his mother and sisters and even his dog. He dismounted and grabbed Emily, who was crying. Luana was also barefoot, as well as his mother and sisters. He hugged them all.

He untied the blanket from his horse and, with a long knife, cut it into make-shift boots.

"Where's Pa and the boys?" said Porter.

"With the other men-folk," said Sarah. "They're supposed to meet us at the river."

"What're you talking about?"

"That's where we're headed," Luana explained. "Orin and the other husbands — and all the older sons — left us so they could find sympathizers among the Missourians to help protect us."

Sarah cut in, "Then the men got separated from us. And when them wolf-hunters found us left behind, they stole our shoes and made us walk through the prairie they'd burned. Most of our people are supposed to be at the river already. I just hope Orin and your brothers are all right."

On the banks of the raging Missouri River, Porter and his family trod through mud, searching for his father and brothers. They were nowhere to be found, although hundreds of families were camped at the river shore. The sight tugged at Porter's heart: His father Orin and brothers Peter, Merritt, and Horace were missing while a mass of distraught humanity sat silently at campfires.

A number of men took turns building make-shift ferries, but the crafts were useless until the churning waters could calm.

Storms rocked the skies above with thunder and lightning. After building a campfire and constructing a tent from an old canvas he found, Porter applied herbs to the feet of Emily, Luana, his mother, and younger sisters. Emily cried from the cuts on her feet, but he was able to stop the bleeding. Tears flowed from his cheeks as Emily cried. And when she finally fell asleep, he held and rocked her in his arms.

"Pa will find us," said Porter to Sarah. "So don't worry, Ma." Actually Porter was more worried than she was. After sunset he ventured out, learning his father and brothers were among 200 men and boys who had not yet returned to their families. He thus began checking campsites all along the shore. What he saw further tore at him: The wives and children of those missing men were, like his family, nursing their lacerated feet at campfires along the river shore. Even older children whimpered for their fathers. Porter wiped away tears. Walking across the campsite on the riverbank, he arrived at the Patten family and there learned his friend David Patten had also not returned;

Patten's wife was worried sick. She cradled two young children, one of whom cried for her father.

Within 24 hours after their arrival, Porter spotted several men arriving up shore, followed by the lost 200. They had walked for two days searching for their families, a day of it along the river bank.

Porter's father, his three brothers, and his friend David Patten were among the first group to arrive. Porter strode straight to his father and hugged him, then embraced each of his little brothers. He observed David Patten's wife discovering her husband, placing the children on a blanket and literally running out to hug him.

Two hours later, as all huddled around the campfires, the rains descended. Their campfires were extinguished. The thundering increased.

Inside their rain-drenched tent, the wet blankets which had served as their covering leaked, soaking the small family — Porter, Luana and Emily. Meanwhile Orin, Sarah and their younger children huddled in a nearby, larger blanket-tent. Luana muttered several complaints so only Porter could hear, but he heard not a word. He hugged Emily to his chest under his shirt to keep her warm.

Finally Luana grabbed his arm. "Have you heard a word I've said?"

"What about?"

She got louder. "If we hadn't stayed in Jackson County we wouldn't be going through this!"

"My parents, brothers and sisters would be. And friends, too."

"That justifies what you've put us through?"

"You wouldn't want me here helping them?" said Porter, incredulously.

"That's not the issue."

"It is for me," he said.

Porter's mother entered. "Son, please come to our tent and join us. We need help for Orin."

Porter gazed at her, frightened.

CHAPTER 39

Porter tromped across the sandy mud of the riverbank and entered his parents' tent. It held an interior equally as muddy and miserable as theirs. Immediately upon entering, he was asked to join in the circle around his father. He anointed his pa's head with consecrated oil. His brother Peter sealed the anointing and pronounced a blessing that declared Orin would recover sufficiently to live through this ordeal. As Peter blessed him, Porter opened his eyes and gazed out the tent into the grey of the twilight rain, a determination sweeping his soul. And this was the scene he beheld:

Along the river shore, babies' crying provided the only chorus in the still, night air. Hundreds of families huddled under makeshift tents of old wagon canvases and wet blankets they had managed to bring, while others shivered under ponchos made from blankets. Still others had nothing to protect them from the cold rain.

Out in the river the wind whipped up waves. Crossing the river by ferry was still impossible.

As the third day arrived, several deaths were reported of those who'd been ill before the expulsion. The hardships of the three days had finished them. Porter could hear coughing across the camp, knowing if the river did not allow passage into Clay County soon, not much of the camp would survive.

The next day he and his family shivered. There were no campfires. The rain would not subside.

Roots and half-edible carp kept him and his family nourished into the sixth day. And finally a seventh.

Several women wandered about camp searching for lost children; all were eventually found. Two were brought in dead and their mother was discovered by a search party two miles into the woods, also dying. She was gone by the time they brought her into camp. Her husband stared at her, then at the lifeless children, and Porter turned his head. He ambled back to his tent with no dinner for his family. Night came and his child cried.

He could not sleep that night. Before dawn he rolled over and faced Luana. She was staring straight at him. Her eyes revealed her love, but her words said only:

"It's silent tonight."

Indeed, the rain had ceased, and so had the wind. Finally. It was November 13, 1833.

Porter gazed out the make-shift tent: The clouds had cleared. Stars were shining and the waters were still as glass. The air quickly warmed and the entire camp was suddenly stirred by an unexpected sight: a shower of meteoric fireworks. The thousand Mormons emerged from their tents to behold an apparent miracle — at least that's how Sarah Rockwell comprehended it:

"Do you see that, Luana? Electa?" she said. "Emily, do you see that? It's a miracle. The heavens are not closed. They are watching. The Lord lives and cares!"

While Luana knew not what to make of the sight, she thought a long moment and finally muttered, "I think you're right. We do have a miracle tonight."

Porter caught the look on her face and noticed for the first time ever an expression of awe, if not downright humility. She gaped at the heavens with eyes wide.

Under the firework showers of heavenly bodies they beheld a show that dazzled them. They ooh'd and ah'd as a polarized audience and, when it had ended, they felt like cheering but didn't. They fell into deep, reverent silence.

Despite Luana's complaining of Porter's over-zealous loyalty to his parents and the ferry operation, and never settling down to become a gentleman farmer of a large parcel of land like that for which she had always hoped and dreamed, she could accept the goodness and dedication of him to their daughter Emily and his sincere efforts to support her. Her parents had taught her to clinically analyze life — including the things of God — by measuring everything with the cold analysis of logic. She knew that process flew in the face of Porter's background, whose parents had taught him the more esoteric values of pure trust and, by her standards, blind obedience — although Porter had made the argument that his faith was not propelled by blindness; rather, it was "revealed" faith by which he ran — but the end result had convinced her until tonight that his and others' "revealed" light was very likely self-induced. Tonight, however, she confessed, upon seeing the rains cease and the stars give forth their splendor, there maybe was more to all this than she had given credit. She had experienced in her misery, and through seeing her own daughter suffer, an openness to prayer, actually hoping prayers could be answered. She also felt she could visualize what the future had in store. She realized life would not go her way as she'd supposed her entire life, and that this man was not the Prince Charming to ride in on a white horse to give her everything she'd longed for and prayed. Her greatest skepticism and even disappointment in life had actually occurred the very month she had married Porter. From there, her negative outlook had blossomed so substantially that she had grown to view "hope" as a mere child's fantasy, which she had, through her few years of married life, completely lost. But her heart was quickened tonight, she felt, and her spiritual eyes opened; she even perceived, in her pondering, a re-birth of hope.

"Porter, I can't promise I'll be perfect, but I think we're on the right road. I think I see that now."

He regarded her, stunned.

"I'm glad we're here . . . together," she added.

It occurred to him that now, finally, they did have a life together. Finally together.

PART III

Reunion

CHAPTER 40

Porter chewed beans. Luana plopped a plate of cornbread beside the beans, Southern style cornbread with white corn and dry innards, surrounded by a tasty, buttery crust on the bottom and sides.

Their cabin was small but comfortable. Luana set a glass of fresh buttermilk on the thick oak table before him. It foamed slightly over the top, just the way Porter liked it. He stared at it and drooled.

"Joseph should be arriving any hour," said Luana. "The messenger said he'd be here before supper."

"It's about time he got here among those who're half-way loyal," uttered Porter, downing the first sips of the luscious, thick drink.

"Half-way loyal?" smiled Luana.

"All right, full blown," said Porter. "I just hope none of the dissenters follow him out here like the rumors said they would."

"Well, they have their point of view," said Luana.

Porter peered at her. "Yeah, I reckon they can follow him or not, or rise up against him with their lies or not."

"That's pretty extreme, don't you think?" she teased.

"I think I've seen those who stick with him versus them that don't, and yeah, they're pretty extreme."

"I mean your viewpoint, Porter; don't you think some folk could look upon it as extreme?"

"Depending on which folk."

"Normal folk."

"My parents are normal folk," said Porter, "and I think they'd agree with me."

"What about my parents?" she smiled.

"What about them?" said Porter.

"They'd side with me."

"Of course — you're their daughter."

"But they'd feel your viewpoint is extreme," she said. "And wouldn't you consider them 'normal?'"

Porter finally caught the twinkle in her eye, and almost smiled. He knew her parents were still not active in the faith, having remained behind at Independence when he and Luana had left three years previously. Luana had substantially changed in her viewpoints and had in fact even been the instigator of daily family prayer and scripture study for a couple years, but both Luana and Porter had recently slacked in that endeavor, and only Porter was attending all his church meetings. He nevertheless felt proud of Luana — she attended most meetings and tried to live their faith. Yet, with the passage of time, she had grown increasingly cynical of life again, and especially where she fit in it. She enjoyed most of her neighbors, although some had begun to grate her the wrong way, as had in certain ways Porter but, unlike before, she did not now voice her dissatisfaction with him.

Before arriving at Far West, Missouri, Porter, Luana and their now four-year old daughter Emily had ferried in makeshift barges with a thousand of their people across the Missouri River and settled in Clay County.

Just when they had found security in their new cabins for almost two and a half years, the same old problems arose. The old-time settlers at Clay feared — from reports of their friends at Independence — that the Mormons would take over politics and spread abolitionist propaganda, as well as making a nuisance of themselves as "Indian-lovers." Their non-traditional religious beliefs did not bode well with some in the community either. And soon, the old mobs began to form.

But when a cholera epidemic struck, they cooled down their climate of criticism. Many in fact accepted Mormon aid and friendship and even appreciated their voluntary efforts to nurse them — until the plague evaporated.

One day David Pettigrew told Porter that Judge Cameron had left the gambling table to talk religion with him during the epidemic, but when it subsided, he didn't frequent Pettigrew's place so often; nevertheless, he'd made a lasting friend with the Mormon.

It was therefore with a certain degree of surprise that Porter saw the same old feelings of animosity beginning to re-ignite by the end of their second year in the community of Clay County, even after the Mormon immigrants had helped their neighbors through the plague.

Luana was once again incensed when she heard her Mormon neighbors complaining of the Missourians' support of slavery. She had thought William Phelps was the only one stupid enough to publicly confront the matter.

"Folks just say what they feel," Porter had said.

"They should keep their feelings to themselves," Luana had countered.

Although no Missourians that she knew owned slaves, most Clay County residents supported the institution and, when the locals felt they were being looked down on, they lashed out at the Mormons' self-righteous attitude, as they felt, and Luana could not blame them.

She was angry at her Mormon neighbors' spurning of the Missourians, and at church she would sit and seethe. After all, she felt, the Mormons compatibility with the locals was a more important issue. "Look at what happened in Jackson County," she complained to a neighbor while leaving church one afternoon.

Later that day, Porter had approached her. "After church today, Sister Peterson told her husband what you said, and he told me —"

"What the devil do you care?" she interrupted.

"Getting along with neighbors is something to care about."

"That's my point!" she said. "Besides, maybe you . . ." She caught herself short.

"Maybe what?" said Porter.

"Nothing."

Porter knew Luana was keeping quiet about something he obviously did which bothered her, and the fact that she would not talk about it — and more especially that she even had a complaint about him after all he did to support her with work that he despised — irked the daylights out of him. However, all she was attempting to do by not opening up her concerns was to live the precepts of their religion and refrain from being critical; additionally, she hoped her neighbors would learn some diplomacy. After their discussion — their first argument in over a year — Porter had taken a walk down a shaded country lane. Pondering the matter and cooling his emotions, he finally realized her intentions. Upon grasping them, he could see the good side of her — the desire for peace and tolerance in their community. With a couple more years of seasoning he had grown to appreciate her more and also accept her desire for Christian tolerance. Her old criticism of their people — which had even included justification of violence against their community — was no longer packaged into her tenets, he observed; indeed, she had mellowed substantially. Upon his pondering the matter one afternoon on a windy walk down the same road, he confessed within himself he had to agree with her: Promoting peace among neighbors was of paramount importance; sharing their beliefs was equally significant, but had to be accomplished with conciliatory tones and kindness, not by emphasizing their differences — especially emotionally-charged ones. He also knew that in the end, the Restoration of the Gospel of Jesus Christ had to be shared — and that precept alone, as he now firmly understood Joseph's teachings on the matter, was enough to incite opposition by those who allowed themselves to be influenced by the Adversary; however, things need not be made worse, he figured, by not reaching out with love and fellowship to all one's neighbors, which he now granted was not always the case in their society but which certainly should be. When he returned to his cabin, he informed her of his realizations. She was elated.

Despite Porter's and Luana's efforts to convey an extension of friendship to their non-Mormon neighbors, a meeting was called by area non-Mormon leaders.

At church David Patten reported to Porter what he'd seen first-hand:

"Reverend Balden's holding meetings. More and more people are coming to 'em. This week they're supposed to bring arms."

After word of the meetings had made its way around the saints, they loaded their weapons. Most had secured arms after a year or two in Clay County — as it had taken that long after they'd been disarmed in Jackson to afford arms — so now they were ready for conflict once again.

On the night of the county's largest meeting in it's history, several ministers addressed the crowd, attempting to rally them to war, but Judge Cameron, Judge Birch, and several other allies of the Mormons who had befriended them during the cholera epidemic made speeches to assuage the mob. David Patten reported the result of the meeting the next day to Porter:

"Our church leaders met with mob leaders after the assembly, and we were given the choice of refusing their offer and risking war or giving in to their agreement."

"Agreement?" said Porter.

"They want to give us the land at the far end of the state — in Caldwell County — as far from Missouri civilization as possible."

Porter was incensed. He wanted to stay and fight. Luana was angry he would even consider it. Just when she thought she had made in-roads on teaching tolerance . . .

"Tolerance ain't the issue any more, once they draw the line in the sand," he said.

But, to Porter's frustration, church leaders ordered their people to put away their weapons and merely move out.

Were it not for the counsel of his leaders, Porter would not have left a home once again. He had kept his gun loaded and perched high on a rack in the front room. He practiced shooting every weekend, using precious seed and commodities cash to pay for the lead balls and powder. Luana never did know how much he spent for the ammunition over the months, but she did not consider it a sacrifice so she never complained, figuring he used shooting as more than a hobby for winning the numerous county shooting contests he won — it was a way to sharpen his skills for needed hunting expeditions in order to provide them with game; so whatever cash was spent on ammo seemed to come back to them fourfold in needed food.

Deep down, he knew he was also sharpening his skills for other uses he might someday need . . .

With troubled heart he had begun packing. When they began their journey afoot, carrying Emily while their horse was loaded down, Porter and Luana spoke little.

While Porter had not wished to move from Clay County, their second Missouri home, he had found it in an obscure way exhilarating, certainly more so than the monotony of day-to-day farming.

The new challenge also gave him purpose. However, he did not know how deeply the forced journey depressed his wife.

Porter and his parents left their small farms unsold and headed with their new herd of three cows, four pigs and two horses between the two families to begin the six-week trek across Missouri. Finally, they had arrived in the spring of 1836 to the western section of Caldwell County at a land far from the outsiders who had so persistently tormented them. They called the land Far West, since it bordered the edge of the Missouri territory.

Meanwhile Electa, Porter's oldest sister still living with his parents and three years his junior, had met and fallen in love with a local Missourian, Samuel M. Ousley. Porter and his parents were distressed when Electa chose to marry this man.

While Porter and his family had moved to Far West, Electa had chosen to stay with her fiance — just as Porter's two older sisters had years earlier in Ohio — and she waved goodbye to her family. As they parted, all were speechless. Her parents knew that, not only might they never see her again but, just as they had witnessed in Ohio years earlier, she was marrying a man who had no interest in the faith. Thus, Porter and his parents felt that her chances of living with them eternally as a family unit in the next life was greatly jeopardized, since their beliefs held that she would have to die active in the faith before she could be worthy to join them there, just as they, too, would have to remain active in the faith to be worthy of family ties in the hereafter. It further pained him to see she had thus trod the same spiritual path as her older sisters.

Porter felt further anguished when he saw his little brothers and sisters waving from the back of the wagon with tears in their eyes, and his parents also in tears. As before in Ohio, he again determined to never disappoint his family by leaving them — either his parents or his children. Ever.

Luana was pregnant with their second child when they left Clay County, and soon after arriving at Far West she delivered their second daughter, Caroline, on May 20, 1836.

Afterwards, back in Clay County, his sister Electa — they learned from a letter — married her young beau on January 11, 1837.

At Far West they built their largest cabins yet, while others built stores and businesses, becoming a self-sustaining community. On December 1, 1836 they petitioned for their own county, fearful of living with prejudiced neighbors as had happened at both Jackson County and Clay.

Luana's uncertainty of being provided for had been alleviated when Porter proved his capability of hunting, fishing, and preparing the ground for the first fall harvest within six months after their arrival. But many crops had been planted too late. That was two years ago when they first arrived. The second year the crops had done well, and now they were planting for this year.

Luana was again content.

Porter meanwhile was becoming disenchanted with his wife's recently resurrected "free-thinking" religious views. She seemed to enjoy occasionally taking sides against him — and he was not used to such division for the past three years since she had mellowed, although in one sense he was: She had never relinquished her ever-present need to express an opposing opinion on secular matters. That, in itself, was frustrating to him and did not flow according to his pre-marital expectations based on what he had witnessed of his parents — with rare exception, such as when his own mother had fought like a mama elk against her equally bull-headed husband when Porter had worked for money to give Joseph for the printing of the *Book of Mormon*, as well as a few other clashes — nevertheless, life overall in the Rockwell household in which he was raised had been serene and solid, where the father quietly, authoritatively had presided, unlike in Luana's.

Now in Far West, despite their frustrated expectations because of growing up in differently-managed households, happiness seemed within Porter's grasp. Nevertheless, he still day-dreamed of life on the river where, for the first time in his life, he had enjoyed true satisfaction. But reality since then had called for his duty to support his wife, his daughter Emily, and the new child, as well as to repay his parents to whom he still felt particularly close and overwhelming indebted. The support to them all came in the form of farm work — the work he most detested. Farm work held no challenge for his sense of adventure, and the scenery was undeniably dull. It was the very opposite of river life. A life still in his blood.

Fortunately, his little brothers and sisters were older and more helpful to his parents now, but Porter was clearly the leader of the siblings, and when his father needed assistance on a major farm task, it was always Porter who was called upon to get it done or supervise its accomplishment.

What bothered Porter most was Luana's increasingly disagreeable nature tugging away at the foundation of solidity and example that he wished to lay for his daughter.

At age five now, Emily was still the entire center of his life.

Kirtland, Ohio meanwhile had proven a disaster for Joseph. He was no businessman. He had begun a bank that eventually slid into bankruptcy. Many of his followers turned against him there and actually formed into a mob that ran him out of town.

In a wagon Joseph and his family had barely escaped and made their way with a few remaining faithful traveling in small and separate groups to Far West to join the Missouri group already established. Joseph was at that moment on his way to the city, and Porter was joyously anticipating his reunion.

It was now the spring of 1838, two years after they had left Clay County and moved to Far West. Porter took a swig of buttermilk and wiped his mouth with the back of his hand.

"I don't know what to do with you, woman," he smiled, "but I reckon as long as you don't talk in front of Joseph like you do in front of me, I'll die a happy man."

"I'll say anything I please, and I have a few things to say to his face," she teased. "When he gets here I'll tell him what he's put us through."

"Luana, he's sacrificed a lot for us and doesn't need to hear that. Please keep your views to yourself."

She grabbed the buttermilk and pretended to threaten him by throwing it at him.

She finally smiled. "All right, I won't embarrass you."

As he lowered the glass to his dog, Ugly took a few laps with his gigantic tongue. Porter petted his head as he spoke to Luana:

"Why can't you be like Mama and not even have anything to want to bring up?"

"Because I'm not your mama."

"You're the only woman I know who's so contrary."

"You haven't figured me out yet," she said, her attractive green eyes shining from her pretty face of long, dark blonde hair. In several years the shade had deepened.

"It's not the church I'm contrary to," she smiled. "You know that. It's you."

"Well that's a relief," he smirked.

"I've reconciled you'll never be the contented gentleman farmer I wanted you to be, and I've come to see that's one thing that may attract me to you, but at the same time it is maddening."

"Well, I wouldn't want you to get bored," he said. "I'm glad I can madden you about something."

Emily sauntered inside with a worn, old doll, and Porter picked her up.

"How's my honey?" he said.

"Fine."

Luana piped in, "I thought I was your honey."

Emily chimed in, "No, I'm his honey, now."

Luana laughed, "I think she's got a point."

Emily turned to face her father. She seated herself on his lap and stared at his nose three inches from hers, "Papa, Grandpa sent me to tell you Joseph is coming into town right now!"

Porter's eyes widened. He excitedly lifted her off his lap and stood, marching out the door. Emily followed, as did Ugly. When he arrived outside he realized he had left Luana in the cabin without asking her to join him. He turned and saw her coming onto the small porch.

"Comin'?" he said.

"I'll be there in a while."

Porter took off toward town square, enthusiastically picking up Emily as he picked up his stride. Ugly trotted along beside them, wagging his tail. Porter and Emily rounded a corner when they spotted Joseph's wagon arriving amidst cheering throngs — several hundred of the Missouri Mormon faithful. Tears sprang to Joseph's eyes when he saw them. It was indeed a dramatic contrast to his Ohio fold. The tall, handsome, dark-featured fellow with receding hairline and energetic charisma then stood atop the stopped buckboard.

"A welcome sight," he announced, "for a not-so-good businessman driven from his own bank!"

The crowd laughed.

Suddenly Joseph spotted Porter coming at him, breaking into a trot. Joseph jumped from his buckboard and bolted briskly toward his old friend. The two stopped before each other, looked over one another's faces and, without another thought, hugged.

"Who's this little girl we're smothering?" said Joseph, trying to hug Porter without crushing the five year old between them.

"I'm the little girl you're smothering," said Emily.

Both men laughed, as did a dozen others surrounding them.

"Maybe I better set you down," said Porter. He placed Emily on the road and hugged Joseph harder, cheek to cheek.

"It is so good to see you, Porter!"

"And you, Joseph."

"And this is your little treasure!" Joseph backed away and picked up Emily. "What's your name?"

"Emily, but you don't have to tell me your name. I know your name. Papa talks about you all the time and says your name so much it makes Mama sick."

Joseph laughed.

"Whoa," said Porter, looking up at Joseph now, "I guess Ma speaks her mind a little more than I'm used to."

"Not much different than Emma, I'm sure of that," smiled Joseph.

Porter cut in, "Emily, why don't you let us get a few words in now."

"But I like Joseph!" she said. "And I want to talk to him!"

"And I like you," beamed Joseph.

"All right, we'll just have to get together and play!" said Emily.

"I think that's what we'll have to do, all right!" said Joseph.

Emma Smith stepped off the buckboard hugging her old friends. It wasn't exactly her nature to hug, but she felt close to many of these people and loved them — as did Joseph.

Joseph's and Emma's children had already descended from atop the wagon.

"I think," said Joseph, "this is the happiest sight I've ever seen."

The growing crowd around him moved in to shake his hand briskly. Many patted him on the back with a royal hero's welcome.

"But I think," said Porter, turning to face Joseph, "you're in for the wrestling match of your life."

They heard a bark. Joseph glanced to the side and saw the huge mut. "What the devil's that?"

"Ugly. He just informed you that I never lose. And he don't lie."

Joseph studied the strange dog and laughed.

Porter continued, "This dog knows everything."

Enjoying all the attention, Ugly rolled on his back and howled.

"See?" said Porter. "He's telling me you ain't got a shot in Hades."

CHAPTER 41

Joseph and Porter both enjoyed reputations of being unde-
feated since youngsters. Neither had ever lost a wrestling match.
While Joseph had pinned him on numerous occasions in New
York, Porter knew they didn't exactly count because he was a
mere boy then, only 17, while Joseph was 24 the last time they'd
wrestled. Now Porter was substantially more muscular.

Porter and Joseph's close mutual friend David Patten presided over the match, outlining the rules to the two participants
and to the crowd which gathered by the hundreds at Patten's
famous pig pens, the fenced area of his prized pigs.

Porter and Joseph stood ankle deep in mud and manure.
The pen had been watered down for the event to create an extra special, earthy soup for the occasion. Porter and Joseph
smiled as they stepped into the gunk at the delight and simulta-
neous disgust of the crowd. Everyone was laughing. Only 30
minutes earlier Joseph had been welcomed by all; now he was
witnessing first-hand their most enjoyable past-time.

"And this is your favorite sport as well, I suppose?" said Joseph to Porter.

"I reckon."

"All I can say is," said Joseph, "this must be an awfully bored group."

The people chuckled.

Emily meanwhile gazed admiringly at her father from the arms of his neighbor, Francis Higbee and his wife.

"You think your daddy will win?" said Francis.

Emily nodded, "Not even a bear can beat him."

Francis smiled at his wife. "Maybe that's who we need guarding our people at the polls in Gallatin soon."

A gunshot sounded. Porter and Joseph leaned forward, hands toward each other, turning in a slow circle, waiting for the other to make the first move.

Suddenly Porter lunged at Joseph, and Joseph stopped him. Neither man could get the other down. Five minutes passed. They released and went for another hold. The crowd cheered. The two contestants leaned for better balance against the fence. The crowd became restless, and goodnaturedly booed. The two men clomped into the middle of the "arena" and grabbed each others' arms again. They circled. Each tried to leverage his weight to throw the other. Neither would go down. Noticeably more tired now, the two parlayed various wrestling holds. Ten more minutes passed. The crowd buzzed with anticipation and began clapping in unison.

"Who's going to go down first?" said David Patten.

"Joseph," yelled David Pettegrew.

"No, Porter will!" said Orin.

"I heard that, Pa — thanks!" said Porter.

And then it happened.

With the crowd cheering them both, Porter and Joseph had each other in a new hold standing up, when suddenly both toppled over with a loud, resounding SSSHPLUNK into the deep, thick mud-manure mixture.

The crowd went wild. They laughed and cheered, then applauded. Joseph stood first, covered with brown gunk, and finally Porter arose.

The two were exhausted. They panted and gasped for air, splashing through the goop to the fence, against which they finally leaned their backs and shook hands.

"You're the only man I've never beat," said Porter.

"As are you," said Joseph, smiling. "I just wonder how Emma's going to take to cleaning this outfit."

"Knowing her," said Porter, "you'll be cleaning it yourself."

"And what about you?" said Joseph.

"I think I'll bury it before I get home," he muttered, dead-pan.

Both men tromped out the open gate. Porter had barely emerged when he noticed Luana striding toward the arena, not knowing of the event. When she beheld him she stopped and gawked at him. Porter feared the absolute worst. He stopped, watched and waited for her reprisal. She stomped to him and stood over him like a hawk waiting to swoop down for the attack.

The crowd silenced.

Luana looked as mean and angry as Porter had ever seen her, then she broke out laughing.

Suddenly she began stripping him right in front of the crowd, pulling off his shirt and ordering him to step out of his pants. The crowd laughed and, a sense of modesty overtaking it, began fading away. She tossed him her apron and he wrapped it around his middle. Ugly, of course, from the on-set, had relished the wind blowing from the pig manure/mud concoction, and could not let such an opportunity pass. He began scampering towards it.

Luana laughed, "Guess who gets to clean him?"

Porter caught sight of him and rushed to intercept him, but Ugly leaped on his back legs, launched over both Porter and the fence simultaneously, and landed with a glorious splash into the soup.

Porter groaned, "Oh, no."

Luana chuckled, "I know it was my turn, but you just lost a couple privileges with this little wrestling match, my dear."

They tried to take turns with this chore, since Ugly had a weekly tradition of finding some abhorrent woodland corpse in which to roll as a sort of indulgent, self-presented gift — much like the rich indulge themselves in expensive body oils and herbs.

"Ugly!" yelled Porter good-naturedly, "get out now!"

Ugly wagged his tail as if to smile at him.

"Ugly, now!"

The huge animal gazed at him, then once again rolled over in the mud.

Luana laughed. "I'm surprised you don't get in and wallow with him," she said. "You know — birds of a feather . . . "

Emma Smith suddenly sauntered past, spotting Joseph covered with mud. Her demeanor dropped. She glanced at Porter, noticed his messy clothes as well, and marched straight to her husband. In Joseph's face she whispered harshly:

"Playing with the ruffians again?"

Porter did not hear her remark but his eyes went wide when he observed Ugly suddenly emerging from the pig-excrement and sashaying directly towards Emma.

Porter tried to yell a warning:

"Joseph, get Emma out — "

But it was too late. Ugly had sauntered straight up to her and stopped, then, seeing her disapproving expression, decided to do the best thing her comment deep down called for:

Ugly shook violently, slinging the pig mud in hundreds of tiny, wet chunks onto her dress. Emma shrieked and stomped away. Joseph fought a smile but Porter shrunk with horror. Not till he would think about it 16 hours later in the middle of the night would he break out laughing.

Luana meanwhile was still walking home with daughter Emily, and never witnessed Emma's travail.

"Emily," said Luana, "would you like to stay with the Higbee children and play?" To Francis, "Is that all right?"

Francis muttered to his wife, "Do we have a choice?" But he said to Luana only what she could hear: "We'd be glad to."

Luana caught the smirk on Mrs. Higbee's face and said, "Is that not convenient?" Luana had babysat the Higbee children twice as often as the Higbee's had taken Emily and Caroline.

Francis responded, trying to hold back his sarcasm, "Of course we wouldn't mind. Mrs. Higbee will be more than happy to watch the girls, but I have to get back to the store." He was a retailer in general goods and interested in the law.

Mrs. Higbee proclaimed, "Luana, you must clean Porter's attire, so I'll watch Emily."

Joseph, meanwhile, walked with Porter and soon caught up to Luana.

She held out her hand to shake Joseph's, and exclaimed, "Since I last saw you in New York, I've learned much about you from Porter and his family. They certainly think the world of you."

Joseph smiled, "Well, I think even higher of them, and I knew Porter would find a diamond of a woman."

"You've hit it right there," said Porter. "Isn't a diamond a hard, shiny rock?"

Luana elbowed Porter good-naturedly.

Joseph smiled and gazed at them both:

"Come by our home tonight, both of you. Emma and I would like to get to know Luana better, and Emily is a doll. I want her to sit on my knee while we have dinner. And bring your dog."

"Despite the Ugly incident?" said Porter, concerned.

"Despite the Ugly incident," said Joseph.

"What Ugly incident?" said Luana, not aware of the altercation with Emma.

"Oh, just another ugly incident," said Porter.

When dinner was served that night, Emma Smith and Luana Rockwell tried to be gracious with each other, but the attempt was apparent. Somehow, with no words spoken, they were critical.

Meanwhile Porter and Joseph laughed and joked.

Emma also kept one eye on Ugly, now clean and lying at Porter's feet. The dog was acting well-behaved, if not downright listless. But when he caught Emma's disapproving gaze, he wagged his tail. Porter caught a gleam in his eye, and knew there might be trouble before the night's end.

"Porter," finally said Emma as dinner was being served, "I would certainly not mind your dog eating outside on the back porch. I'll feed it left-over scraps."

"He eats what I eat," winked Porter to Joseph.

Joseph spoke up, "I think he's fine, Emma."

Emma glowered at the animal, and Ugly wagged back. Emma, serving a pot of gravy, "accidently" bumped the animal with her shoe, and Ugly glowered at her. When Emma maneuvered to the far side of the table, the animal casually arose, began wagging its huge tail, and knocked over a large swatch of butter. Before Emma could grab it off the floor, it disappeared.

Porter held back a smile as the dog ambled out of the room, smacking his lips.

As Emma cleaned up the grease mark left on the floor, Ugly sauntered into a bedroom and returned awhile later wagging his monstrous tail. Emma shot a suspicious glance at him, but would not know of his deed until the next morning when, entering her closet, she would discover the dog had deftly lifted a leg over her newest pair of shoes. Now, however, Ugly returned to his master's feet and laid down, acting as if nothing had happened. Porter, staring down the hallway from which his dog had returned, suspected Ugly had, with his unusual sense of humor, played some sort of nasty little practical joke, and for a moment the thought flashed across his mind precisely what he had done; but he dismissed the thought with a silent chuckle.

'Emma,' thought Porter, 'needs to loosen up, and Ugly has prob'ly just done her a service.'

Porter now turned his gaze to Emma, thoughtfully studying her, with a small smile. She caught his stare and felt disconcerted, retreating into the kitchen for the last food to serve.

Luana was embarrassed at Porter's unintentionally amused smile, and she glared at him. He caught Luana's sharp, silent retort and straightened his shoulders. He tried to suddenly get serious and listen to Joseph, who meanwhile had been walking about the table, assisting his wife in serving Emma's hot beef, biscuits and gravy while detailing to Porter and Luana the story of his Ohio bank failure. Business affairs were not particularly interesting to Porter, but out of respect he tried listening as best he could to his friend.

Joseph then sat, and turned to Porter and Luana and asked them what had been happening at Far West.

Luana told him the community had prepared for Joseph's arrival weeks earlier, and had been animatedly anticipating him. Porter then brought Joseph current on family and community news:

"Francis Higbee and his wife are real likeable in some ways, but I get the feeling they look down their noses at me. They and a few of their friends are good folks that I just don't like being around that much."

"They're fine folk," said Joseph. "With the strains of what we've all been through and where we came from before we joined together, we're bound to have some differences among us. I suggest we all now look for common ground."

"And you'll die the eternal optimist, Joseph," said Emma. "I've still never seen anyone like you. Not even Porter!"

They all laughed. Then Joseph crawled onto the floor and began playing with Emily and her doll she had brought.

Luana was amazed, finding Joseph more personally likeable than she had imagined, having met him only briefly years earlier. She almost invited them to dinner next week, but her eye caught Emma gazing at her. Though a smile was on Emma's face, Luana felt uncomfortable by the look beneath the smile, and decided to say nothing about the dinner invitation.

It was the last time the two women ever ate together.

Luana, though charmed by Joseph's kind demeanor and concern for others, actually felt envy. She knew Porter did not confide in her even half what he did with his old friend. When Luana prepared to leave with Emily and Caroline, Joseph invited Porter to stay. That both intrigued and bothered her, wondering what in tarnation Joseph actually saw in her husband.

When they were alone Joseph reported:

"Dissenters are our greatest problem, Porter — not riled up ministers and magistrates — but dissenters. And pride is their Achilles Heel. Pride and greed."

Porter learned how Joseph's patience from the Ohio experience had been tried. He had to excommunicate several once-close associates. "Including John Whitmer and William Phelps for misuse of church funds, and Oliver Cowdery for urging vexatious law suits against the brethren and for attempted counterfeiting."

"But I'm here for you, Joseph."

"Some of the dissenters in Ohio couldn't leave it alone there, so they've followed me here."

Porter had occasionally seen a disagreeable cock-eye in Whitmer and Cowdery, but the news about Phelps shook him.

"You're one of the few I could trust with such confidences, Porter. I would not even hint of this to others."

"My mouth is sealed. You know who you can trust."

Joseph confided more information to him.

Porter's concern grew for his friend as he learned of others on the Prophet's list: David Whitmer and Lyman Johnson were two others he would never have foreseen as unfaithful, so when he learned they had been "disfellowshipped" — a less harsh ecclesiastical disciplinary action — he was equally surprised. Later that evening he walked home, his mind awhirl over Joseph's problems.

He felt sick over the idea of having traitors in their midst. So it was only natural that one night he was stirred by a lecture given by Sidney Rigdon, a high official in the church. Rigdon began with the text from Matthew, "Ye are the salt of the earth, but if the salt have lost his savor, wherewith shall it be salted? It is therefore good for nothing but to be cast out and trodden under foot of men." He proceeded to point out that the dissenters had scandalized the church, prejudicing the minds of non-Mormons in surrounding counties.

Porter was fired up. When Rigdon drew up a petition days later to rid the county of these "problem-makers," Porter was anxious to sign. He placed his "X" (with his name printed beside it by a friend) as 69th on the list. Rigdon received 14 more before signing his own, and hoped his expulsion order would rid their people of these dissenters once and for all.

However, at his cabin several days later, Porter was exasperated to hear Luana complain:

"Sydney Rigdon has made not only a fool of himself, but of everyone else who signed the petition."

"Why do you say that?"

"Learn to read and find out for yourself," she said.

"Thanks for the insult," he said, "but what are you talking about ?"

"It's in the newspapers. Across several counties the dissenters have gone and told the Missourians of their being forced to leave us."

"I signed it too, Luana."

She gazed at him incredulously. "I thought you'd learned acceptance of our neighbors — and extending kindness at all odds."

"Dissenters are a different breed," he said.

She shook her head disbelievingly.

In his heart he knew better, but turncoats against Joseph frustrated him with a special intolerance because, unlike Missourians, they were simply rebelling. They had apostatized against the cold light of truth and he did not want them living in their midst, much less criticizing them to their neighbors with false claims.

Luana blew out a sigh. "Porter, I read you're now on the dissenters' target list."

"Well that suits me fine, and believe me the feeling's mutual."

"What I'm afraid of, my parents in Jackson County will hear of this."

"Good."

"They'll think I believe in this nonsense along with you."

"That don't bother me."

"It doesn't bother you what we support now — vigilante-style justice?"

"Rigdon seems to know what he's doin'," said Porter.

"Well Sampson Avard doesn't. Once he heard that the Missourians got heated up like a hornet's nest, he decided to retaliate against the dissenters. First, it was Rigdon's fanaticism, and now it's Avard's insanity."

"Well maybe he's right. Somebody oughta make an example of the dissenters."

"Are you serious?"

"We should keep our problems among ourselves," he added. "The dissenters had no right going to the Missourians. They'll just turn them into mobs! Look what the mobs did at Independence! I feel like whippin' a few apostates myself!"

"They have every right to complain — everybody does!"

"But they lied!" he said.

"So?"

"I have half a mind to shoot the fools!"

"Porter, do you know what you're saying?"

———————

Porter learned what he was saying a week later. Joseph came by and helped him chop wood.

"What Sydney said was flat-out wrong, Porter. I never authorized such a document of retaliation, and then what Avard did is the worst possible thing. I'm preaching peace and he wants war!"

Porter quickly melted from his previous, bellicose position.

"Avard started a band called 'Danites,' but most of his people walked out of the meetings when he called for secret passwords and even murders. I excommunicated him when he refused to back down."

"Where is he now?"

"Typically, he went to the Missourians. He told the Fifth Circuit Court I was the prime mover of the 'Danite' band, and now the Missourians are doubly riled up!"

Porter was triply riled up. He had supported Sampson Avard, thinking him a defender of the people, but it was obvious now Avard was only out for his own glory. Porter felt so humiliated he had supported Rigdon and Avard — and with such enthusiasm — that he could not even admit it to Joseph. Joseph knew anyway, but never mentioned it.

To Luana, when he walked home that evening he simply mumbled, "Joseph has exposed Avard and Rigdon." That's all he said.

Luana saw Porter's embarrassment and turned away, knowing she need not say another word. She felt compassion for Porter's hurt pride, and never again brought up the subject.

CHAPTER 42

Porter and his daughter Emily played horseshoes outside their Far West cabin. Ugly was busy burying a large ham bone for future feasting. The sun cast bright orange hues across their yard and cabin. Inside, Luana cooked a turkey with fresh herbs, producing a scintillating aroma. She was assisted by Porter's mother Sarah and his younger sister Mary. From little Caroline's small bed at the other end of the home, an occasional cough broke the silence. Outside, Emily threw a horseshoe from three feet away. It hit a bucket of grease, which flew into the air and backwards onto Porter.

"You won! You've beaten your daddy!" cried Mary out the window, watching the contest and laughing.

"Just mind your own business!" called back Porter, wiping the mess from his shirt.

Orin rode up and dismounted. "I got here as soon as I could." He noticed Porter's grease-covered shirt. "But it looks like you've already had dinner."

"Very funny," said Porter.

The others laughed.

Suddenly Luana screamed inside, "I burned the turkey!" All the women laughed. "Porter, get a new one!"

"Ugly," said Porter to his huge hound who, lying lazily in the sun, merely moved an eye to see what he wanted, "why don't you go sneak up on some fat turkey feeding in the marsh and bring him back, then you can have this nice black one."

Ugly assessed him a moment and figured his idea a waste of time. He immediately went back to sleep.

"I think," said Orin to his oldest son, "you're about to go hunting again."

"Can I go, too?" said Emily.

"I don't think so," said Porter. "When I hunt I walk a long ways. It's no place for little ones." He went inside the cabin to retrieve his rifle, mumbling.

Meanwhile outside the cabin, Orin played more horseshoes with Emily who, after a minute, suddenly broke out crying.

"What's the matter, Emily?" said Orin.

She would not answer at first, but after some probing, her grandpa dug out a response.

Porter clomped outside the cabin, carrying the blackened bird and muttering, "They want me to stay here and just pull the burned skin off this thing. No hunting till another day." He dropped the turkey into a pan on the porch.

"Son, I think we've got a problem here," said Orin. "Emily feels left out, I do believe. She wanted to go hunting with you."

Porter studied Emily, who smiled at him through her tears. He picked her up and gazed into her sky blue eyes, then he melted. He gave her a tight, heartfelt hug. "Emily, next time I go hunting, I'll take you. And you never have to worry about one thing — I will never leave you. Not for more than a little while. I'll always be here for you. You remember that the rest of your life."

Luana sauntered outside and grabbed the turkey pan. "Better take care of this later. You and your pa are needed inside to give Caroline a blessing. Her cough is getting worse."

Porter and Orin stood over young Caroline who lay asleep in her small bed. Luana and Porter's mother Sarah sat nearby. After Orin administered a drop of oil to the top of the child's head, both men placed their hands over Caroline and Porter blessed his child to be rid of the disease. He also blessed her to grow up with good health and a long life, "to a ripe old age."

Afterwards, Orin turned to his son: "I reckon you musta been inspired on that one, cause that's a pretty gutsy thing you said. This has been the most sickly child I've seen in years, and with other little ones sick like this, I've seen eight in ten not grow to their teens before they're called home to their Maker."

"You're right," said Porter. "I was inspired." He glanced at his wife, whose eyes were gleaming with tears.

Outside they heard horse hooves. Porter and Orin strode to the door and noticed nine horsemen approaching, reining to a halt.

Their spokesman hailed Porter and his father, and asked if they were joining the group to go vote at Gallatin. Luana appeared in the doorway and immediately handed Porter the turkey pan again, so he could pull off the skin.

"Can't this minute," said Porter, holding up the blackened turkey. "I've got more important business."

They glanced at the darkened bird and chuckled. Porter shook his head, smiling:

"You best be riding before the polls close," he told them.

Their spokesman was candid: "It'd feel a whole lot safer if you was riding with us. But charcoaled turkeys do take precedence at the family hearth."

They laughed again and turned their horses. Porter watched them pull away and felt a sudden solemnity overshadow him.

"Be careful, boys."

CHAPTER 43

The same nine riders arrived at Gallatin to vote, when they found themselves smack dab in the middle of a downtown whiskeyfest. Fifty locals were getting soused as they observed the nine newcomers arriving, sober, distant, and determined to vote.

"Boys," spoke up one of the locals as the strangers hitched their horses and strode to the voting box set outside the general store, "I'd stick to my own kind if I was you."

The nine said nothing in return, which angered the crowd.

"What do you think you're going to do?" said a Missourian.

The nine Mormons ignored them and began voting at the box.

The locals began closing in on them.

"Can't you be a little friendlier than that?" spoke another.

One Mormon said merely, "Mornin'."

The nearest Gallatin citizen glared at him, surprised at his response.

A state election official boomed his voice at the locals. "Now you let them be, boys. They can vote just like you."

The nine quickly voted, dropping their cards into a voting box slot, then began striding back toward their horses.

Five of the Gallatins stepped in front of them.

The nine Mormons stopped, eyes widening. One observed several boards of lumber next to the adjacent hardware store. "Now I do wish Porter was with us," mumbled one of the nine.

Twenty others of the Gallatins suddenly joined the five, stepping in front of the nine outsiders.

One spoke up, "Ain't you gonna apologize for not talking to us?"

One local by the name of Durfee suddenly shouted to the others, "I think we oughta teach them Mormons manners!" At that, he lurched forward to launch a fight.

But the nine ran to the adjacent boards, grabbed them, and began whacking away. Durfee went flying. Ten others ran forward and also got leveled.

The other 40 were angry seeing their fellows helplessly scattered, so they began charging the nine.

But all who attacked them — being rendered useless by too much liquor — were whacked senseless, and the nine Mormons dropped their boards, mounted up, and rode off in a hurry.

One still-conscious local sat up, pulled out a pistol, and fired.

He missed, but shot out the lantern of the barber shop. The barber ran out, spotted the culprit, and backhanded him. The fellow flew back into the road as a puff of dust flew up around him.

———————

Fearing retaliation by state officials, Joseph that night sent for Porter and asked him to recruit 16 others. The contingency of 18 riders, including Joseph, Porter and David Patten, rode three hours that evening. They arrived at the home of Judge Adam Black where Joseph dismounted and went to his door.

"I've heard the rumors already," said Black, greeting them with eyes wide.

"Rumors?"

"That your nine people at Gallatin routed the entire town and planned to burn the city."

"That's why I'm here," said Joseph.

Judge Black regarded him curiously.

"To put an end to the rumors," added Joseph. "That's not what happened." He handed the judge a sheet of paper. "This is a petition we wish to have you sign. It declares our desire only for peace and shows your intention to also keep the peace."

Black read it over. "I don't like the wording."

Joseph sighed, "Then what do you wish it to say?"

Black thought a moment, scribbled a few words and handed it back.

Joseph read it aloud. Porter noticed hardly a syllable of difference between the first and final versions, realizing the man was simply acting contrary, like old Cecil Pritsimmons had at the Big Blue barge. The agreement promised to Joseph the courts would "support the constitution" and "not instigate further violence against the Saints."

Black gazed at him a moment and smirked. "Hand that back to me." He took it and, with Joseph's pen, signed it on the door.

Hours later under a midnight moon, a door knock awakened Porter. His friend David Patten stood in the framework and nodded him to come into the chilled air.

"I didn't want to disturb your family," said Patten, now walking with him to the well 20 yards from the cabin.

"What is it?" said Porter as they approached the well.

"Judge Black must've gone the next morning to see Boggs."

"What're you talking about?"

"After he signed our petition he must've gone straight to Governor Boggs," said Patten. Since Porter's last seeing Lilburn Boggs in Jackson County, he had been elected governor of the state.

"The judge told Boggs we harassed him and forced him to sign the petition!"

Porter was shocked.

"I imagine," continued Patten, "Governor Boggs sees this as a chance to rid himself of us. He ordered 400 militia to arrest Joseph and scare us out of the state. And he also asked for volunteer civilians from 11 counties. An assistant came to us on the sly and told us, cause he likes us."

"Then Joseph knows?"

Patten nodded, "Joseph just sent me here. He wants me and you to spread the word."

Porter rushed inside and caressed Emily's and Caroline's foreheads as they slept in bed. Then he whispered to Luana:

"I'll be back in a few hours."

"Of course," said Luana.

"What do you mean by that?"

She didn't answer. She studied Porter with cool, assessing eyes as he prepared to leave.

Porter and 10 others waited behind a thick grove of trees. This was his first leadership assignment.

A look-out ran to them:

"They're coming."

Porter nodded to his men and they all took positions.

CHAPTER 44

$\mathbf{A}$ supply wagon rolled down the road from Independence.

On Porter's signal, a tree fell across the road, the wagon halted, and Porter's force galloped in, intimidating the two guards on horseback into dropping their weapons.

Two of Porter's men tossed back the wagon canvas, uncovering 20 wooden rectangular cases. Porter used the stock of his rifle to smash open a case. As the top popped open, he beheld 20 rifles inside.

"All right, boys," said Porter to the two militia guards. "I don't reckon these weapons are going to be used to drive out anybody tonight."

The two guards glared at him.

From behind the clump of trees, his men brought their own wagon and began loading the cases.

One of Porter's men grabbed a case and mumbled, "I just wonder what we've done now."

———————

Porter and Emily sat at a dinner table with friends David Patten and David Pettegrew. Orin Rockwell was seated next to Joseph Smith. Emma brought in apple cobbler she had made.

"This is the best-looking crust I've ever seen," said Orin.

"Can I have some too?" said little Emily.

"Honey," said Joseph, "you can have all you want."

"It sounds," said Porter, "like her mama never feeds her. But she does a great job with the girls."

"How is Luana?" said Joseph.

"A little weak from the ague. Caroline's a lot better, though — she's like a new girl since the blessing. My mama's got her a couple days at her cabin."

"Well Luana needs her strength to take care of both girls," said Joseph. "I admonish you, old friend, to take care of Luana. I don't want you leaving your property for a few weeks till they're better."

"With all the good adventure going on around here," smiled Porter, "I don't know about that."

"Porter, that's an order."

They chuckled and Porter dove into the apple cobbler. "Em! This is the best . . . really the best . . . apple cobbler I've ever had!" Porter delighted in the freshly cooked, slightly spiced apples floating in delectable filling and perfect, flaky cobbler crust cooked to a golden brown.

Emma smiled. Though she looked upon him as a ruffian, she did like compliments when she knew they were sincere.

And despite her problems with Porter's overall lack of civility, she did know Porter was good for his word.

"I think that deserves seconds," said Emma.

They all laughed.

"I've never had apple cobbler before," said little Emily, "but it's the best I've ever had, too! Can I have some more?"

They all laughed again and Emma scooped up more.

"I think," said Orin, "this is about the best I've ever had!"

"Indeed!" said David Patten.

"The very best," said David Pettegrew.

All were chuckling as they received seconds.

"Emma," said Joseph, "I'd prepare a round of thirds if I were you."

They all chortled harder. Suddenly they were interrupted by a messenger knocking.

"Yes?" said Emma to a 17 year old neighbor boy, a red-haired, shortly packaged lad of five feet. "Would you like to come in for cobbler?"

"It's the best in the world, lad!" laughed David Patten. All broke out laughing again.

The boy's countenance portrayed sobriety and they all put down their forks.

"What is it, boy?" said Joseph.

"The Missourians — they've attacked two villages!"

Porter turned to gaze at the boy and lost his smile.

The Mormon villages of DeWitt and Adam-Ondi-Ahman, the boy explained, had been attacked by Missouri riders in retaliation for Porter and his men stealing the 400 rifles meant for the state militia who were to attack Far West.

As for Porter taking the rifles, Joseph had hoped this action would send a message to the governor that, unlike their pacifism at Independence, they would now stand up for themselves and force the locals to regard them as a people with which not to be trifled.

But Boggs, rather than throwing his hands in the air, had ordered an attack on the two villages outside town. The boy messenger reported what he'd just witnessed at DeWitt:

There, he'd found a scene he had not been expecting — the village was in ashes. Buildings still smoldered and over a dozen men lay stretched out on the autumn leaves, whip marks on their backs, their wounds being treated with herbs by their wives. Cattle had been scattered, and two Mormons had been taken prisoner and ridden out of town on a cannon. The mob had bragged to the villagers that the two would be executed the next morning at Crooked River.

Responsible for this plan was Samuel Bogart, a Methodist minister who had promised to shower Far West "with thunder and lightning."

Joseph, hearing this report from the boy, walked to the doorway and stared off, thinking. He could then see in the street 30 families arriving at the far end of town, ragged-looking and exhausted.

Joseph turned to David Patten:

"Gather all able-bodied men who'll volunteer. I want you to lead them before dawn to rescue the prisoners." Joseph immediately ran outside to comfort the homeless families trudging into the city.

Outside, Porter also stared at the incoming refugees. He

was torn as never before: Should he join the force marching tomorrow to rescue the prisoners, or stay home with his family as Joseph commanded? He felt sick to miss out on the chance to save others, and was convinced David Patten needed him. But he could not in good conscience leave his sick wife. He picked up Emily. "Let's go, child, and figure out what we're going to do."

CHAPTER 45

Luana lay in bed. At 3 AM a bell tolled on the town square. She opened her eyes. Porter was gone from her side. Ugly lay in the spot where Porter always slept, and was snoring. Startled, she sat up. Darting her eyes about, she caught sight of Porter in a chair rocking Emily.

"What's wrong?" said Luana.

"Couldn't sleep."

"Why?"

"That," he said, nodding toward the still-tolling bell.

"What is it about?" she said groggily.

"It's about me."

She awakened more. "A call to arms?"

"A call to me." He arose and set Emily down beside her. He slipped his arms into his coat and lifted his rifle.

"What're you doing?" she said.

"Going to rescue two young men the Missourian pukes kidnapped."

"You're leaving us?"

"The boys need my help."

"And what about us?"

"I just threw some cut logs on the fire. If it gets low, I put extras beside the fireplace."

"What if I get the chills again and can't get up?"

"The fire will last. I'll ask Sister Patten to come see how you're doing in a couple hours. I fed Emily, and breakfast is on the table for you."

"So you're just going off like this?"

"It was a hard decision."

"Without including me?"

"People's lives are at stake." said Porter.

"So you don't care what I think?"

"I've said my peace. I don't wanna fight."

"Porter, it's not your war."

"Every war for this people is my war. I will be there."

"Then I've got my own decision to make. If you'd leave us like this, it is surely clear to me where I belong."

"What're you talking about?"

"Among folk who love me," continued Luana.

"Are you loco?"

"So if you leave, I am taking the children with me to my parents back to Independence. It's not only safer there — what with all the war here which you seem so excited about — but it's where I'm loved."

"Luana, you can't take these babies from me."

"Why shouldn't I?"

"They're my life, Luana."

"Where you're going is your life. And even if it wasn't, didn't you just reveal your feelings for me in all this? They're your life?"

He stared at her a moment.

"If you head out to join another battle, you will prove everything I suspect about your feelings for me."

He studied her, thinking, then turned and opened the door.

CHAPTER 46

Porter arrived at the town square. Sixty volunteers stood in loose formation. His mind whirled over Luana. Obviously she would not be leaving him during her sickness, but when he returned, he was not certain. He hoped to have time to soften her, but he wondered how deep a wedge he had hammered between them, and felt fearful of the long-lasting resentments he may have caused even if she did not leave immediately. Certainly she had seen his growth toward tolerance, he thought, but when anyone stepped over the line to join the ranks of avowed enemies out for their blood, he operated at a different level of peace-making than Luana, so much so that he knew he enjoyed the "blood rush" — the adrenal flow that came with a call to arms. The protector within him was undoubtedly disproportionate to the "patient gentleman" within him, which her father seemed to be — pacifistic at all costs — and which she wanted him to be; nonetheless, he knew he was doing the right thing, especially since their safety and very freedom was on the line; therefore, he was frustrated by Luana's lack of support — even her opposition to him. He shook away his thoughts and stepped onto the town square.

David Patten was the assigned commander of the rescue force assembling.

Most wives came out to see them off. The "soldiers," every bit as ragtag as the bunch at Independence he had ridden with, held clubs, pitchforks and rifles. David walked in front of the group. They formed a quasi-position of attention out of respect for him, standing straighter and taller when he appeared.

"Brethren," he barked, "we will march out immediately and ambush the militia at Crooked River. There, we shall rescue the prisoners."

The men, rather than cheering as Porter expected, began mumbling, doubtful. He studied their uncertain countenances. He wondered if there were anything he could say. Many of the men were gazing at their wives, knowing their children were sleeping and could awaken in the morning with no father. Porter realized they needed a burst of encouragement, so he broke ranks. He walked down the line in front of them and raised his voice:

"And why are we marching out to fight, brethren? For our own families. Like the folks in the *Book of Mormon*, we are fighting for our wives, our children and our freedom!"

The men forced themselves to stand straighter. Many began looking a bit more determined.

Patten proudly watched him.

Joseph, outside his cabin, regarded Porter's attempt and, though he'd admonished his old friend to remain at home, he rubbed moist eyes as he muttered to Emma in the cabin behind him:

"I'm not sure we've got a more loyal friend. And I must join them."

"No, Joseph, if something happens to you, our whole city would collapse."

Joseph nodded, realizing Emma was right. Patten had likewise admonished him earlier in the evening.

In the pre-dawn woods Porter marched at the forefront of the men. Beside him was his friend, fishing partner, and leader David Patten. Owls created strange sounds in the night, while the sky was filled with stars. Porter gazed up at the firmament, wondering what lay ahead the next few hours. Could they free the prisoners or would all their force be massacred by the immensely larger, trained state militia?

Patten ordered them to stop and load their weapons.

"Wouldn't it be safer," muttered one in the ranks, "if we were closer to them to do this — just before we attack?"

"If their guards spot us we'll have no time to load up," answered Porter before Patten could speak.

The river shore to which they were marching was 12 miles ahead. Suddenly the sky lit up with thousands of shooting stars and whirling constellations — it was the *aurora borealis*. For a few minutes they all stopped and stared. "I think," said Patten, "this is going to be a significant day!"

"I do believe you're right," said Porter, hoping to find something on which to hinge a doorway of hope in order to encourage his fellows.

"It's a miracle!" called out Parley Pratt, one of the soldiers.

One of their group explained the *aurora borealis* occurs rarely but certainly on schedule, yet that did not dissuade the force from seeing it as a sign to them. Porter saw it also as a sign to give them confidence.

As they resumed marching with the light blazing overhead, the tinkling of swords and the clunking of horsehooves mesmerized Porter as he marvelled at the scene before him. Soon they trod across thick prairie grass, and the heavenly lights faded.

The first signs of dawn appeared. Dead ahead were shadowy outlines of tents. They heard the crackling of campfires and the whinnying of horses. Commander David Patten raised his hand. The company halted.

They had arrived at Crooked River.

Patten motioned to his men flanked out behind him to crouch low, then he waved them slowly forward.

Fifty yards from the tents they stopped. Enemy guards posted about were listlessly gazing off. Nowhere in particular, just off.

Patten glanced at Porter beside him and sighed:

"I suppose this is it, old friend. I'd rather be on your old river barge fishing, with not a care in the world."

"I'll second that," said Porter.

"We're at the crossroads of destiny for some of us," whispered Patten.

"And maybe all of us."

Patten gazed down and slowly blew out another sigh, fighting his own fear. He peered through the mist and descried the two Mormon prisoners tied to a tree, standing behind tents near the river. He glanced around and observed a number of his own men having second thoughts. One mumbled to another, "We're only farmers, and facing a trained army twice our size?"

Patten trembled slightly. "Do you think many will die today?"

"Maybe."

Porter sniffed at their consternation.

"They say," said Patten to Porter in hushed tones, "you see your whole life in front of you when it happens. I just saw half of mine."

Porter studied him, concerned, knowing they needed absolute confidence at this moment or they would buckle in battle.

"What do you see?" said Patten.

"I see a hot breakfast waitin' for us when we get back. So the sooner we get this thing over with, the better!" He stood with his rifle raised. "Seize the enemy, boys. Drive them clear out of the county!" And then he yelled like an Iroquois warrior.

The force of 60 Mormons arose, standing in place, and Porter beheld a dozen Missouri guards before them, whipping their heads around with eyes wide.

David Patten suddenly stood and shouted, "The sword of the Lord and of Gideon!"

Their men shouted in turn and Patten pointed his sword at the enemy. He then ordered, "Charge!" The Mormons sprang towards the river; Porter felt his feet flying forward. He and 60 others ran through tall grass and brush, charging past trees, shouting and waving swords, rifles and clubs.

The 140 militia soldiers poured out of their tents and grabbed their swords and rifles. The first six Missourians to load aimed directly at Porter Rockwell.

CHAPTER 47

Eight Mormons suddenly opened fire and shot all six rifle-men aiming at Porter. On the run he pointed his rifle and fired. A Missourian jerked his right shoulder back and made a complete turn, his pistol flying into the mist. Another militiaman fired at Porter — but missed by inches. Porter rushed at two others and swung his rifle — both ducked, then rose again, and Porter whacked them off their feet.

Several of Porter's comrades fired, then began swinging their rifles. The Missourians defended themselves, but seemed surprised at their ferocity.

Porter clouted one in the stomach, saw another running at him from the side, ducked, and bashed him squarely in the chest. He ran forward to another militiaman and swung his rifle stock into the man's thigh, then kicked him in the abdomen.

David Patten deflected sword blows from two Missourians. Porter ran at them and smashed his rifle stock across one militiaman's sword, knocking it clear, then clouted both fellows backwards over the river bank. He heard a splash, and saw both men swimming away. He cheered.

He then perceived a general panic among the Missourians. About 20 broke ranks and took out running into the river.

Porter yelled across his men to Patten:

"We're now only outnumbered by 50. I like the odds!"

Patten smiled and yelled for another charge.

The remaining Missourians were overrun by the charging rescuers.

Porter stopped before the Missouri commanding officer and ducked from a sword swinging toward his head, then he rammed his head straight at the officer's belly and yelled like a wild hog. He knocked the man over and, in one motion, took from him his sword then kicked him in the rear.

"You best retreat toward that river," yelled Porter, "less you want your ears chopped off and fed to the wildcats hereabouts."

The officer's eyes widened and he took off disarmed, diving into the water and swimming away.

A dozen militiamen saw what Porter had done to their commanding officer, and in fright they also took off running.

Other Missourians at a tree grove were braver however; they determined to stick it out till the end. Three of this squad did, and were practically trampled by 30 other Missourians beating a retreat for the river.

In a gully stood Porter beside David Patten. Both warded off blows from the final three militia swordsmen.

David got the best of one and stuck his shoulder. The man dropped back, wounded, and retreated, shouting obsenities.

Porter, facing another militiaman, sliced his sword down

while ducking a thrust. The sword flew into his contender's boot, sticking a toe. The man shouted and hobbled toward the river.

When the third militiaman realized he alone from his platoon now faced the two invaders, he bravely took on both.

David shouted to Porter, "He's yours. I got others up on the bluff to take care of!" He turned to his men and yelled, "Lads! Follow me!"

Porter butted his foe unconscious with a blow from his sword handle, then glimpsed back at Patten. He was proud of him, watching his friend leading their force of 60 fearlessly up the bluff. There, the last 50 Missourians gathered to attempt one last effort to fight back.

When the Missourians saw the force of 60 coming with Patten screaming, they fired. One Mormon was hit and fell. Two other Mormons opened fire and one Missourian was hit. Most men of both forces had spent their only loaded shot, so both sides now resorted to swords.

Patten and his men charged them with swords. Five Missourians were immediately struck on their arms. The remaining ones retreated and regrouped 30 yards downhill, beside the river.

Patten was relentless: He led a final charge, enclosing them in a wedge, with Porter's men swinging rifle butts at the forefront. This technique so surprised the Missourians with swords — and the effect was so stunning to the enemy — that Patten yelled for all his men to use their empty rifles.

They scabbarded their swords and unslung their arms, then on Patten's order began charging with swinging rifle stocks.

Eight Missourians were immediately leveled to the earth.

The other Missourians, so staggered by the sight of the effort, panicked and extended their swords too far from themselves; thus the Mormons' rifle stocks began whacking their swords away even more effectively. Patten's men smacked away the more vulnerable swordsmen's weapons, and most Missourians were soon left completely defenseless.

As David led the force still forward, with all his men still yelling and their rifle stocks still swinging, 20 Missourians tried one last counterattack — but all were whacked by rifles and half fell unconscious. The other half arose, turned and took off running.

Patten yelled, "Drive them into the river!"

The Mormon force kept up their attack and the last Missourians made one final effort of fighting back but, seeing the futility of standing against the riled up invaders who now outnumbered them, they turned to retreat. However, the militia company sergeant, seeing their defeat, ran in front of his force who had retreated and shouted at them to turn about and mount bayonets. This re-grouped force of 50 Missourians mounted the small swords at the end of their rifles, then took strategic positions behind trees to face their enemy.

But the invaders' sheer confidence gave them the power of stampeding cattle.

Porter saw the extended bayonets of the enemy, and shouted at Patten to halt their men. They came to a stop just 15 yards from the waiting weapons.

Porter stepped in front of the Mormon force, turned and faced them:

"Boys, Remember bayonet offense!" He shouted to the 57 remaining Mormon fighters behind him:

"Thrust forward!" he yelled. "Then to the side!" he shouted. "And when they're about to see their own bayonet knocked off their rifle by your stocks — like this — " he said, knocking a bayonet off a surprised Missourian's rifle into the green meadow, "and you see the fear on their face as they know they're about to lose their heads — like that," he said, seeing the same Missourian's eyes darting about for an avenue of escape, "then you take your rifle stock like this to commence swinging, and off he runs! Like that!" And the Missourian took off running.

Porter's force cheered. Then he commanded them to commence the same drill on all the militiamen before them, and half the remaining Missourians took off running.

Porter whacked one stubborn militiaman and went to the next, fending blows of the bayonet with his rifle stock, then knocking him off his feet — right in the midsection — watching him fly eight feet back into the river.

Patten next yelled, "Get the prisoners!"

Four Mormons ran to the two prisoners tied at a tree and began cutting ropes.

Porter scampered across the woods beside Patten and beheld no Missourians remaining. The last 10 state militiamen were charging into the river and diving in.

At last, Porter felt the time for celebration had arrived, and he broke into a cheer. His 57 fellows joined in. He continued gazing into the mists, where he could barely see across the river, and he felt a smile sweeping his face.

Across the narrow river the last Missouri militiamen were arriving on shore and running away. But the battle was not over:

Five of them hid behind trees and reloaded. Then, surprising to Porter, opened fire. Porter espied among the thick trees a column of smoke as he heard five loud booms. Suddenly he caught from the corner of his eye his old friend David Patten flying off his boots, six feet back, and crashing to the ground. The few Missourians left across the river cheered.

Porter and a half dozen others ran to his side. Patten was bleeding in the abdomen. He was clutching the earth and moaning. Porter peered across the river and observed those five Missourians now taking off running away, but still celebrating.

Porter knelt closer to Patten, who was now in both pain and shock. "I had a count made of our men just before that last volley," said Porter. "Only two of our boys are down. And none wounded seriously."

"I guess," Patten grimaced, trying for a smile, "you can make that three."

Porter wiped Patten's forehead with his hand, pushing away beads of sweat and tears from his face.

"You'll make it, David."

"I remember one really good morning when we caught a dozen catfish, Porter. We feasted like overfed pigs on that barge."

"That we did."

Patten tried for a smile. "Reckon we can do that again? Maybe you'll even get another barge. I'll help you build it."

"You better. I can't do it alone."

"Then again, maybe you'll have to, old friend."

"How come?"

"You know what we were talking about before the battle? Where I saw half my life before me?"

"Yeah," said Porter, still rubbing Patten's forehead and now fighting his own tears.

"I think I just saw the other half."

Porter looked up at the field and viewed bodies scattered everywhere. "David, we whupped 'em. We whupped 'em good. And we freed the prisoners."

But when he glanced down he saw David Patten's eyes glazed and staring upwards.

CHAPTER 48

The whole town of Far West greeted the returning troops with cheers. Appearing around a woodland bend on the main road, however, the Mormon soldiers walked tiredly, distraught over the loss of the three among them. Yet they hadn't been routed as some predicted. Nor had they been made an example of by the militia as others had expected. They had in fact won.

Now, women and children cheered as they approached the city, and a small brass band broke into music.

When they reached the business district where the crowd was now gathered in considerable numbers, they beheld the townspeople all throwing hats into the air.

Wives and children rushed to hug husbands and fathers. Soldiers dropped to one knee to hug their children.

As the two rescued prisoners appeared at the back of the pack, their families cried and ran to them. But as Porter appeared, tears flowed freely from his face. An excited teenage boy, the youngest of the returning force, ran up to Joseph and announced:

"We won! We freed the prisoners!"

Joseph ran out to Porter and hugged him, elated, only to discover Porter in tears hugging him back. Joseph gazed at him as if to ask, "What's wrong?"

"Joseph," answered Porter to the silent question, "three of our men were killed, including David Patten. They're coming in on that wagon."

Joseph stared at the wagon and looked like the wind was knocked out of him. Patten had been a loyal brother to them both, and a humble apostle of their faith. "Somehow," said Joseph, "I expected a miracle, with no one dying."

Porter wished to support him, "It was still a miracle."

Joseph could not look into his eyes, and went to find the families of the three men killed in battle.

Luana, still weak, spotted Porter in the crowded street. She carried Emily. Little Caroline was across the street with Porter's mother and sisters. Luana wore a smile, relieved that he was safe, despite her anger with him.

She immediately perceived his remorse. She ran to him and hugged him. Porter was surprised. She uttered, "What do you feel like for dinner?"

"What're you doing here?" said Porter. "You belong in bed!"

"It's a small miracle, but I woke up at dawn, and the ague was gone! Do you believe in miracles? I believe in miracles again. I had forgotten that I do!"

Porter almost beamed, despite the distress over his old fishing buddy, David Patten.

"It's all over?" she said.

"Yeah, the battle is."

"I said all over?"

"I think so."

"Don't you think this aggression policy was all a mistake?"

Ever defensive, Porter roared, "You tell that to the families of the two boys we rescued!"

"And to the families of the three who were killed?"

Porter gazed at her a moment, and stepped back a foot, literally taken back.

Lilburn W. Boggs gazed out his third story window at the autumn leaves floating casually to the ground. As an unseasonably warm October in 1838 it was a good day to go fishing, an event he'd planned with his relatives for weeks. However, he was frustrated by the day's activities and knew he'd have to cancel his participation in the reunion. Angered, he whirled his turnstile chair around and gazed across his massive oak desk at the two Caldwell County men facing him.

"You're telling me," said Boggs, "that what you saw at Crooked River was a complete massacre?"

The men nodded slowly. One said, nodding, "They took 'em all prisoners, then killed them."

"And to think," said Boggs, "that I hand-picked the militia myself." He pounded his fist down.

"I know that's humiliating for you, governor."

"Don't tell me what I think is humiliating."

"Yes, sir."

"Is there anything else you learned?"

"Joseph Smith's soldiers right now are marching on Richmond to lay it in ashes," said the taller of the two.

Boggs gazed at the two men assessingly. "You wouldn't be making any of this up?"

The shorter glanced at the other, his eyes darting back and forth. "No, sir!"

Boggs turned to his aide sitting adjacent to his desk:

"Issue these orders immediately to General John Clark: 'The Mormons must be treated as enemies, and must be exterminated or driven from the state if necessary for the public peace; their outrages are beyond all description.'" (Author's note: This was the actual transcription of the order.)

At Joseph's house Porter ate dinner in silence. Both Joseph and Porter were consumed with concerns as Emma served boiled potatoes, cabbage, beef, and fresh rolls and butter. Porter did not even realize what he was eating; he simply ate. Joseph finally broke the silence:

"Since the battle at Crooked River, the account of our victory has been blown all out of proportion." He glanced at Porter and saw his eyes burning. "And we've got other problems now. Apostles Orson Hyde and Thomas Marsh have apostatized from the church and gone to the Missourians. And they've taken another rock to toss into the hornet's nest: They claim we passed a decree to kill all dissenters, then march on the Gentiles and make it 'one gore of blood from the Rocky Mountains to the Atlantic Ocean.' I defended myself to the press against this charge, but I'm afraid it's too late," he confessed to Porter. "I don't know what to do. The lies of dissenters are our greatest enemy."

Later that night just before falling asleep, Porter heard horsehooves in the distance; he arose to the reports of gun-shots. Ugly jumped from a dead sleep and walked curiously outside. Porter followed. His neighbors were all inspecting their property. They found no one, but all their cattle were dead, and the one cow and two bulls Porter owned were wounded. Luana's eyes moistened when she saw the sight. She was angry with herself for getting too close to the animals, and as she stared at the scene, Porter went to each animal and, wiping away tears, shot them. First the cow which he'd nurtured and stayed awake nights to keep alive when it was sick and but a calf, and then the larger, older of the two bulls which he had often gazed upon proudly, fond of their innate beauty and gentleness, and finally he loaded his weapon for the youngest bull, which months ear-lier he had bought as a calf. He was unable to pull back the hammer, and Luana looked down. He finally turned his head away and began to squeeze the trigger. He heard the weapon fire, and now all three of the animals lay perfectly still, free from suffering.

Several neighbors gathered in the road to trade informa-tion, when a woman in the distance screamed that her main source of food for the children — the old family cow — was dead.

The air was dense with smoke from outlying farms still burning. Porter sat alone before the fireplace. He stared at the flames. His dog lay asleep by the fire. Luana sat in a back room, quilting. Porter wanted to visit Joseph, but was afraid to leave his wife and the two girls unprotected. He realized that village leaders would get word to him on some course of action, but waiting for the news was agonizing.

"How do you know Joseph's even alive?" said Luana.

"I don't see him ever getting killed," he replied. "Do you?"

Luana snorted a skeptical sigh.

"What does that mean?" he said.

"Please understand — if he does, I won't move again," she muttered.

"Not even if commanded by the Lord?"

"He'd have to tell me himself, and then I might not."

"But you see it daily," he moaned.

"I see what?"

"The signs," he said.

"Like flames, smoke and blood?"

"Other signs," said Porter. "You've seen the light."

A long pause settled in the cabin before either spoke again.

"Porter, what could happen to Emily and Caroline?"

He pondered at the two girls sleeping, then floated his look outside the window to the moon.

CHAPTER 49

A peaceful morning at Haun's Mill, Missouri awakened 40 men, women and children. Soon they were working in fields and at the mill next to the stream. After a few minutes one of the young workers turned and beheld 240 Missouri militiamen approaching horseback across the meadow, pulling out rifles.

One of the militia leaders bellowed, "Boys, remember Crooked River!"

The horses broke into a gallop.

The 40 Mormons simply stood in their steps, disbelieving what they beheld. Then broke for cover.

Eight of the boys in the field ran to the mill. The horsemen swept past them, firing, and mowed them all down.

The women screamed and ran for the woods. The horsemen rode past them but shot only near their feet, barely missing.

A small band of militiamen dismounted, and walked among the boys lying on the ground whom they had shot. Finding several alive, they grabbed the boys, carried them to a nearby out-building, and commenced throwing them against a wall over and over to die in misery. A number of the mobbers watched, laughing.

The last 12 boys and men ran into a storage shed, hoping to find safety.

One man at the shed saw his wife rushing toward the cover of trees. "Get to Far West! Get help!" he said, then he slammed the shed door behind him. Through one of the many cracks between boards he noticed a 10 year old boy running toward the shed. The horsemen were right on his heels. The man at the shed opened the door for him, and the boy ran inside to the relief of those already there.

Casually, a hundred horsemen dismounted and with smiles on their faces sashayed up to the shed.

The 12 boys and men inside gaped at several dozen rifle barrels slowly poked inside the wide cracks of the boards. "Ready," said the horsemen's leader.

A quarter mile away the women in the woods heard the report of a hundred rifles firing almost in unison.

Eighteen bodies of boys and men lay about the deserted mill area, 12 of them in the shed. While the horsemen rode away, the women and girls returned from the woods, opened the shed and beheld a sight they would not soon forget.

Not much later, thousands of armed state militia arrived at the woods outside Far West.

"Remember Crooked River!" was the marching cry of militia leaders. They were ordered to halt and load weapons, then wait for the order of attack.

Just outside the city Porter rode beside Joseph. They surveyed their force of 450 men who were laying breastworks to act as a protective barrier. Volunteer women, boys and old men were on hand to reload, and would give them a slight chance against such a superior force.

Porter heard distant drums in the woodland wind. He thought of himself more a fighter than an officer, so he had declined any leadership offers. Certain commissioned officers obviously underestimated his talent and did not push the matter, or he may have been.

Joseph was staggered when Colonel Hinckle, his appointed leader of the Mormon brigade, rode up, having just met with the leaders of the invading force:

"They're 6,000 of them, Joseph," said Hinckle.

Porter blew out a silent sigh. Joseph glanced down, thinking. The three men were still horseback.

"I have volunteered a peace proposal," said Hinckle. "And the enemy has agreed to it."

Porter and Joseph regarded him curiously. Joseph finally said, "What is the proposal?"

"That you surrender, Joseph, along with several other church leaders."

Porter stared at Hinckle, shocked. As did Joseph.

Hinckle continued, "They in turn will not attack the city."

Porter exploded, "Are you crazy!"

"Calm down, Porter," said Joseph.

Hinckle, defensive, spoke louder, "Even warriors must save lives."

"Warriors!" said Porter. "You call yourself a warrior?"

"I know battle strategy," shouted Hinckle, "and what 6,000 trained soldiers can do to a group like this!"

Joseph shook his head, confused.

"Just look at your men, Joseph," continued Hinckle. "Old men, farmers, boys. What chance have you got?"

"The same," said Porter, shouting in his face, "as we had at Crooked River! Don't you believe in miracles? Or is one miracle the limit you can expect to see against the pukes?"

"On what grounds," said Hinckle, "do you base your preposterous assumptions!"

"Common sense, General," said Porter, "which I fear is more than what you've got at the moment!"

"I take that as a challenge!" said Hinckle.

"Take it anyway you wish!" exploded Porter.

"Brethren!" said Joseph. "We have a war in front of us!"

"If you can call it that," shouted Hinckle. "This is a massacre in front of us!"

"It is a war we will win!" exclaimed Porter.

"All right, Joseph," said Hinckle, "what do you wish me to report to their commanders? That you will fight them to your deaths or follow the terms of my proposal?"

Joseph scanned his men lining the breastworks and studied their appearance.

"Joseph," pleaded Porter, "we cannot lose."

"Let him decide for himself," said Hinckle.

Joseph looked at Porter. "He's right. We cannot hold off 6,000 trained soldiers."

"Why not?" yelled Porter.

"Perhaps we could have another miracle, but I cannot risk the lives of so many people. If I could even save one life by surrendering . . . "

"No!" said Porter.

Joseph disregarded him:

"Colonel Hinckle, you have my response to your proposal, and I congratulate you for your foresight."

"The foresight of a coward," mumbled Porter.

Hinckle smiled, "Let's not be sore losers, Mr. Rockwell."

Porter pulled a sword from his scabbard.

Joseph grabbed his arm:

"Put it away, Porter."

"He's betrayed you. The man has just — "

"He's doing his best," interrupted Joseph.

"But that's not enough!"

"It's the right thing for now! I believe that," said Joseph. "So I certainly don't see betrayal here."

"Well, however you see it, it's what's just happened," Porter exclaimed, then he rode his horse away to be alone.

CHAPTER 50

Four hundred and fifty Mormon soldiers stood in two lines at the town square of Far West, Missouri. Under a flagpole, walking past a table in one line, the Mormons had to surrender their weapons. In the other line they were forced to sign away their real estate deeds "to pay the expenses of war."

Across the street Joseph and numerous church leaders were shackled in hand and feet chains, ready to be led away. All the Mormon soldiers' wives and children were being rounded up and brought to town square.

Suddenly an officer with two guards arrived and quickly dismounted. This young captain possessed dark eyes as spirited as his gait. He strode with long steps in his tall, lanky frame and finally arrived at the feet of the militia commander, General Alexander Doniphan, a stately, dignified gray-haired gentleman.

"Sir, I have orders," he said, handing a document to Doniphan, "from the governor himself, saying you are to have Mr. Joseph Smith lined up at dawn before a firing squad . . . and shot."

Doniphan ripped the orders from his hands and read them. He gazed at Joseph thoughtfully. Finally he turned to the young officer sent by Boggs.

"The man in question," said Doniphan, "is not guilty of such a punishment." Doniphan knew Joseph previously, having performed for him as an attorney to help incorporate Caldwell County in a manner to the Mormon leader's liking. From his personal dealings with Joseph, he remembered him in a far different light than what Boggs was claiming.

The young officer, intoxicated with his own authority, shouted at Doniphan, "Do you understand what the governor says? He orders you!"

Doniphan was quite aware his decision could amount to nothing less than career suicide, and he knew he'd have the rest of his life to relive the choice of this day. He could see his dreams crashing into ashes. No one dared disobey the powerful Boggs, a man the newspapers supported and who controlled the state political machinery. Doniphan stared down at his shoes, wishing such a choice had never been thrust upon him.

"You can tell the governor I refuse to obey his orders."

The young officer stepped forward. "You say you refuse Governor Boggs' military authority, sir?"

"No, I refuse to shoot an innocent man in cold blood."

Porter entered his cabin and slammed the door behind him. His dog, uncomfortable with the loud noises and all the tension, arose from sleeping on the porch outside and decided to leave for several days, as he for years frequently had.

"What's the matter?" said Luana.

"Hinckle betrayed Joseph right into their hands, and our entire force is giving up their weapons."

"'Betrayed's' an awfully strong word."

"Are you ever going to side with me?" he said, putting his rifle down and sitting at the dining table while placing his face in his hands.

"What does Joseph say about this?"

"He let himself get betrayed."

"Let himself? You think he's stupid enough to let himself get trapped — or 'betrayed?'"

"I know what I saw."

"Maybe there's another way to look at it."

"You can't even agree with me just once?"

"I wasn't there," she said.

"That's my point — so how can you argue?"

"But I know if your whole army is back there surrendering weapons," she said, "then you must also support Joseph and get back there to join them."

"And surrender my rifle? After that militia colonel in Independence smooth-talked us into giving up our weapons? That's when the mobs ran wild!"

"So what do you plan to do? Fight the entire state militia yourself?"

"If I have to."

"Go surrender your rifle!" she demanded.

"Not in this life."

"I assume you're the only loose cannon to run off this way?"

"There were others."

"What others? What're you talking about?"

"Some who were at Crooked River with me left the breast-works an hour ago, just before the militia marched in. I told them to head home and hide their rifles and themselves while they're at it, 'cause some of the militia might recognize them from Crooked River."

"You honestly think the other deserters would join with you to fight the militia?" she smirked.

"Deserters? Are you as crazy as Hinckle? We're the only ones willing to fight! That makes us deserters?"

"To Joseph's plans. And here I thought you were his big supporter," she said, turning her back on him to pull creamed corn from the oven.

He picked up his rifle and headed for the door, having come to a decision on who he would shoot first if given the chance.

"The other boys who took off with their rifles may not join me to fight," he said, "so you might be right, but I can do damage on my own."

"Where're you going with that thing!"

"I got a score to settle." He looked over at Emily and winked, then shut the door firmly behind him. "No Missouri pukes are going to hold me down," he muttered.

"Porter! . . ." Luana felt the wind knocked out of her and stared at the closed door.

CHAPTER 51

$\mathbf{A}$t the Far West town square the disarmed Mormons and their families were paraded before a speaker standing in the back of a wagon, a smirk sweeping his face. It was the same young officer who had brought Doniphan his orders from Governor Boggs. He announced they were completely at the mercy of 12 Missouri committeemen to judge what they could keep as necessities to help them move out of the state, and they had $4^1/_2$ months, until April 1, 1839, to leave.

From his hidden position behind a clump of trees, Porter winced at having to desert their hard-worked farms once again.

On the platform also stood several smartly-uniformed militia officers. General Doniphan had meanwhile retreated to a tavern across the street to observe the scene and make certain no officers attempted to counter his orders by killing Joseph.

Porter ran from the clump of trees to the side of a building where he spotted Joseph and the other church leaders being lined up, still in chains, beside a heavy guard. He removed his rifle and took aim at the speaker. The young officer looked like a Missouri puke, if ever he saw one, with all the trappings of a genuine roughneck — scraggly mustache and thick southern drawl that held no attempt to mask his prejudice nor the enjoyment he received at hearing his own words:

"Citizens of Far West, do not think — do not even consider — do not even let it enter your minds even for one second — that you will see your leaders again!" (Author's note: This was the actual proclamation.)

Porter eased his finger toward the trigger. He knew if he missed, there'd be thousands of soldiers on him before he could reload for a second shot.

But his rifle was rock steady and his aim deadly sure. He wondered for a moment if he should instead shoot Colonel Hinckle, "the betrayer" with whom he was still angry, but in his heart he figured Hinckle was either a coward, or simply stupid, or perhaps indeed did have Joseph's and the city's best interests in mind, despite his arrogance, but certainly he was not a cold-blooded enemy like the Missouri puke on the platform. His thoughts ran wild as he tried focusing on his plan. After he would dispatch this young officer to the Spirit World, he'd slip through several buildings and head into thick woods for assured safety.

The young officer continued:

"Oh my dear citizens, I regret to inform you that now is the hour to prepare. But for what? To meet your Maker? No. To leave? Yes! You must prepare to leave this glorious state of citizens who abide by the laws. And where will you go without your leaders? Whoever knows! Furthermore, whoever cares!" Several hundred of the militia chuckled, then applauded. "But wherever you decide to go, you must leave by April 1st! Get home now and pack your belongings right away!"

"I'll pack his belongings," said Porter in a mumble, his finger now touching the trigger. Then, just as he was at the instant of firing, a thought shot into his mind. What about Joseph and all their people? If he picked off this puke now there would be Hades to pay.

Porter never wanted to fire a rifle so badly in his life. The satisfaction would be immeasurable. He took aim again just to feel what it might feel like — to imagine the enjoyment of eliminating this lunatic bully, who now represented to him all the tyrants he had ever faced since a kid back in Manchester, New York.

He glanced at Joseph again. He realized he could not pull the trigger on this man, and he lowered the rifle. 'He's not even armed,' he thought to himself. 'What have I almost done?' He trembled and broke into a sweat.

At that moment he heard a command from the platform:

"Guard detail, take the prisoners to Liberty Jail, and report back immediately!"

Joseph gazed across the square at his wife and children, who were as forlorn-looking as Porter remembered ever seeing them. From his hiding place he watched helplessly as Joseph and about 45 other church leaders were escorted away under the "protection" of 200 soldiers, down a muddy road and away from Far West.

Porter snuck into the woods and gathered his thoughts a moment, watching Joseph being led away. He could quickly recruit his Battle of Crooked River comrades who, like he, had fled with their guns, and they could ambush Joseph's guards but, with Joseph and his followers shackled in hand and feet chains, would get practically nowhere before being mowed down by surviving militiamen like a turkey-shoot. He realized he would just have to rescue Joseph some other way.

Porter's children were playing in the woods behind the cabin when he came upon them. They screamed with joy and ran to his legs and clutched them as, one at a time, he picked them up and hugged them. His dog Ugly then jumped on him and knocked him over. Wrestling with him on the ground, Porter finally pushed him away.

"Get him off me!" laughed Porter. "He's got the breath of a buffalo! I can't breathe!"

The children laughed as Ugly licked him on the face, then left, wagging his tail.

"I think," said Porter, "I'm going to die — get me a wet cloth!"

Emily brought him a wet towel from the well and Porter washed his face quickly. "My goodness, that dog's a weapon."

Inside, Luana assessed him coolly. "The militia will be checking houses for those who haven't signed over their property yet, I heard. And I'll have to sign our house over to the committee."

Porter broiled with anger but, after seriously reflecting a moment, nodded.

Luana walked outside to be alone. She was still frustrated at his not abiding with her demands of surrendering his rifle, fearful of the potential retaliatory repercussions by the militia against her family. The Haun's Mill massacre had sent a strong message to the saints that a brutal Boggs regime ruled with an iron fist. When Porter passed her in the garden, he glowered at her. She was frustrated by his anger. After all, she felt, she was merely a mother bear protecting her den; however, she knew Porter saw her as merely a bear, period, critical of him for no justifiable reason. He shook his head, kicking himself for not heeding his mother's advice years earlier. For his children's sake, he would just have to make the most of it. He sat down and ate, angry at himself more than at her.

Porter moved along the roadside under the cover of thick trees. Two local Missourians approached horseback, and he froze. They did not recognize him and rode silently past.

Several minutes later he arrived at the cabin of Brigham Young. After greeting him, Brigham sat him at his table for supper. His wife was cordial but quiet, as the stocky, charismatic apostle to Joseph chewed on stale bread crusts and drank buttermilk, his life-long favorites.

"Joseph has been sentenced. Sampson Avard and others testified against him and the others. They claimed the "Danites" attacked Missouri homes — whereas the homes were actually attacked by Missourian mobocrats in order to frame us. When we tried to counter their charges, they aimed their guns at us in court and told us to shut up. Nevertheless, the judge released forty of our leaders — all except for Joseph and five others. They've been taken from Independence Jail and are on their way to Clay County to await some other bogus trial."

"Do you have plans to free 'em?" said Porter.

"Have you seen the jails here? They're like small fortresses."

"So what're you going to do?"

"Nothing," said Brigham. "This town is the most demoralized I've yet seen it."

"Why can't we stay and fight?"

"With what — clubs?"

"Rifles," said Porter. "Some of us have rifles."

"You're talking about six thousand militia and hundreds of armed civilians chomping at the bits to invade us."

"So we're just gonna sit back and watch?"

"I've signed a pledge of rebellion to Boggs' Exterminating Order," said Brigham. "Other than that there's not a great deal we can do, frankly."

"How many signatures have you got?" said Porter.

"239."

"Make that 240."

Porter headed into the dreary frigid air to find his family, parents and siblings. His thoughts were also riveted to helping Joseph. But then he realized the cold fact that they first had to flee the territory to save their own lives.

CHAPTER 52

After hours of walking, Joseph and his five fellow prisoners arrived at an open courtyard in the rain. Their militia guards commanded them to lie down for a night's sleep, but the cold October storms pelted them and they slept a matter of minutes on the cold, wet grass.

The next morning they were led by the guards to Liberty Jail at Liberty, Missouri. The jailer unchained the prisoners and placed them into the dungeon, a room so small they could not stand. The room was barely large enough to fit the six men. A swill bucket served as their bathroom facility. The only light came from cracks in the uneven trap door in the ceiling. This door connected to the main floor above, where the jailer resided.

When the guards left, the jailer stared down at the wet prisoners, shook his head, smiled, and slammed the door shut on them.

The frozen Missouri tundra seemed endless. The Mormon immigrants drove their wagons Eastward across the entire state of Missouri to Western Illinois. Porter walked beside Luana, each carrying a child. Despite Luana's earlier claims to never again move, she once again was moving with her husband to yet another home in the wilderness. Porter's parents trudged in front of them, beside his brothers and sisters. None of the clan had a wagon since theirs was burned at Independence half a decade earlier. He noticed his father growing weaker, aggravated by the cold, 300 mile journey. His deteriorating condition kept the going slow for the Rockwell families. Porter's brothers — Peter, Merritt and Horace — remained close to help their pa. On the trek, the brothers — including Porter — took turns hunting and fishing to keep the clan fed. They mostly traveled on muddy roads and bumpy fields.

At the Mississippi River they finally arrived. It was a long-welcome yet dreary sight. Their people quickly built barges to cross it.

Across the river at Quincy, Illinois the citizens welcomed them with open arms. They wished for the Mormons to build a new community there. "We're opposed to slavery here — you folks won't have such troubles with us," one of the land-owners told them. Accepting his graciousness, they borrowed his land to erect temporary shelter. Immediately they built cabins and lean-to's, and lived with many of Quincy's families.

Porter constructed a lean-to like the Jackson County version — with a roof and three covered sides — for his family, while aiding his brothers in building a cabin for his parents next door. Orin was visibly worn. Porter and his brothers continued to hunt and fish for their survival. Porter meanwhile could not get Joseph out of his mind.

As they retired at twilight one day, the four brothers gazed over the settlement. Though it was far better than their encampment at the Missouri River shore, it was still a disheartening sight. They were a displaced people with no leader, no land, and no money.

The next few days went fast. While the prospects of Porter's people appeared promising, he still worried incessantly about Joseph.

After completing his parents' cabin and stockpiling firewood at break-neck speed, Porter entered his open-air home one afternoon and gazed at Luana.

She had become quieter the past couple months, overwhelmed by the relocation. She discovered the whole ordeal especially disconcerting when, just after she had exhausted herself this particular day bathing the girls by herself, she observed Porter enter the door, stand there, and stare at her, as he announced:

"I'm headed back." Those were his only words. She waited for him to explain. He didn't.

"What?"

"It's that unfinished business I told you about," he said.

"You're going to take on the Missouri militia?"

"No, just rescue Joseph."

She gazed at him, stunned. "Are you certain you should try this? It seems to me some devil-may-care single men out there without families would volunteer in your place."

"Which friends would you want to see if you were held in a pit?"

"What do you mean?"

"Joseph has known me since we were boys. Maybe it means a little more, having some people there — those he could trust as steady shooters — that's all."

She studied him, aghast, as he requested her to package wild game jerky and hard rolls for him to take to Joseph and the other prisoners.

"Are you actually planning to give them all our jerky?" she demanded.

"Of course."

"What about food for our family?"

"We'll make do."

"With what?"

"I'll hunt something up."

"Then hunt something up for Joseph."

"Don't have time."

"Make time, Porter. I can't have you giving away our last food."

"We don't need it as bad as him. Don't you have faith we'll be looked after?"

"I've seen what's happened from it, yeah," she snorted. "What do you expect the children to eat — air?"

"Luana, package it up now."

She caught the anger in his eyes, but was not intimidated by him, now or ever, unlike most men who saw that look. After pondering a long moment, she softened, sighed, and declared,

"We do have to save Joseph. At the very least from starving. You're right. I'll pack up what we have for you to take."

Porter appreciated her usually coming around after she thought something like this through — especially when it affected the welfare of others. He then recruited his brothers Peter, Merritt and Horace to finish smoking and jerking wild turkey for the clan to stockpile until he returned.

He left his parents with the final words, "At least you'll be out of the cold, and Peter will help you with firewood. I've chopped a month's worth already."

Later that evening he returned to his home. He held Caroline, then commenced to pack. Emily watched, consumed with curiosity.

"Where're you going, Pa?"

"Out to see Joseph."

"Coming back alive?"

Porter gazed at Luana, concerned over what she must've told her.

"I'll be home in a few weeks," he clarified.

"Is that a long time?"

He looked into Emily's eyes. "I'm afraid too long."

"Can I come, Pa?"

Porter turned and faced her. He studied her face and his heart melted. It had not even occurred to him that such was a possibility, but it suddenly dawned on him that there was no reason why they should be apart. He finally smiled:

"I don't reckon why not."

Luana exploded, "You most certainly are not taking her! Not only is it dangerous, she'll slow you down. You need to get the food to Joseph, then head back here as fast as you can! I am outraged you would even think of taking her — or that you would even allow yourself to be slowed down! We need you back here to build us a better home!"

"Better home?"

"A real cabin."

"The place here is only temporary till we re-locate," he said. "I've told you that."

"Who says we'll re-locate?"

"Brigham and the others."

"I don't care what they say," she said. "There's no reason you can't make us a better home here."

"It's a decent enough one for now."

"You call this decent?" she said.

"Decent enough for hundreds of other folks."

"I am not hundreds of other folks."

"Maybe you oughta think about becoming one."

"And maybe you ought to just settle down for once," she said, "and support your family the way we're entitled!"

"We'll see you in a few weeks," he said, grabbing a pack of Emily's things he'd gathered.

"You're really serious about taking her?"

"Of course."

"That is completely crazy."

"What's wrong with it?"

"Taking a little girl into the heart of your enemies? You

don't see what's wrong with it?"

"Your enemies? You can't bring yourself to say our enemies anymore, can you? So if they're not your enemies, why should they be mine? Emily and I are heading right into the heart of our friends, right Emily?"

"Porter, you'll only take her over my dead body."

"Well I'm taking her whether you care to live or not." At that he grabbed Emily, his rifle, and both their packs, then hauled everything out to his horse, saddled and ready to ride.

Luana grabbed his shotgun from a make-shift dresser, and as he walked outside she pointed it at him from the open entrance.

"You turn and face me!" she shouted.

"I know you wouldn't shoot me in the back," he said, "but I can't guarantee you wouldn't shoot if I faced you, so I'd be a lunatic to turn and face you now, wouldn't I?" he smiled.

That caught her sense of humor. The preposterousness of the situation and what she was doing with the gun, despite her anger, pulled at her emotions from every direction. She began laughing, and as he rode away with Emily she finally broke out simultaneously sobbing. She stared helplessly as they rode away, still holding the shotgun but pointing it to the ground. She re-entered the lean-to and threw it down, grabbed little Caroline, and hugged her.

CHAPTER 53

Porter and Emily set out on their journey with all the meat jerky they owned. It was a curious assortment of opossum, squirrel, porcupine, rattlesnake, venison, and beef. All delicious stuff, according to Porter. Emily had to agree. Anything he said, in fact, she agreed with.

Riding through the badlands of Missouri with Emily was a risk for the five year old which even Porter was now wishing perhaps he had not made.

The long ride was precarious enough, but traversing the land of his most vituperous enemies with her made him begin to doubt his own sanity. He simply could not say no to this child who so completely dominated his heart. Whenever they saw riders approaching from the distance, they would dart into the cover of woods to travel awhile before re-emerging onto the road. At night Porter would build a small lean-to for cover and a campfire for warmth. Each night he'd snuggle her, validating his feelings he had discovered when she was one hour old, re-

alizing now that he still loved her more than anything on earth.
Two weeks later they arrived at Liberty, Missouri.

Immediately Porter searched for and found a woodland
pond. There he built a camouflaged lean-to. He bundled Emily
comfortably. They were safely concealed in the woods a mile
from the nearest Liberty, Missouri farm.

"Where're you going, Papa?"

"I'll be back in a while."

"Can I come?"

He looked into her eyes, wishing more than anything he
could bring her.

"It ain't safe," he said.

"But it's safe here?"

He nodded and smiled. "I reckon no one comes here more
than once every four or five years, judging from the footprints."

"Can I drink that water?" she said, nodding at the pond.
"I'm thirsty."

"This stream water we got is cleaner." He poured her a
drink from one of the canteens.

"Can I take a walk through the woods? I wanna see all the
streams and trees around here."

"You're like me, ain't ya?" he said. "Most kids would want
to stay here where it's safe, so they couldn't get lost."

"I just want to see everything around here."

"No, you stay put."

"Will it be dark when you get back?'

"If it is, wait for me," he said. "Now if something happens to me and I don't get back before morning, you go through those trees into town and ask for the sheriff. Then give this paper to him and say your grandparents are over there in Independence. Your Grandma Sarah wrote this out."

"What's it say?"

"It gives George and Olive Beebe's name and address in Independence. The sheriff would take you there if he got this note."

"What's gonna happen to you?"

"Nothing."

"Then what's the paper for?"

"In case something does."

"But what could happen if you say nothing will?"

"A falling star could hit me."

"In the daytime?"

"Yeah, only you wouldn't see it."

"How come?" she said.

Porter blew out a sigh, exasperated. "You ask too many questions."

"What would it look like if it hit you?"

He feigned getting hit by a falling star. He crossed his eyes and fell over backwards.

Emily began chuckling, then laughed harder and harder as he rolled around, dying from the meteorite. He finally stopped and looked up at her.

"That's what happens," said Porter, "when a falling star hits you."

"Papa?"

"Yeah?"

"Do you ever act this silly when you're alone with Mama?"

"No."

"How come?"

"Because she don't laugh."

"So you're silly 'cause I laugh?"

"I reckon I like to hear people laugh. Especially you."

"Papa?"

"Yeah?"

"Do you love me?"

"Honey . . . " said Porter.

"Yeah?"

"Do you know what I looked like when that falling star just hit me?"

"Yeah?" said Emily, wide-eyed and wondrous.

"That's the way I feel every time you smile at me."

She smiled and hugged him.

Liberty Jail lay dead ahead. Porter, ever conscious of certain ironies in life, did not let it pass him that "Liberty" was in the same name as "Jail." He lowered his leather hat over his brow so no one could recognize him in case any veterans of the "Jackson County Wars" might be milling about. He strode confidently toward the door of the main floor which housed the jailer.

He was determined to rescue Joseph if it meant getting jailed himself.

CHAPTER 54

Porter entered the jailer's office.

"You still have the prisoners?"

"We always have prisoners."

"Joseph Smith and company?"

"We'll have them awhile."

"A long while," added the jailer's friend.

The jailer opened the trap door. Porter was met with an overpowering stench. He descended below by performing a reverse pull-up, dropping into the dungeon.

Joseph greeted him with a handshake. Porter noticed the men with vomit on their shirts from sickness, and learned they'd also been fed rotten horse meat and human flesh, taken from the bodies of several Mormons murdered in recent days — those who'd not fled to Illinois. The prisoners had refused, of course, to eat it. In one corner was the swill bucket of human waste which was taken out occasionally to be emptied in the outhouse, a task paid by the jailer to the town drunkard with a pint of cheap moonshine. But it too often overflowed.

"Porter, it is so good to see you," said Joseph. "You have no idea."

"Where's Sidney?" said Porter, noticing the sixth man among them missing.

"He got too sick," said Joseph. "So he's on his way home with friends who came for him."

The prisoners Porter found were Joseph and Hyrum Smith, Lyman Wight, Alexander McRae and Caleb Baldwin.

Lyman Wight took a handful of beef jerky from Porter. "You don't know how I live for food our people bring us. Trouble is, we have to split it five ways," he smiled.

"So you're all right?" said Porter.

"Perhaps," mentioned Baldwin, staring off at one of the walls, "there is no deeper feeling of hopelessness than not knowing when or if you will see your wife and children again."

"Or freedom of any kind," added Wight. "It could be years before we ever even see a trial. And then they could frame us on anything."

Porter sensed the pressure on Joseph to maintain a semblance of sanity among them.

"Does it ever get warm in here?" said Porter.

"Warmer. We could use new blankets. As you see, these old ones aren't in the best of shape." They were ragged and filthy.

"So what do you need?" said Porter softly, knowing the jailer above could hear if he spoke in full voice.

"Food, and something for this." Joseph pulled from behind his back a small shovel, then revealed a hole in the wall against which he had been leaning.

"You're digging yourselves out?"

"Were. 'Till the handle broke."

"I'll get you another," said Porter. "Here's a present for you." Porter withdrew from his coat a bag of small cakes and breads. The men attacked them like wolves, except for Joseph, who was more anxious for news.

"How's Emma and the children?" said Joseph.

"I stopped by their place near Quincy on the way here," said Porter. "Quincy, Illinois is where we've located till we find another place to settle, if you get out." He corrected himself: "When you get out." Joseph smiled and Porter continued, "She wanted you to have this." He handed Joseph a letter that would be read a hundred times in the future when the trap door would be opened for meals or swill bucket-emptying, or at anytime there would be light.

"Any news for them?" said Porter.

"I wish I had," said Joseph. "Just my love for each. Give them all a hug for me, will you, Porter? Especially Joseph III — he's very sensitive and I know must be taking this exceptionally hard."

All five prisoners questioned him during his allotted 30 minute visit for all the information he could provide on families and friends.

The jailer shouted down he had two minutes left.

"Any word on the trial?" finally said Porter.

"It should have been months ago," said Joseph. "Who knows if and when they'll convene."

"Don't worry," said Porter. "I looked over the building here

441

pretty good, and I figure with a surprise attack at night we could get you out. I just need to bring back a dozen men to help me."

"I won't hear of it," said Joseph.

"Why not!"

"It's not worth losing a single life over, and most certainly that would happen."

"What if I just took on the jailers myself right now, and — "

"How would we all get to safety?" said Joseph. "We can't run, because our legs muscles have softened so much. But I do have an idea. Why don't you bring something with you next time?"

A dim sparkle of hope shone in the other prisoners' eyes.

"Something," continued Joseph, "that could really help us out."

Porter gazed at him knowingly.

"Twenty feet *that* way," said Porter. "I noticed on the way in."

"And I did, too," smiled Joseph, "Months ago."

"Don't worry, brethren." Porter regarded each of them. They looked in his eyes and saw even more hope.

"Hurry on up here now, boy," said the jailer. "Your time's up."

Porter gave Joseph a long hug. He then shook hands with each prisoner, and started up the ladder. He glanced back at their anxious, gleaming eyes set in sallow faces, and immediately he began to weep. He wiped away the tears so the jailer would not see his emotions, then pulled himself up onto the main floor.

But see him they did. And his tears.

The jailer and his friends, the "assistant jailers," who used the jail as a hang-out to get away from their wives and share a little booze and conversation every night, gazed at him a moment, then broke out laughing. Porter felt for the first time in his life like strangling several human beings in the same room at the same moment.

At the pond outside Liberty, Emily was enchanted by falling snow flakes. When her father came tromping through the white wilderness, she was intrigued by the fact she could hear him 300 yards away. Sound travels in such a unique manner in the white cold that it seems to make time stand still.

"Are you all right, honey?" said Porter, arriving at the lean-to and dismounting.

"Yeah, but can I go with you next time?"

"Honey, as your smart mama would say, there's a 'probability' I'll get shot at next time."

"What does 'pro-bility' mean?" she said.

"Good chance."

"So can I come with you?"

Porter gazed at her and smiled. "You are just like me. It's amazing."

"So what do you say?" she said.

"Maybe in a few years."

"Promise?"

Porter thought a moment. "I'll have to think on it."

Emily added two seconds later, "So, did you decide?"

"No."

"When will you know?"

"In several years. Why do you ask so all-fired many questions?"

"Cause I want something to look forward to."

"You look forward to being shot at when you're older?"

"Yeah, I reckon," she said.

"You've got so much of my blood in you it ain't even funny."

"Don't know why that would be funny. I got enough of my own blood."

Porter leaned down and gave her a big kiss on the forehead. He then pulled two fresh pastries from his pocket and handed her one.

"Where'd you get this?" she said.

"Bakery in town."

They lit into them.

"I love this!" she said.

"I'll get you another," said Porter. "Soon as I get back from town." He wrapped her in a blanket again and left her at the lean-to.

"I'd build a fire for you, honey," he said, "but we can't attract attention this close to the city. You'll be plenty warm till I get back in an hour or two. Here's some jerky to tide you over."

At that he took off, and she watched him ride across the snow and away.

Through the trees Porter discovered a farm ahead. He dismounted and hitched his horse to a tree. Keeping hidden by traversing between thick groves, he made his way to a tool shed. Not seeing anyone through the farm house windows — because of there being rippled glass through which one could only see movements of people — Porter snuck carefully toward the shed, then made a dash for the doorway.

Inside the shed he found on first inspection no tools. But, as he was leaving, there in one corner leaned two shovels. From the handle of a tall shovel his eyes went downward. And there it was. Just what he needed. A short shovel. He felt the blade. Plenty sharp, he figured, and the handle seemed rugged. The tall shovel suddenly fell over with a clang. He grabbed the short shovel and two saddle blankets off the ground, scampered to the doorway, gazed at the cabin 30 yards distant, and took off running for the woods. Not 10 feet out the doorway he heard a shotgun blast.

CHAPTER 55

The buckshot whizzed over Porter's head. He ran a jagged line toward the woods. He heard the shout of a man, followed by another shotgun blast.

The buckshot wiped out a branch beside him. He was now at the edge of the woods. As he entered the thick brush he knew he was safe: The farmer would have to reload.

Suddenly another blast. A rifle ball whizzed over his head and struck a nearby tree. The farmer's wife, he assumed, must also be armed. And then another rifle shot. He dove as the ball hit the heel of his boot, the impact knocking him over.

Two more rifle shots came — this time into the dirt beside him. He rolled over and up and ran for the cover of thicker trees.

Another shot, then another. Chunks of wood shot out of trees beside him. He figured a whole clan must be back there aiming at him, and they must have an arsenal in there.

He ran deeper into the woods now, and heard one more rifle shot, which hit a tree 10 feet behind him.

He sighed and kept on running, finally making it to his horse.

The jailer played solitaire with an old pack of greasy cards when he heard a knock.

Porter stood in the framework.

"We're closed now," said the jailer.

"It's still daylight."

"Not for long."

"Well, can't I see them?"

"You heard me."

"Look," said Porter, "I've come a long ways."

"Haven't we all," he chuckled. "You've already seen enough of them."

"I need just a short visit — I've got these blankets for them."

"I'll give 'em to them," said the jailer, taking the blankets from him.

"But I still need to see them. I left out something important."

"You heard me. We're closed."

Porter sighed, frustrated with the man. The jailer's two buddies ambled in, sporting pistols in their belts. Porter tried to be diplomatic, "Look, I got my little girl waiting for me outside town. And we came all the way across the state together just so I could see the prisoners."

The jailer studied him a moment and softened. "You've got three minutes with them."

As Porter thanked him, he caught himself nervously grasping his coat pocket. His eyes must have widened when he spoke — he noticed the jailer scrutinizing his face.

"All right," said the jailer, "take it off."

Porter felt like kicking himself. He'd made it this far, only to show his nerves at the last second before entering the dungeon. He opened his coat and a corn dodger fell out.

"All right," said the jailer, "I think we better let the food stay here with me this time."

"My wife cooked it for them."

"So?" said the jailer.

"I don't reckon she'd take to anyone else gettin' a hold of her corn dodgers," said Porter. "If somebody has to break a tooth on it, we'd just as soon it be among friends."

The jailer wasn't buying it. "Open the other side of your coat."

Porter did, and each passing second seemed like an hour. Then the hand shovel suddenly crashed to the ground.

All three men stared at him, then broke out laughing. The jailer's taller "assistant," a huge gruff fellow in his early 30's who resembled a giant, chuckled, "What else you got up your sleeves?"

The other assistant, a trim, good-natured older man who wore a perpetual smile, said, "Question is, boy, how much lighter are you gonna weigh when you come out compared to you going in?" The others laughed harder.

The jailer shook his head. "Nice try."

Porter sighed. "I'll just be five minutes."

"You'll be zero minutes. Pulling a stunt like that makes me want to lock *you* up. Now get out of town."

"I'll just be one minute then."

"I said get out. And take your blankets with you." He threw the two blankets back at Porter.

Porter also grabbed the shovel and headed for the door.

"Where do you think you'd be taking that?" said the older assistant.

"If it was any of your business, I'd tell you," said Porter, striding to the door.

"Don't come back here, son," said the gigantic muscular assistant. "We don't want to see you again."

"Feeling's mutual," said Porter, slamming the door behind him. "Filthy pukes."

The door opened and the giant bellowed out, "What did you call me?"

"You're a filthy Missouri puke, and if you take one step towards me I'll take your head off."

The huge, surly man at the door roared back, "That's what I thought you said!" He closed the door and Porter heard all three men laughing inside harder than ever. "I don't wanna lose my head over this," said the giant to the others, then they all broke out laughing even harder. It was obvious they had downed a couple drinks and were feeling no pain.

Outside, Porter was distraught.

Then he discovered his horse missing.

CHAPTER 56

Porter searched the town for his horse. Nothing. He had left it hitched just outside the jail. He made his way past the jail and church, and spotted stables ahead. The stable boy was shoeing an old mare when Porter approached and inquired about his animal. The young fellow seemed nervous, but said he did not know where such a horse was or who stole it.

Porter searched the town, and finally discovered his lost roan. It was on a nearby farm tied beside several others. He was actually angrier when he realized the thieves had not even bothered to unsaddle it. Then he spotted the robbers — apparently two brothers in their mid-twenties — playing poker in the barn.

Fifty feet from them Porter loaded his pistol. He snuck to the two men's horses and with his knife severed the ropes, smacked the two animals — which took off running — then climbed his own. He broke into a gallop. He glanced back and noticed the two robbers running after their own stampeding horses, shouting and swearing, but to no avail. Their horses escaped.

Porter galloped toward the jail. He arrived at the building, hitched his horse to a pole, and burst into the jail office, this time with his gun flashing. The jailers gasped and jumped back against the wall.

"Give me the keys."

"Won't do you no good," said the chief jailer.

"I'll decide that — now give 'em to me."

"I said —"

"Shut up and hand 'em over."

The jailer nodded and handed him the keys. The gigantic assistant chuckled nervously and his older skinny buddy said, "Shut up!"

The gigantic fellow quit giggling.

Porter opened the dungeon grate and glanced in. The prisoners were gone. He slammed the grate down and rushed to the jailer. He stuck his pistol to the man's throat.

"Why didn't you tell me!"

"I tried, but —"

"Where are they now!"

"I ain't sure."

Porter pulled the hammer back.

The jailer cleared his throat. "They've taken 'em to court at Gallatin.

Porter left the jail, jumped on his horse, and quickly rode out of town.

"I believe that boy means business," said the big surly fellow.

"I do think you're right," said the jailer, and they all broke out laughing again.

Arriving at the same farm where he'd taken the shovel and blankets, Porter snuck toward the shed again, ran inside, and propped the shovel in the same corner as before. He hung the blankets on a nail, then ran out the door and — once again — heard a gunshot.

"I don't believe this," he muttered aloud to himself. "They're shooting at me for returning their stuff!"

Suddenly he turned a corner and found himself face to face with the farmer's oldest son, a strapping, good-sized fellow with more muscles than brains.

"Well what've we got here?" said the 16 year old boy.

"Just returning your shovel and blankets."

"So I saw. You know, we shoot thieves in these parts."

"Thieves steal stuff," said Porter, hoping to buy time by talking with him till he came up with a plan to escape. "But I ain't a thief — I'm returning your stuff."

"Don't that still make you a thief?"

"An honest thief I'd say," said Porter smiling.

"An honest thief?" said the boy. He looked confused. Suddenly he called out, "Pa!"

Porter's eyes widened. The last thing he needed was a make-shift court convened in the farmhouse of a clan of Missouri roughnecks.

"What's your pa's name?" said Porter to the boy.

"Juke Segans."

"Juke!" yelled Porter, calling after the father.

"Pa!" shouted the boy.

"Juke!" said Porter again. He then turned to the boy, "I'll tell you what. You go that way to find him, and I'll go to the cabin."

The boy nodded, turned and walked five steps, then realized this might not work. He suddenly turned and realized . . . his captive had bolted.

As he stared into the woods, he stood there scratching his head.

"What's the matter, boy?" said the boy's father walking up to him.

"Oh, nothing, Pa, just talking to myself."

Porter then had a choice: He could follow after Joseph and his guards on the road to Gallatin — and then attempt to rescue him and the others — or return to Emily at the pond. If he left her awhile longer, the darkness closing in might frighten her — plus, what if he were killed or even wounded? She would be terrified until morning, waiting to walk into town to find the sheriff as instructed by her father, and worried sick over being away from her ma and wondering what happened to him, and then crushed for years if he were dead. He knew he had to return to his little girl.

Porter arrived at the woodland pond a mile away.

"Papa," said Emily, dropping her blankets and running toward him from the lean-to.

Porter dismounted and ran to her, picked her up and hugged her. "Too many close calls out here, honey," said Porter. "Even for my liking. I guess I'm gettin' old."

"How old is old, Pa?"

"Well, I'm 25 and 25 must be old."

"I reckon so," said Emily.

They went eastward horseback.

Emily held onto his waist, sitting behind him. They had only been on the road a half hour when she spoke up.

"Did you get Joseph out?"

"He got taken to Gallatin right under my nose, honey. I just plain failed him."

Emily wanted to say the right thing, knowing her pa was unhappy inside.

"You wouldn't have even failed if you hadn't tried. So it's good you went and tried, huh?"

Porter thought a moment and almost smiled. While he had failed Joseph once, he figured, he never would again. Ever, in his life.

At a campfire that night, Porter stared at the burning embers. Emily sat facing the heat, seated in front of her father and snuggled with her back into his chest. She felt his chin resting on top of her head.

"I reckon," said Emily, "you'd do anything for a friend, huh?"

"A true friend would also do anything for me," said Porter. "Joseph's proved that ever since he was a kid."

"Like you'd do for me?"

"How'd you know that?" said Porter.

"Just do."

"You're too smart for your own good."

"I know."

Under the stars and deep in the woods, a half mile safely away from the road, he stared at every twinkling light in the firmament. He never slept a second. There had to be a way to rescue Joseph, he figured, and simultaneously not put Emily in harm's way. There just had to be. He pondered it for hours. And finally he offered a little prayer — actually a mighty prayer — for help. He pled as he rarely had in his life. Despite his weaknesses and mistakes, he wished to help the Lord, his Kingdom, and his own best friend more than anything. He knew he was in a position to help more than anyone else, or at any time in his own life. It was perhaps the most pivotal point in the church's and Joseph's existence. If only he could figure out how to rescue the Prophet. He prayed even harder. Outgunned and outmanned by an armed guard, and with Emily at his side, it seemed absolutely impossible.

Then an idea struck.

CHAPTER 57

On their way to Gallatin, Joseph Smith and his four fellow prisoners rode beside Sheriff William Morgan and three guards.

"Looks like this is your lucky day, boy," said the sheriff.

"On the other hand," said one of the guards, "at court in Gallatin, you're likely to find it ain't your lucky day."

The others chuckled.

"I'll wager," said another, "you'll get 30 years — if you get out alive!"

The guards laughed harder.

Joseph was never happier than to be released out of Liberty Jail into the company of these pirates. Truly, freedom from the dungeon, no matter the prospects ahead, made it a glorious day, and he could only smile with gratitutude.

On horseback they rode — Joseph and his four fellows — and they were taken to court at Gallatin. There, they stood before the judge and were declared guilty of murder, treason, and larceny by a grand jury. The jurors were so inebriated and the crowd so hostile that their attorney prevailed upon the magistrate to transfer them to another court — the one at Boone County — for sentencing.

On their journey to Boone County Joseph was surprised to see a horseman approaching with a little girl. He suddenly recognized them, and ascertained Porter and Emily must have followed them since even before the court at Gallatin!

Joseph and the other four Mormon leaders held back their surprise as the two figures approached from the opposite direction, having ridden ahead through the woods and circled back. Therefore, Joseph and company regarded Porter as a mere stranger when the man with the little girl began befriending Sheriff Morgan, stridling up to him horseback.

"My, my, my what a fine day," said Porter to the sheriff. "You look awful tired toting these prisoners about."

"Are you up to something, stranger?" said Sheriff Morgan.

"Just gotta celebrate a little," said Porter. "Say, you wanna join me?"

"No thanks," said Sheriff Morgan, "We're a little busy transporting these prisoners."

"Well don't pay no mind to them," said Porter, nodding to the prisoners. "Cause what're they gonna do? Escape? They're still in handcuffs!" He laughed hard and long. The deputies smiled, amused by this bizarre fellow. "So, if you just imbibed with what I've got here to imbibe with," he continued, "what are they gonna do? Take it away from us?" He howled at his own joke. "Yes, sir, it is time to celebrate!"

"Why celebrate?" said the sheriff.

"You'd celebrate too if you'd have just won a contract to supply the entire state government with 100% prime, brain-stifling nectar. In fact, I'm willing to celebrate with any soul who finds the good fortune to come across my path today."

"Well, I hate to see you celebrate alone, stranger," said Sheriff Morgan, eyeing the liquor.

Porter held out a jug to Joseph. "You gentlemen care to join me?"

"Sorry, stranger, but no thanks," said Joseph. "I suppose we're hungrier than we are thirsty.

"Well, I've got some beef jerky on me if you'd care to indulge," said Porter.

"They don't get nothin to eat'," said Morgan. "But me and the deputies here will join you under them trees for a spell if you don't mind. I'm gettin' saddle sores already." They rode slowly to a grove beside the road.

Porter had purposely picked the noon hour. The sheriff and his men would have their stomachs empty by now and it would not take long for the liquor to take effect. He had bought the strongest alcohol he could find in Gallatin with his last money.

"Whew! How potent is this stuff?" said the sheriff after a swig.

"Oh, it's more water than nothin'," said Porter. "I've had a whole fifth since mid-mornin' already — and I ain't even woozy."

The deputies grinned. They knew they were going to enjoy the next couple of hours.

They sipped the liquid and found it scrumptious. They'd never tasted such delectable, watered-down whiskey.

After twenty minutes, the sheriff was beginning to sense something strange about the happiness he felt with life. It dawned on him he was not under any real pressure to deliver these prisoners at the break-neck speed he had supposed. They didn't seem like vicious chaps; certainly they had seemed cooperative and had hurried along before now, so why wouldn't they keep cooperating? They could still all arrive by sunset. He glanced at his deputies, laughing and enjoying this remarkable juice. "Well," he finally muttered to Porter, "I reckon we oughta be leavin' in a couple minutes here . . . "

"What's the hurry?"

The stranger's look of disappointment pricked the sheriff's conscience. After all, this person was kind enough to share his nectar of the gods with them, and the guards did happen to be the only humans on the woodland trail who could celebrate with this lonely fellow and — what the devil — here we are all in this together . . . Why not help each other out? He smiled at the stranger.

The stranger grinned back and handed him another bottle.

"Life's too short not to celebrate," said the sheriff.

"Especially at times like this," added the stranger, smiling big now and taking another sip.

Sheriff Morgan took a long pull on the bottle and soon began to enjoy April more than he had ever imagined. The wind whistling in the trees above and the chirping birds sounded farther and farther away, like an enchanting melody from a distant, fairy-tale forest with each passing second. The last conscious thought he had was how harmless, watered-down liquor could taste so darn good, and isn't this an interesting, enjoyable human being sitting next to him, and —

Minutes later, Sheriff Morgan awakened to the sound of horsehooves.

He looked up. The prisoners were gone. The stranger was gone. His own horse was gone.

His deputies were sound asleep. He kicked them and one urinated on his own boot. They finally awakened amidst cajoling, yelling and threats from the sheriff. They groggily arose and fired rifle shots. But to no avail. Joseph and company were not even in sight.

When the four guards ran to their horses they were disconcerted to discover they had a long walk ahead of them.

Joseph and friends were well on their way to freedom.

And Porter was laughing so hard, one could hear him a mile in every direction . . .

CHAPTER 58

Porter and Emily studied the moon glistening on the Mississippi River. It was two weeks later. Emily looked over at Joseph and the other freed prisoners now hard asleep, then back at her father.

"Papa?"

Porter shifted his look to her.

"If I was a boat in the Mississippi, and I got caught by a current, how far would you go to get me?"

"As far as I needed."

"And what if it took me to the end of the river?"

"I'd follow you."

"What's after that?"

"The ocean."

"Would you follow me across that?"

"Even if I had to swim it."

"You'd do that to find me?"

"Without a second thought."

"So would you ever leave me?"

"Never."

She smiled.

The next day they crossed the wide Mississippi River on a barge and made their way to Quincy, Illinois. By now, sixteen hundred saints had settled there. Emma Smith and her children were living at the Cleveland home four miles outside of town. The citizens of the city were still feeding and clothing the displaced Mormon immigrants.

As they approached shore, Joseph observed camps of his people scattered along river banks in and near Quincy. He and his fellows were suddenly greeted with cheers. Emma Smith cried when she beheld her husband striding along the river bank towards her. Joseph's children ran to him and grasped him, Joseph III broke into tears. Joseph fell to the ground and wrestled them all playfully, not even fighting his own tears of joy.

Luana was laundering, stirring clothes in a pot of hot water over a campfire, when she looked up and spotted Porter and Emily. She ran at full speed a hundred yards to Emily, hugged her, and picked her up.

"Mama, guess what? I stayed by a pond and men shot at Papa."

"Sounds like a safe, family outing to me," said Luana, glaring at Porter.

Porter went straight to the lean-to and saw little Caroline under her blankets. Her hair was sticking out, and it seemed longer. He realized he had been gone quite a while from home.

He picked her up and hugged her. She groggily awakened a moment, saw him, and smiled. "Papa!" she said, then fell back asleep in his arms. As he strode out to Luana, holding young Caroline, Emily came up to hug her little sister.

"I suppose," said Luana, happy to see him safe, yet miffed, "you determined to not leave Joseph until you rescued him?"

"What are friends for?" he said. "He'd have done it for me."

"But would you have done it for me?" she said.

"Why would you even ask that?"

"Why do you think?" she said.

"That's fool's talk."

"Fools speak the truth at times."

"At times, but this ain't one of 'em," he said.

Realizing they were again at one of their famous impasses, she changed the topic. "Porter, I miss my parents. Could we get a message to them to come visit?"

"Ain't safe. Horsemen are all over Missouri."

"But it's safe enough to carry your little girl?"

"We needed to be together."

"You didn't answer my question," said Luana. "Could we get a message to them?"

"If you want me to fetch 'em, I'll go see them."

"At least I know someone who really loves me," she said, feeling challenged and jumping back to the argument.

"Your parents?"

"Who else could I be talking about with feelings for me?" said Luana.

"Me."

"Well, that's nice. Once a year now you've let me know you have feelings, and I appreciate that," she said dryly. "But I happened to have meant real feelings, so, yeah, we are talking about my parents."

"I'll set out tomorrow to get them," said Porter.

"They won't leave the farm very long — but it makes me happy to know I can see them even a little while. I've dreamed of this for months."

"Well, you dream all you want," said Porter, feeling slighted, "but I'm going to see my pa now."

"Can I go see him, too?" said Emily.

"Of course you can see Grandpa," said Porter.

"Of course she can't go!" exclaimed Luana.

"Why can't she see him?"

"She just got back."

"So?"

"You can't just take her off again!"

"Is that right?" He picked up Emily and began walking 200 yards through the meadow to his parents. Not breaking stride, he turned back to Luana. "And could you unsaddle the roan, brush him down and feed him?"

"Am I your slave?" she said. "I've got enough laundry to do!"

"Forget the laundry, the horse is more important," he shouted.

Luana sighed and glared at the horse. "Caroline, when you're old enough, will you help me, since big sister will always be off with Pa?"

Two year old Caroline looked at her curiously and said, "Yep."

Luana, doubly resentful over Porter taking off with Emily again so soon, entered the lean-to, picked up a butcher knife and stabbed it into the table.

Porter shook hands with his father and reported his mission. Orin tried holding in a cough.

"Is that the same cough," said Porter, "you had when I left?"

"Prob'ly just a little winter exertion."

"It's gotten worse since Far West," spoke up Sarah, entering with kindling. She set down the wood and hugged Porter. "How did it go, son?"

"My boy rescued the Prophet!" said Orin. "Porter, you tell us all about it but first let Mama catch you up on the family."

"First," said Sarah, "tell me how you and Luana are getting along."

"You've never asked that before," said Porter.

"I'm just concerned about the girls," said Sarah. "You two don't fight, do you? At least around them?"

Porter glanced with a smirk at his pa. "Never."

"Well," said Sarah, knowing the answer as a mother often can, "I want you to be civil around the young 'uns."

"Yes, ma'am," said Porter, knowing civility was not particularly his premier trait.

"They need two parents who they know respect each other. I used to think it was all about love. But, if you're building a cabin, love is really nothing more than sand. It shifts, it gets loose. It gets hard and crumbly. It falls. It's got good seasons and bad. But you take respect. That's a rock. That stuff stays. That's a foundation for a cabin."

"Yes, ma'am."

CHAPTER 59

Joseph had arrived from jail in April 1839. A few days later at a church conference in Quincy, he decided to purchase two parcels of land northward: one in Commerce, Illinois and the other across the river in Iowa. Meanwhile, Porter watched and admired Luana working around the cabin when he was not working the fields for farm produce. He appreciated her sacrifices and told her so.

"Then build me a cabin," she said.

Porter knew the rainy weeks ahead would be trying for Luana in her lean-to, even though they were on the verge of moving northward.

"All right," he sighed. "I'll build you a cabin." He felt defensive whenever she confronted him, but left alone to his own thoughts, he would often find his conscience pricked. "I reckon she does deserve a cabin," he mumbled to himself, "even if we are heading out in a few weeks."

And so he did. It wasn't much larger than their lean-to, but

Luana liked the comfort and protection from the elements it afforded. He built it in the evenings after fishing and hunting for their food, and he completed it — with the help of his brothers — in just two weeks.

Joseph sat at their table, eating Luana's dessert specialty: bread pudding, which neither man enjoyed that much — especially as much as her true specialty — fried catfish cooked in an old family recipe batter — but the pudding was the item on which she most prided herself, so Porter pretended to enjoy it.

"Great stuff," he muttered.

"We're ready to make the move," said Joseph, forcing the last swallow of pudding down his throat as well, "to our new settlement northward."

"You mean the swamp?" said Luana.

"I mean the swamp," said Joseph. "But we can and will drain it. I see no other alternatives, do you?"

Luana glanced at Porter. "You're both crazy if you don't see alternatives. I worked myself to death on this plot of land — I thought it was our last move," said Luana.

"You hoped it was our last move," said Porter.

"And it is," she said.

"I told you weeks ago it was only temporary."

"What isn't temporary of everything we do?" she responded. "We'll die from malaria at Commerce — I've heard stories it's the most diseased spot in the state."

"I'll personally drain the swamp if I have to, but we're going there," said Porter.

"This squash casserole is awfully fine," said Joseph, trying to calm them down. "Yes, Luana, I believe it is among the finest I've ever had."

"That's bread pudding, Joseph."

The next morning Porter awakened and found breakfast prepared for him the first time since his return. Luana never again said a word on the matter of moving, but he knew she would be prepared to make the short exodus to Commerce within the week. That's the way she was, and he appreciated that about her. Unbeknownst to him, she appreciated that very same trait of his — of usually coming around, even if it were after a display of initial intransigence. Ironically, she realized, they were two stubborn peas of the same pod. And that deep, deep down, they loved each other dearly.

Trekking northward, Porter and Luana led their horses, upon which rode their two children, Emily and Caroline. It was a 43 mile trip from Quincy to Commerce, Illinois, and their dog Ugly trod beside them, anxious to find a place to settle and sleep in the sun. However, he especially anticipated the exploration of the glorious, highly heralded swamps, to find an even more varied habitat of dead creatures and their exotic perfumes. The best things of life, he realized, were indeed worth rolling in and relishing.

As they began the journey, Porter glanced back one last time at another cabin over which he had developed more than a few callouses, and then he gazed again at the long road ahead.

THE END.

EPILOGUE

$\mathbf{A}$ll the major events in this novel are historically documented in the author's book, *Porter Rockwell: A Biography*. What differentiates this work is an exploration of the characters and their relationships through dramatic scenes. While most scenes in this series are historically accurate, a few incidents are fictionalized, yet completely compatible with historical characterizations.

For example, in this first volume, the reader should note that while Joseph was indeed Porter's best friend, the following specific scenes were fictionalized: the fishing hole account and the outdoor picnic disruption event at Manchester, New York, the mud wrestling scene at Far West, and part of the rescue scene of Joseph Smith in Missouri. (Regarding the latter, while Joseph did escape Sheriff William Morgan *en route* to Boone County via the sheriff's inebriation, Porter's participation is speculative (although it was likely he that did attempt the futile rescue attempt at Liberty Jail involving the shovel handle).

Another point of fiction is the location of Luana Beebe's parents who, from a recent discovery by the author — since this book was written — likely never lived in Independence, Missouri, but rather, probably died in Ohio, contrary to what has been historically accepted for decades.

Most other events in this series are accurately portrayed, including the battles and conflicts in which Porter and his people participated.

In summary, the events and relationships depicted herein are based on years of research, and from that the author has attempted to now capture the period, the characters, and their motives with as much truth as possible for a work of fiction; consequently, he hopes the reader will enjoy this series as much as he while researching it, wherein history, for a time, came alive for him.

Heber C. Kimball Home, Nauvoo
by Al Rounds

Full-color, 25" x 15" signed-and-numbered, limited-edition art prints of *Heber C. Kimball Home, Nauvoo*, depicted on the front and rear of the dust jacket of volume 3 of *The Porter Rockwell Chronicles*, are available from the publisher at the price of $150.00 each plus shipping and handling.

Shipping and handling charges are $15.00 for the first print, plus $1.00 additional shipping and handling for each additional print ordered at the same time and shipped to the same address.

As the 700 limited-edition art prints sell out, the collectors' value may substantially increase.

The Porter Rockwell Chronicles, Vol. 2
by Richard Lloyd Dewey

Hardcover, $23.88 (Reg. $27.50)   ISBN: 0-9616024-7-3

The true-life adventures of Porter Rockwell continue in this exciting, second installment of the Rockwell saga. The sacrifices he makes for best friend Joseph Smith cause increased tension with his wife, while his unusual, heart-melting relationship with his oldest daughter Emily develops even further.

His character as a man in his twenties is unveiled in this volume to help the reader understand his future, miraculous career as a gunfighter, U.S. marshal, and bodyguard to Brigham Young.

Porter's first years in Nauvoo — including a brief history of the city and an artfully rendered photo essay of Nauvoo by the author — are also contained in this volume.

**Look for it in your favorite bookstore,
or to obtain autographed copies, see last page.**

The Porter Rockwell Chronicles, Vol. 3
by Richard Lloyd Dewey

Hardcover, $23.88 (Reg. $27.95)   ISBN: 0-9616024-7-3

Readers claim this is the most exciting, engrossing volume yet about the true-to-life adventures of Joseph Smith's bodyguard.

All 526 pages are packed with powerful storytelling by a writer whose work *U.S.A. Today* calls "riveting," and *The Midwest Book Review* rates "superlative."

The Nauvoo period is wrapped up in this heart-wrenching, spell-binding true story that pits Porter against leaders of mobs and against his own, conflicted character, which is richly revealed by the choices he makes. He protects his neighbors but in the process sees he is losing his wife. In the end, Porter makes all necessary sacrifices for the person he loves most — his eldest daughter, Emily — while he stands tall as "The Mormon Protector."

Porter was an eyewitness to most scenes in the early Mormon days, so this series details an accurate account of many little-known events and establishes itself as a basic text of LDS history.

**Look for it in your favorite bookstore,
or to obtain autographed copies, see last page.**

Porter Rockwell: A Biography
by Richard Lloyd Dewey

Hardcover, $22.95   ISBN: 0-9616024-0-6

The epic biography that traces Porter Rockwell from turbulent Eastern beginnings to battles with Midwestern mobs to extraordinary gunfights on the American frontier. Quotes hundreds of journals, letters, and court records. Illustrated by western artist, Clark Kelley Price.

**Look for it in your favorite bookstore,
or to obtain autographed copies, see last page.**

Porter Rockwell Returns
by Clark Kelley Price

36"w x 24"h, $30.00   ISBN: 0-929753-0-6

This classic color print of the painting by renowned western artist Clark Kelley Price depicts Porter Rockwell coming home at night in a lightning storm through downtown Lehi, Utah.

In this vivid scene, Rockwell is returning from a hard day's work, with an outlaw draped over the horse he has in tow.

**Look for it in your favorite bookstore,
or to obtain by mail, see last page.**

ORDERING INFORMATION

☛**All books ordered by mail are autographed.**

The Porter Rockwell Chronicles, Vol. 1   (Reg. $27.95) **$23.88**
by Richard Lloyd Dewey. Hardcover, 490 pp. ISBN: 0-9616024-6-5

The Porter Rockwell Chronicles, Vol. 2   (Reg. $27.50) **$23.88**
by Richard Lloyd Dewey. Hardcover, 452 pp. ISBN: 0-9616024-7-3

The Porter Rockwell Chronicles, Vol. 3   (Reg. $27.95) **$23.88**
by Richard Lloyd Dewey. Hardcover, 527 pp. ISBN: 0-9616024-7-3

Porter Rockwell: A Biography   **$22.95**
by Richard Lloyd Dewey. Hardcover, 612 pp. ISBN: 0-9616024-0-6

Porter Rockwell Returns Art Print   **$30.00**
by Clark Kelley Price. 36"w x 24"h, unsigned. ISBN: 0-929753-0-6

Utah residents, add 6.25% sales tax to price of items
(before shipping & handling).

SHIPPING & HANDLING:

For books, add $1.00 for first item and $1.00 additional shipping and handling for each additional book sent to same address.

For art prints, add $15.00 for first print and $1.00 additional shipping and handling for each additional print sent to same address.

Send check or money order to:
Stratford Books
P.O. Box 1371, Provo, Utah 84603-1371

Prices subject to change.